CITY

OF

LIES

CITY

OF

LIES

A Novel

Peter McCabe

WILLIAM MORROW AND COMPANY, INC.
NEW YORK

It is the policy of William Morrow and Company, Inc., and its imprints and affiliates, recognizing the importance of preserving what has been written, to print the books we publish on acid-free paper, and we exert our best efforts to that end.

Library of Congress Cataloging-in-Publication Data

McCabe, Peter, 1945–
   City of lies : a novel / Peter McCabe.
     p. cm.
   ISBN 0-688-12118-7
   I. Title.
   PS3563.C33373C58   1993
   813'.54—dc20   92-16733
                                   CIP

Printed in the United States of America

First Edition

1 2 3 4 5 6 7 8 9 10

BOOK DESIGN BY M.C. DE MAIO

For Yvonne,
Madison, Jason, Nicholas,
Alexander, and my parents

ACKNOWLEDGMENTS

I wish to thank a number of people who
have encouraged me: my wife, Yvonne, a wonderful
reader and guide; friends and colleagues, Sally
Helgesen, David and Sandy Peckinpah, Nancy
Evans, Ken Gross, Jane Gaynor, Tom and Ellen
Werts, Mike Fisher, Pete Bonventre, Cyrus
Nowrasteh, Art Monterastelli, Beth Polson, Nancy
Meyer, Richard Dilello, Barry Golson, T. D.
Allman, and Mike Ahnemann. And I especially
wish to thank my literary agent, Loretta Barrett,
who sold this book, and Lisa Drew, who bought it.

Men are the sport of circumstances.
                                    Byron

CHAPTER ONE

My FATHER WAS an engineer and very circumspect, and when I first told him I intended to become a reporter, his response was "Why would anyone want to make a living snooping around in things that don't concern them?" At the time I thought he demonstrated a marked lack of curiosity about the larger world. Lately, I've been thinking, maybe he had a point.

Certain events that I pursued have led me to conclude that there is a perverse side to my nature. What is reporting, after all, but a curiosity about the dark side of life? It's true that I went beyond proscribed limits and in doing so ran into the unexpected—but isn't this what reporting is all about? Isn't this where it's supposed to lead?

I find myself asking, how did I come by this impulse to want to peek and poke at the world's underbelly? Was it an errant mutation of my father's scientific bent—his need to know? In the end, I guess it doesn't matter how I came by it. The fact is, I was curious, and I let my curiosity run away with me. I'm not making excuses here. I'm merely getting this on the record. There's no reason for me to blame myself for what occurred. These events were under way long before I entered the picture.

As for the outcome . . . well, if this is a trap I dug for myself, so be it. All things considered, it's not an unpleasant one. In many ways I'm better off than I was before. There are a few scars, I won't deny it, and a sense of loss—a loss of innocence. But if that's the worst of it, I guess I can live with myself. Losing one's innocence isn't so bad.

I was still an innocent, however, when I moved out west after college and cut my teeth at a small California daily, where I met Maggie Linear, a free-lance artist. We got married and moved into a terra-cotta apartment a few blocks from the Pacific. A year later, our son, Jackson, was born. Life wasn't bad—in fact, it was about as pleasant as it could be for two people living on tight incomes—but it didn't take long for the local niceties to wear on me. After a time I wanted the rush of working at a major metropolitan paper, and I convinced Maggie it was important that I return east, where I grew up.

I sent off my clips to various papers. Six weeks went by—then I got a call out of the blue from a Ted Cantor, the city editor at one of the New York dailies. I flew east for an interview, and two weeks later, after I'd given up hope of ever hearing from him again, he called to say there was a job open for me. We sold our furniture and moved to New York.

Our new home was a two-bedroom apartment in a prewar building on Manhattan's upper Upper West Side. It was not what Maggie had in mind when she agreed to move. But I heaped on her promises of eventual change, and in the meantime I knuckled down at my new job and put in the hours. When I'd been at the paper a few months, Cantor began sending me out on crime stories. He liked what I wrote, and he kept me on the crime beat for a couple of years, then he switched me to the court beat. I wasn't thrilled at first. The job involved hours of tedium for a few moments of drama. Eventually, I hit on the idea of writing about the court system itself. After one false start, I turned in a piece Cantor reacted well to. He suggested I do a series, and six months later I was promoted—to feature writer.

But a few cracks had appeared in my world by then. Instead of capitalizing on the gains I'd made, I found myself riding the slippery slope toward divorce. Maggie and I had married young and we were growing apart, and although we did our best to avoid a breakup, we had both come to recognize that we were unsuited. For one thing, I loved New York. Maggie hated it. We muddled on for a year, then we split up, and she and Jackson moved back to California. I stayed on. I saw Jackson three times a year, and told myself Maggie and I had each given the other the opportunity to find greater happiness. But it was a painful time nonetheless.

I took solace in all the predictable antidotes—and when the worst of the pain wore off, I began doing free-lance pieces for magazines. The work filled the hours, and I threw myself into it, enjoying writing at greater length than I could for the paper. After the fourth or fifth of these articles appeared, an old friend, Virginia Danbury, the associate publisher of *City Magazine* called me. She said *City*'s editor in chief, Jack Rosenberg, wanted to talk to me about becoming a regular contributor. Virginia was offering me a leg up. I said, "Sure. Why not?"

Things had been frustrating at the paper lately because of budget cuts, and I was back on the court beat again, at least temporarily. Cantor had asked me to cover the trial of Lou Koslo, a Mafia boss. It wasn't my job to file the day-to-day testimony—Cantor had assigned a young reporter, Al Killion, to do that. But that week Killion came down with the flu, and instead of writing colorful backgrounders, I was doing journeyman work again.

By Friday afternoon I was bored to death. The trial had bogged down in recesses, and the prosecutor, Jim Danziger, was on his feet every five minutes objecting. The lawyers were going up to the bench for sidebar after sidebar, and I was sitting on the hard bench where I'd spent too much of my working life, thinking only of myself and the weekend ahead, when Harry McLaughlin, the court official in charge of the pressroom, came in and handed me a message. It was from Virginia Danbury, and when I called her back, she said, "You are coming to this thing, right?"

I'd forgotten.

She'd invited me to the fourth anniversary party for *City Maga-zine*, which was being held that afternoon in the main suite of the Stanhope Foundation, three floors above the *City* offices in midtown.

I said, "Do I have to?"

13

"Mike, don't wimp out on me, you promised you'd come."

I told her I had planned to go upstate for the weekend and wanted to get an early start.

"But it wouldn't hurt to show your face before you talk to Jack. It's been ages since you've seen anyone."

She was pulling for me. And the alternative was to go back upstairs and be bored along with everyone else. I told her I'd be there, then I went back to the courtroom and asked a UPI reporter, Larry Laub, if he'd mind covering for me. He asked where I was going and I told him, and he promised he'd call me if someone shot Lou Koslo on his way out of court. I thanked him and told him I owed him one. Then I packed up my stuff and headed downstairs to the subway.

That afternoon, I recall feeling a vague anxiety about the fact that I might be taking a new career step. I remember thinking I'd grown comfortable with the honest malice of the guys on the paper's rewrite desk. *City Magazine* would be a different game, with higher stakes, and I wouldn't be able to ease back on the job as I'd been doing at the paper lately.

It was time for a challenge. I guess I recognized that. But I sure as hell wasn't thinking of that day as one that would mark a total change in my life.

CHAPTER TWO

SINCE ITS RAPID rise to success, *City Magazine* had moved to a new high rise on Third Avenue. Originally, it had been housed in a building in the garment district where you used to have to fight your way through racks of flannel nightgowns to get in. But now, instead of nightgown manufacturers, *City*'s neighbors included law offices, ad agencies, and the Stanhope Foundation. Lately, everyone wanted a piece of *City*. Even the foundation was kissing its ass, asking for the honor of hosting the party. The magazine, chock-full of ads, and offering a mix of solid stories, gossip, outlandish fashion and photo spreads, had become the darling of that group of people who believe they're at the forefront of taste and opinion in New York.

My connection to the magazine dated back to its early days. Three years ago, I'd covered the trial of a woman named Mavis Allen, who'd been convicted of murdering the wife of a married man she'd been involved with. Shortly after the verdict, I got hold of some information that suggested the husband's testimony was perjured, and I did a piece for the paper about the case. Then Virginia called and said Rosenberg would be interested in me writing a feature-length piece for them. Cantor gave me his blessing, and a month later, I handed in six thousand words. The story ran with a cover line, and later that year, when the New York Supreme Court threw out the Allen conviction, Rosenberg put my piece up for a National Magazine award. It didn't win—pity—but the nomination did get me noticed, and it did earn me a first-rate lunch, courtesy of Virginia.

She and I had been in touch since then. I'd known her since college—we'd even gone out on a few dates our senior year. Nothing came of them, there was never any blood-and-guts between us, and after a few futile efforts to kindle passion, we settled for being friends. Lately her mission had been to "rehabilitate" me. Since my divorce, she'd drag me out to parties—in a sense her inviting me to the *City* function was part of this process. Still, when I walked into the foundation's suite that afternoon, I didn't see her; I recognized only a few editors and the literary luminaries who had banded together out of fear of getting stuck talking to a nobody. Then, as I was moving away from the bar, I felt a tap on my shoulder. Virginia, wearing an elegant tailored suit and clutching a large vodka, was at the center of a group of fresh faces who could only have been advertisers. I listened as she prattled on about some full-bleed four-color ad, flattering the silly bastards; then, as I started to walk away, she made the abrupt "excuse me" of a party pro, and demonstrating her relief with a quick roll of the eyes, she dragged me off to meet people.

As usual, she knew everybody. Within five minutes I met the Stanhope Foundation's directors, two members of the New York City Board of Estimate, and the ex-wife of a real estate magnate, whose autobiography *City* was excerpting. I was introduced to Milo Stacovich, an inventor who owned a lot of stock in *City Magazine*, and to Virginia's boss, Dick Bruton, the publisher. Bruton wasn't publisher when I wrote the Allen article, so Virginia told him who I was. She said I was interested in flexing my muscles again for *City*. Bruton smiled a tight smile. Stacovich chimed in that his favorite crime writer was Ross Macdonald. He and I talked, and I saw Bruton shifting his feet, as if impatient to resume his conversation. Eventually, Virginia caught on too.

As we moved away I told her, "Bruton seems like a hell of a guy."

"Dick gets that way sometimes . . ."

She craned her neck above the crowd until she spotted someone else I needed to meet. Then, as we crossed the room, I ran into a reporter friend, Matt Shaw.

Shaw was a saloon acquaintance, an ex-war correspondent who had signed on with *City* at its inception. He was with Henry Drake, the senior editor I'd worked with on the Allen story, and a woman I didn't know. Virginia said, "You're among friends," and promptly abandoned me.

I hadn't seen Henry since he and I had gone over the Allen story line by line. He was a tall guy with a faintly arrogant stare, and I'd since heard he was being groomed as heir apparent to Rosenberg. He asked how I'd been, and I said, "Well enough," then he introduced me to the woman. Her name was Lisa Dennison, an associate editor, and when she'd pieced together enough of the conversation to deduce I was a reporter, she asked what I wrote. Before I could answer, Henry said, "I told you about Mike. He's the one that got away." I figured it still galled him a bit that they'd dangled the carrot three years ago and offered to make me a contributor, but at the time I didn't bite.

"Can't blame him," Shaw said. "None of us were making a living here back then."

Henry rolled his eyes and said, "I notice you haven't been complaining lately."

Shaw grinned. A number of his stories had recently been optioned for movies.

He and Henry got into a harangue about writers' compensation, and I stayed on the sidelines and tried not to stare at Lisa Dennison. It required an effort. She was about twenty-five, with long dark hair, high cheekbones, and green eyes with a hint of cobalt blue at the iris. Eventually, Henry drew me out of my reverie by asking what I was doing here. I said I was here to keep an eye on Virginia.

She returned, on cue, and pried me away, and as we crossed the room I asked her about Lisa Dennison. Virginia said, "Forget it."

"Why?"

"Because she's seeing Mitch . . ."

I guess my surprise showed. Mitch was Virginia's older brother. It was his venture capital firm that had raised the money for *City*, which was how Virginia got her job. The last I'd heard, Mitch had been dating an analyst at Salomon Brothers. I'd met the woman once; she was very intense and, well, financial—certainly not a dish like Lisa Dennison.

We were hovering, waiting to talk to Rosenberg. Virginia arched her eyebrows and said, "What?"

I said, "Nothing," and a moment later Rosenberg was free and Virginia buttonholed him.

Jack Rosenberg was a rumpled figure in his early fifties. To me, he had always seemed to be a man at ease with himself, confident of his worth. He greeted me like a lost friend, which was encouraging, and we chatted for a while. I told him what I'd been up to, then someone else wanted his attention, and as we shook hands, he said, "Are we on for next week?"

Virginia said she'd set it up, and as we moved off, she insisted this had all been worth it. I said, "I guess so," and we were on our way to the bar when Virginia tugged at a man's sleeve. She said, "Stephen—remember Mike."

I remembered him. But it took Stephen Lister a moment. He was in his early thirties, fair-haired, a good-looking guy wearing an expensive leather jacket. He'd been the photo editor when I'd written the Allen article. In the meantime he'd become a name around town and a power at *City*—he'd gotten the credit for giving the magazine its look.

I'd never cared for him. Back when I'd met him, I'd gotten the impression he viewed my article as fodder for his own brilliance. I listened as he and Virginia chatted. Then someone interrupted to say there was a phone call for her. She went off to take it, and Stephen Lister was cornered by the two women he'd been talking to previously. I heard him say something about a well-known model who had turned camera-shy, and having no interest, I drifted away.

I'm not much at parties. Put me in a roomful of people, and I tend to squirrel myself away in a corner with a drink. And I was heading into one of these modes when Henry Drake sidled up to me. He propped one foot on a planter and asked me the real reason I was here, and I saw no point in not telling him. I said Jack wanted to talk to me about contributing some articles.

"Well, that's a first step." Henry seemed pleased. He tossed down his drink and said, "Let's hope it works out. I always thought you'd fit in here."

"Why's that?"

"Thick skin." Henry grinned. "Like me. Not everyone works out . . . there's a lot to contend with here . . ."

"Like what?"

Henry tilted his glass in the direction of the party. "Bruton . . . he's a beauty . . . Stephen Lister's another. I guess you've noticed we've become a more *visual* book." He laced the word with sarcasm.

"Lot of politics?" I suggested.

"*Lots* of politics . . ."

We talked for a few minutes about stories I might write. Then Henry looked at his watch and said he had to run. He asked me what I was doing for the weekend, and I told him I owned a place upstate and I planned to go up there and watch the deer. Henry set his glass down, rested a hand on my shoulder, and said, "You're saner than I thought." Then he made his way to the door.

It was a little after six. The party was already thinning out, and the event began to seem overblown for people who wanted only a few belts before getting away for the weekend. I looked around for Virginia but didn't see her, and as I drifted around the room trying not to look lost, a young woman caught my eye. She started over to me. She was nice-looking, with deep hazel eyes, and it occurred to me it might have been worth coming here after all.

She approached and said, "You're Mike Kincaid?"

I nodded.

"Virginia needs to talk to you. She's in an office along the corridor."

I felt a twinge of disappointment.

Virginia was prone to theatrical gestures, and I figured this was one of them. But this woman was offering to show me the way at least, and so I followed her out of the room. She said her name was Ann Raymond. I asked her what she did for the foundation, and she said, "I don't . . . I'm a writer."

"For *City*?"

"I've written one article for them."

We walked a few more yards to another corridor. Then Ann Raymond stopped, indicated a door, and said, "Think you can find your way from here?"

To my surprise, she stuck her hand out, and maybe a corner of her tongue as she smiled, and for a second there was a wickedness in her eyes that made my blood jump. Then she turned and headed back to the suite, offering me a little wave, like I once saw Judy Holliday do in a movie. It was funny, and sexy, and as I glanced after her, I liked the way she walked. There was something limber and athletic about that walk, and I liked the way her jacket hung on her shoulders, which she held back, like the shoulders of a young cadet. Then I walked into the office to find Virginia leaning against a desk, in a real funk.

She said, "Are you still going upstate?"

"Yes."

"Do you have a date?"

"I'm picking Cheryl Tiegs up at the Waldorf."

"Then invite me."

"Fine."

"You're a prince, Mike."

Then she let fly with a string of expletives, and in the midst of these I caught the name of her brother, Mitchell. I told her to cool off, and when she did, we took the elevator down to her office so she could collect her bag. Her answering machine was blinking when we walked in, and when she played back the message, the voice was Mitch's. She turned off the tape and said, "Fuck you, dear bro," then she picked up her bag and we left.

I walked out with her, asking myself why I'd agreed to her coming. I guess it was a spur-of-the-moment thing after I'd had a drink or two. Nothing more than that.

CHAPTER THREE

As WE DROVE upstate that evening all Virginia did was complain about her brother. She began railing about him in the cab on the way to my car, and she was still going at it as we drove north on the Taconic Parkway in the thick of the Friday traffic. She was incensed and I was a captive audience.

It had been a long week. I wanted to relax and think about nothing—now I had to listen to this. She told me she and Mitch had had a fifteen-minute argument over the phone, at the end of which she had hung up on him. Since a phone hang-up is a reporter's least favorite sound, I guess I was feeling some sympathy for Mitch.

I asked her what the argument was about, and she said Mitch had accused her of indiscriminate socializing and suggested people were getting the impression she was shallow and flighty. I said, "What else is new?" She didn't smile. She lapsed into a sullen silence, then she started in again, and finally I said, "Why should you give a fuck what Mitch thinks?"

She tossed a cigarette out the window, uttered a derisive snort, and repeated for the tenth time what Mitch had said, "I don't want people getting the impression you don't deserve the job!"

This time I offered no comment. I'd already conceded it was tactless of him.

I'd known Mitch almost as long as I'd known Virginia. He was a few years older than his sister, but they had the same shock of fair hair, the same broad face, the same square Danbury chin. Virginia had introduced us years ago, and although Mitch and I were never close, I always felt he approved of me in some harsh, defiant way. Ten years ago, when I'd first met him, he had just gone to work on Wall Street. In the interim he had gotten rich, formed his own company, and raised the money for a number of ventures, of which the jewel in the crown was *City*. He'd retained a stake in the company and obviously thought enough of his sister at one time to install her in her job. Around the office, she was known as Mitch's eyes and ears, a label she resented, even if there was some truth to it, but Mitch wasn't merely being nepotistic. Virginia had abilities, and a certain flair, and Mitch was modest enough at least to stay away from the "creative" side of magazines.

Virginia started in again, this time about an argument she and Mitch had had at their Memorial Day weekend party, at a summerhouse they shared on Long Island. I'd been invited to it, but I'd passed.

"I don't know why he bothered to come. He doesn't like my friends. He doesn't want my friends to like him. Since he's been seeing Lisa, he's not interested in meeting anyone new."

I said if I were seeing Lisa Dennison, I might cut down a little on socializing. Virginia glared at me as if I were taking Mitch's side. I said I wasn't and she let it go.

I'd never understood the reason for the sharing arrangement in the first place. Virginia was a dedicated social whirlwind and Mitch wasn't—his idea of a good time was to sit out on the deck of the Southampton Golf Club and compare vintage wines with like-minded friends. They were brother and sister, but their life-styles were incompatible, so why the hell didn't they rent separately? I asked Virginia this, and she conceded I had a point. The summer rental was a habit from years ago, one that no longer made much sense. She lapsed into silence again, then she said, "It's the hangers-on he doesn't like. At least that's what he calls them."

22

"Who?"

"Stephen and his friends."

"Stephen Lister?"

"Mitch doesn't like the crowd Stephen brings around. He doesn't want him at the house anymore—he's made that clear."

I said, "I wouldn't either," and Virginia glared at me again, as if I were trying to start something.

Eventually, she said, "Based on what?"

"Gut. I know he's a friend of yours. But I don't like him."

"Well, *you* don't have to like him, but he and Mitch have a professional relationship, so you'd think Mitch could at least be civil."

I said, "Maybe Mitch doesn't think it's civil of him to bring around a lot of unwanted guests."

Virginia rolled her eyes, and we drove a number of miles in silence. Finally she changed the subject and started to tell me about a new apartment she was buying in the city. She was still talking about it as we drove up the steep road in the western Berkshires that led to the cabin. I stared through the headlights, watching for deer, vaguely aware of Virginia rambling on about mortgages and maintenance fees and other items I couldn't afford. Then we turned off the road and pulled up on the patch of gravel outside the cabin. Virginia said, "Gee, it's cute," and that was the sum total of her appraisal.

We opened up the place and aired it out, then took our drinks out to the porch. And as soon as we sat down, Virginia started in on Mitch again.

"You know what I can't understand?"

"What?"

"Why Mitch is so down on Stephen when he's benefited from Stephen's impact."

I was getting tired of hearing this.

"Can we talk about something else?" I said.

Virginia swatted at a bug and said we could talk about whatever I wanted to talk about. Then she brought up the subject of Milo Stacovich and asked if I found him interesting.

I said, "Why—because he's got forty million in the bank?"

Virginia took a moment before replying.

"No . . . because of who he is—how many inventors would buy into a magazine?"

I told her that rich men who invested in media ventures didn't necessarily meet my definition of interesting. For this, I was told I was being an asshole.

"Milo's very smart," Virginia insisted. "He made the corporate world pay for what came out of his lab."

"Good businessman, is he?"

"Oh stop it . . ."

I told her I thought we'd exhausted the subject of Milo.

She got up off the porch glider and went inside to get a beer. I leaned back in a rocker and gazed at the night sky. There was still a faint glimmer of daylight in the west, but once this faded, the only light would be the moon and stars, and the reflected glow of a few communities in the Hudson Valley. After a week in the city, I'd grown to love this splendid isolation. My nearest neighbor was a half mile away, which was fine by me. Usually while I was up here, I'd read, or walk the perimeters of the property, maybe fix a screen or two for the exercise.

Virginia returned, cracked her beer, and asked what *I* wanted to talk about, since I seemed to be exercising veto power over the conversation. I said, "Let's talk about Ann Raymond."

For a few seconds the only sound was the sound of crickets. Then Virginia broke into a trill laugh. "Well, well!" she exclaimed. "The reticent one."

She was pleased about this. She wanted to know more. I said there was nothing more to tell.

"Bull*shit*. What happened?"

"An exchange of glances."

Virginia insisted that was enough. "I'm going to get you two together. I'll have a dinner party."

Already I regretted bringing this up. One of Virginia's dinner parties, complete with place settings, wasn't my idea of a first date. I said if I wanted to ask Ann Raymond out, I'd ask her myself.

Virginia gave me her maiden aunt look and started to tell me how highly Ann Raymond was regarded at the magazine.

24

"She's really an interesting writer. Jack says it's rare to get someone in the social science field who can actually write. She's smart . . . classy . . ."

"Spare me," I said.

"Well, not too classy. I imagine she could get pretty trashy, just like you."

"Did you go underwear shopping with her?"

Virginia grinned and offered nothing more, and I asked if it was a setup, her sending Ann Raymond out to get me. She refused all comment. Then she stifled a yawn, stood up and announced she was turning in.

"Have nice dreams about Ann," she said. "I think she's a wild one."

I showed her to her room, gave her some clean sheets, and said good-night. Then I stacked the cushions at the end of the porch glider and stretched out, gazing at the darkening silhouette of the Catskills. Life could be worse . . .

I watched the last traces of vermilion disappear from the sky, then I got up and took a short walk down to the field below. I stood there, gazing back at the cabin. In some respects this place represented a demarcation point in my life. I'd grown up thirty miles from here, but after I returned from California I only came up here to see my parents. They'd lived here all their lives. My father had been born in the next county. To him, this was God's country, and he never understood why I chose to live in the city once I moved back from the West Coast.

At the time I told him being a reporter wasn't the only way to make a living, but it happened to be the way I'd chosen. So I had little choice but to live where there were newspapers and stories. My father shook his head and gave my mother a dirty look when she observed that stubborn independence appeared to be a Kincaid family trait.

A year later, both my parents were dead—my father six months after my mother. To my surprise, my father willed the family home in Hudson to me and left my brother his bank account. Maggie and I were still together then, and we didn't have many free weekends, but when we did, it was always strange coming to my parents' place. I sold the house eventually. The town was growing out toward it and a supermarket chain had bought the vacant lot across the street.

Then one weekend two years later, Maggie and I came upstate to visit some old friends of mine. It was late July and the corn was ripening in the fields, and as I drove around the familiar lanes, I felt a regret that I no longer had any attachment to this area. That weekend I made a decision. I bought this cabin with my parents' hard-earned money, and it was to Maggie's credit that she laid no claim to it when we divorced. I'd been spending more and more weekends here since then, enjoying what I grew up with and often wondering what my father would think if he could see me. And it did occur to me that night as I stood gazing back at the cabin that maybe he was onto me, before I was on to myself.

That weekend, Virginia slapped at a lot of bugs, all the while insisting that the R and R was doing her good. She was not good in the country. She fidgeted constantly. Once she'd finished the work she'd brought with her, she began scanning the local paper for a movie, but there was nothing showing she hadn't seen already. She tried to get tickets for the Berkshire Theater, only to discover that it was sold out, and when she asked about Tanglewood, I told her the season hadn't opened yet. Finally, she settled for dinner at the cabin.

That night it rained, and it was still raining the next morning when I drove to the village to buy the Sunday paper. When I got back, Virginia was up and making calls. We ate breakfast, then we divided up the paper and read for a few hours as the rain dripped steadily from the roof onto the mountain laurel. When it was still raining around two, Virginia started to get restless again. Eventually, she asked if I'd mind making an early start back to the city. I said it was fine by me. I had a phone interview to do anyway and my notes were in town. We were agreed then. I set about closing the place up, and half an hour later we were headed back to New York.

We were quiet in the car. Virginia was working on the *Times* crossword. For a while the rain eased up and the fields shone radiant beneath oblique shafts of sunlight. Then the car swept around a long bend in the parkway, and the rain started to pour down. We were about halfway through Dutchess County, when Virginia looked up from her paper and said, "Ann Raymond has a place up here somewhere." I looked over at her and didn't say anything. Virginia said, "It might prove convenient." Then she chuckled and went back to her crossword.

We got back to New York around five. As we turned off the West Side Highway, the crack dealers slunk toward us, fingering their wares. "Why do we do this?" Virginia groaned. "Why don't we just stay in the country?" She draped an arm across the seat behind me. "I think I'll buy a place near you, that's what I'll do. I'll join a local theater group and introduce you to all the local nutty actresses."

I said that sounded great.

"Okay, we'll get old together and sit in our rockers. I'll become obsessive about my rose garden. You can write irate letters to the local paper. How would that be?"

I said I'd think about it.

I dropped her at her apartment on Seventy-sixth Street. Then I turned the car back onto Broadway and drove uptown.

I still lived in the apartment I'd lived in when I was married. It was on Riverside in the 100s, in one of the few buildings on the Drive that was not either a co-op or owned by Columbia. The living room had a view of nearby rooftops, one of the bedrooms no view at all, but the other bedroom faced west, and it had a view of the river and the Jersey Palisades.

Since my divorce I'd used it as an office, and when I got to it that night, a lone green light stared back at me from the answering machine. I started sorting through the mail, and among the bills I came across a notice from a glassware store in Hudson. I'd been in the store once, years ago, to buy Maggie an anniversary gift, but things like this were always turning up and giving me a jolt.

I poured myself a drink and shook off the relapse into gloom. Then I did the phone interview I'd come back to do, and when I was

27

done with it, I lay on the couch and made some preliminary notes. I was dozing when the phone rang, and when I picked up, the voice I heard was strained. It took a second before I recognized it as Virginia's.

"Mike . . ."

Virginia started to babble. I told her to calm down, I couldn't hear what she was saying.

"The police are coming over . . ."

"Why?"

"They wouldn't say . . . can you come over, I can't reach Mitch?"

I thought, "Shit, I really need this." Then I thought maybe someone in her family had died, and so I told her I'd be there. I figured I might be in for a long night, so I swilled some coffee and hauled out some dry sneakers and a slicker, then I went out and walked up the street to Broadway and waited for a taxi in the rain.

There wasn't a yellow cab in sight, and five minutes went by before a gypsy cab showed up. The driver was Russian, and he took about ten minutes to get the address right, then he tried to go the wrong way to Amsterdam, and I wound up yelling at him as a truck bore down on us. He grunted and nearly hit another cab, and finally I got out and took a bus down Columbus. As I headed across Seventy-sixth Street, I saw a Chevy Caprice double-parked outside Virginia's building. Her apartment was on the ground floor, and when she came to the front door, her face was white. She squeezed my shoulders.

"You're not going to believe this . . ." She was trembling as she leaned against me. She took a deep breath. "Stephen Lister's been killed . . ."

It was strange, I tell you. Hearing it like that. Having seen this guy large as life just two days ago.

Virginia was still squeezing my shoulders.

"Not an accident?" I said.

Virginia moved her head side to side, and I felt her tears on my cheek.

She stepped back and stared at me. Then she told me the police wanted to ask her some questions. I told her to take her time. She nodded and opened the front door of the building to get some air,

28

then she turned and stared at me in the vacant way people do when they're trying to come to grips with the imponderable.

After a few minutes, we went inside. Two detectives were seated on the couch, engaged in a conspiratorial mumble. The nearest one was a stocky guy with a wrestler's physique, and when he looked up and saw me, his jaw dropped.

"Mike . . . ?"

Phil Gutierrez stood up and banged his knee on the coffee table, and didn't even seem to notice. He faced Virginia and said, "*He's* the guy?" Virginia said, "Why . . . ye-es . . ."

Phil started to shake his head. I'd known him several years. He was with the 20th Precinct. He glanced at his partner, a younger guy I didn't know, then he turned to Virginia and said, "You mind if Mike and I talk for a minute?" He indicated the bedroom door, and Virginia stared at him blankly for a moment, then in a startled voice she said, "Go ahead."

I caught the look on her face as we left the room. She had no idea what to make of this.

Phil closed the bedroom door. He stared at me, then he shifted toward the bed as if to sit down, but he seemed to think twice about parking his bulk on it. Amid the lace touches of Virginia's bedroom, he looked about as out of place as anybody could be.

"Okay," he said finally. "Who is she?"

"She's a friend."

"She told you about this?"

"Just now, at the door."

"Are you and she . . . ?"

"No . . ." I said wearily. "I've known her twelve years. She works for *City Magazine.* They're talking to me about a job."

"You're quitting the paper?"

The question contained a note of concern. I told him I hadn't made up my mind yet. Then I glanced back at the other room and asked if he'd care to tell me what happened.

"The guy got shot in his apartment. About three hours ago."

"Robbery?"

29

"Doesn't look like it."

"How come you knew he knew Virginia?"

Phil stared at me a long time. Finally he said, "Her message was on his machine."

Before I could ask anything else, he asked me, "She says she was with you all day?"

"Until about five-thirty."

"And this guy worked for her?"

I nodded.

"You knew him?"

"Only slightly."

He took his notebook out of his pocket, glanced at it, then he put it away, and I watched his eyes dart around the room, taking in everything. Then he stared at the wall for a long time as if it might contain a secret passage. Finally, he sighed and said, "Okay. Give me a minute."

He went back into the other room. I sat down on the bed and waited. After a while Phil stuck his head around the door again and beckoned me, and when I went back in the living room, Virginia was sitting stiffly on the sofa.

The other detective was asking her, ". . . And you were here from five-thirty until now?"

"Yes, I was asleep."

"You didn't make any calls?"

"In my sleep . . . ?"

Virginia was definitely recovering. I saw Phil scratch his nose to conceal a smile. He sat down opposite her, and for a moment I thought he was going to pat her hand.

"Virginia," he said. "One question . . . when did you last speak to this guy?"

"Friday." Virginia frowned.

"You're sure about that?"

"Yes . . . I tried to call him this morning . . . from Mike's place. He wasn't in. I left a message."

Phil took out his notebook and read from it, " 'When do you

30

want to come by and check out the stuff?'—that was your message, right?"

Virginia nodded.

"What stuff?"

Virginia stared at him, uncomprehending. Then she said, "He was thinking of buying some of my furniture. I'm moving."

Phil glanced at his partner, nodded slowly, and put his notebook away. Virginia stared at him, then she said, "What did you think I meant?"

Phil Gutierrez shrugged. He looked at me as if to ask, "Is she really that naïve?" Then I watched him glance around the apartment. I saw him take in the pictures of Virginia's parents in their oval frames. I saw him take in the *City Magazine* projections on the computer. And when he'd finished checking out the room, I saw him conclude that, yes, she probably was that naïve. But she was no longer a suspect.

CHAPTER FOUR

A FEW MINUTES later, Phil took me aside and told me that drugs and pornography had been found in Lister's apartment. Before he could elaborate, Virginia interrupted with a barrage of questions. Phil turned the tables on her. He asked her if she'd mind telling him a bit about Lister—background stuff, "stuff that might help"—since she was a friend.

Virginia's mouth wavered. She looked at me and got no reaction, and eventually she said, "Okay. Of course."

The cops took a seat on the couch and opened their notepads. Virginia sat in a wing chair opposite, her shoulders hunched forward as though supporting added weight. The weekend already seemed far behind us.

I sat in the far corner of the room and listened. Virginia kept looking to me and making repeated expressions of disbelief. Nothing like this had ever crossed her doorstep. She inhabited a world where death was a whisper about elderly aunts and uncles who had slipped away.

First, Phil asked her if she could shed any light on what Lister might have been up to that weekend. She said she had no idea. She vaguely remembered him saying he was planning to stay in town.

Other than that, she hadn't a clue. Then the other detective, whose name was Ray Larsen, asked her about Lister's work, and Virginia became a bit more animated. She said Lister had started out as a photographer, then he became photo editor, then senior art director. "But he was really more than that. He was the designer of the magazine."

Virginia took it upon herself to elaborate, and Phil scratched his earlobe and sat patiently throughout this until Virginia lapsed into a despondent silence. The detectives glanced at each other's notes. Virginia chewed her lip, then she asked how Lister had been killed. Phil kept his eyes lowered and said, "He stopped two bullets."

I saw Virginia flinch. When Phil next asked her about possible enemies, she began to cry.

I asked if I could get her anything, but she shook her head. She dabbed at her eyes with a tissue and said, "It's just the shock. I can't believe anyone would want to kill him . . ." Phil told her if she didn't want to continue, he'd understand, but she said no, she'd just as soon go on—if it would help. Phil gave her an encouraging smile and said any time she needed to take a break, she was to say so.

She nodded. Then he asked her, "Where was he from, Miss Danbury?"

"Glenville. Long Island."

"Does he have family there?"

Virginia said she believed his parents were dead. She had heard him mention an uncle once. She thought he might live on Long Island. Phil made a note, then he floated the question that didn't get him an answer the first time, "Anyone you know really hated the guy?"

Virginia hesitated. "Some people disliked him . . . people who resented his success . . ."

Larsen finished the answer for her. ". . . But not enough to kill him?"

Virginia shook her head. She was adamant.

Larsen gazed at her a moment, then he asked bluntly, "Did you know he took drugs, Miss Danbury?"

Virginia's mouth made an involuntary twitch. She didn't answer

34

right away, and when she did, she said, "No, I did not." But she was looking at Larsen as if to say, "So what?"

"Well, I guess you wouldn't know if he was dealing then?"

The question threw her. For a moment she looked panicked, then she said, "I told you, I didn't even know he *took* drugs."

There was a short silence. Phil said, "We found half a kilo of coke in his pad, Miss Danbury."

Phil made a slight movement of his shoulders. Virginia stared back at him and didn't say anything, then as Phil flipped his notepad to a new page, she said, "I can't believe he was dealing. Why should he be? He made enough money."

Larsen was looking at Phil, and I saw Phil nod slightly. Then Larsen asked her, "Did you know anything about his interest in pornography?"

Again, Virginia seemed thrown by the question. She looked as if she were the one being accused. Eventually she said, "He was a photographer. If he took pictures of naked women, it doesn't surprise me."

Phil waited to see if Virginia had anything more to say, and when she didn't, he said, "You mind giving us some names—people who knew him best?"

The question guaranteed we would be here a while. Virginia was on safer ground now, and within minutes the cops were scribbling furiously as she began to reel off names of people Stephen Lister knew: people in the SoHo art crowd, the photography crowd, fashion magazine editors, models, gallery owners, people who hung out in the clubs he frequented. It was a tribute to his social talents. The list continued—Virginia said at her own Memorial Day party, Stephen Lister knew more people than she did.

"Sounds like he got around," Larsen said.

Virginia gave him a baleful look, then she said, "He was very committed to his career, if that's what you mean."

I saw Phil look at me, and I had the feeling he couldn't wait to get me alone.

The questions continued a while longer. Then the room fell silent. The detectives glanced at each other's notes. Virginia blew her nose and said, "I need a drink. Anyone else?" Larsen declined. Phil said he'd take a soda. I said I'd have whatever Virginia was having.

She got up and squeezed by me on her way to the kitchen. Phil lit a cigarette and eased himself up from the couch. For a moment he gazed at the damp patch his raincoat had left behind, then he asked Larsen if they'd missed anything. Larsen studied his notes and said he had nothing else right now. Phil reached for a piece of Italian pottery and used it as an ashtray. After a moment he looked at me and said, "You're pretty quiet, Mike." I told him murder generally had that effect on me.

"Anyone hear the shots?" I asked.

"Not as far as we know."

"You found the body pretty quick."

"One of those things," Larsen said. "He left the bedroom window open. Rain starts pouring in, the woman downstairs' ceiling starts dripping. She goes upstairs, knocks, can't get no answer, so she calls the super. Super goes in with his key. He finds him . . ."

The phone rang. Virginia came in and picked it up. The call was for Phil. She handed him the phone and went back to the kitchen, and Phil tucked the receiver against his ample neck and listened for a moment before uttering a few monosyllabic grunts. He glanced at me, and for a moment I thought he was trying to discourage me from eavesdropping on his conversation. Then he said to the caller, "Guess who's here?" He tossed out my name, then he turned to me and said, "It's your pal, Richie. He's over there right now."

I nodded. Rich Bianco was with the Midtown Task Force. On cases like this, which were sure to generate press, he was brought in and paired with the precinct detectives.

Phil talked for a while longer, then he handed the phone to me. I said hi to Rich.

"What the fuck you doin' there?"

I told him the world was getting ever smaller.

"Did you know this guy?"

"Only slightly."

"What if I told you he made snuff films."

"Are you kidding me?"

"He was rigging 'em, looks like." Rich chuckled. "What's up, Mike, did you think he was a stand-up guy?"

I said, "I hardly knew him."

Rich asked if I planned on stopping by. If so, he would hold off phoning this in. I looked at my watch. It was eight-forty. If Rich were to hold off, I'd have an exclusive. I told him I'd come back with the other detectives.

When I hung up, Phil asked me if Rich had mentioned the films. I nodded. In the kitchen I could hear Virginia cracking ice. I wasn't sure how she'd take me leaving, but I had no choice. This murder was newsworthy.

When Virginia came back in, she handed Phil his soda and started to ask questions. I interrupted and said I needed a moment alone with her. We went into the bedroom. I didn't mention the films. I told her I needed to call this in to the paper, and I didn't want to do it from her place. I said it would be better if I left with the detectives. She sat on the edge of the bed, giving me a strange look, then she said, "Do you need to bring in the drugs?" I said from the sound of it, I didn't have much choice.

She nodded morosely, then we went back to the living room. Phil and Larsen were waiting, holding their raincoats. Phil thanked her and said he was sorry about what had happened to her friend. She asked what the chances were of them finding the killer and Phil told her, "Miss Danbury, right now you know as much as we do." Then he and Larsen walked out of the apartment ahead of me, and I told Virginia to fix herself another drink and take it easy. There wasn't much else I could say, and I felt like a creep for leaving her.

The rain had stopped, and after the warmth of Virginia's living room, the night air felt cool and pleasant. I waited at the side of the car, as Phil cleared some space in the rear seat. Then I got in and closed the door. I asked Phil where Lister's apartment was, and he told me, "West Eighty-eighth."

Larsen started the car. Phil lit a cigarette, and Larsen lowered the car window and wafted out the smoke. Then he turned the car north onto Central Park West and we drove the twelve blocks. Phil draped an arm over the seat back.

"You really thinking of quitting the paper, Mike?"

I told him I'd been there six years.

"I guess you guys can move around, huh?"

Larsen said he could use a transfer too—to some place where he could breathe clean air. He lowered the window again and wafted out the smoke, and Phil glared at him and said, "Listen to this shit . . ."

Larsen squared the block and drove back east on West Eighty-eighth. Halfway along the block, two radio cars were parked outside a building, their dome lights painting a row of orderly brownstones on the opposite side of the street. We parked behind them. Phil asked me what I'd been working on, and I told him I'd been covering the Koslo trial. He sneered and said, "That piece of shit," then the three of us got out and walked past a uniformed cop lazily twirling a nightstick.

I checked out the building as we went inside. It was a ten-story prewar, well-maintained aside from a few stains on the marble floor, and a couple of chips in the alabaster of the ceiling moldings. There was no doorman on duty. A sign in the lobby warned tenants not to buzz people in unannounced. Phil pointed to it and said, "Think anybody listens?" Then we took the elevator up to the seventh floor.

On the way up, Phil asked me again, "How well did you know this guy?"

Again, I told him, "Only slightly."

"What did your gut tell you?"

"He was a prick."

Phil shook his head and sighed wearily. "Friggin' playboys. I hate these cases."

The elevator wheezed to a halt at the seventh floor. We stepped off into a knot of cops. One of them was posting yellow tape around the apartment door. The others were discussing pension benefits. I could smell a trace of gunpowder in the air as we went in.

Phil said, "One second," and I waited in the narrow hallway as he and Larsen went on ahead. Then Rich Bianco appeared, stroking his mustache. He said, "Jeez, Mike, you know all the right people."

I'd known Rich four years. I'd first met him when I wrote a front-page story about a case he was working on. The day after the story ran, he'd invited me to his house in Queens, where his wife, Jeannie, cooked one of the better meals I've ever eaten in my life. Since then, he and I had been having drinks off and on. We'd become friends, and on a number of occasions he'd proved to be a valuable source.

He waved me in, and I stepped gingerly around Stephen Lister's body which was covered by a tarp and was already giving off a noxious odor. Phil crouched next to it and with a faint smile said, "Take a look, Mike. The only other ID we got's the super's."

Larsen grinned and said, "Give the guy a break." Then he wandered off into a bedroom.

Phil lifted the tarp. Stephen Lister's eyes were closed, but the lines on his face were etched in a look of shock, as if he had not expected to be shot. The face was handsome even in death, the blond good looks marred only by a trace of spittle that clung to the side of his mouth. There were two holes in the front of his shirt. He had been shot at close range—traces of unburned powder had tattooed the edges of the chest wounds. The shirt had inched up on the right side, exposing a small stab wound—the mark of the coroner's investigator— a light touch with a scalpel, a thermometer inserted and pushed down hard and then up into the liver, where the temperature would establish the official time of death. Then I noticed the faint red marks on the forearm.

"He shot up?" I said.

Rich leaned forward. "Skin-popper, looks like. Recent."

Phil was still holding the tarp. He said, "It's him, right, Mike?"

I nodded, and Rich said, "Keep this guy company. Then we'll show you his whole bag of tricks." He followed Phil into the kitchen.

I stayed where I was and looked around. The living room furnishings were expensive. A black leather couch occupied the center of the room. A polished granite table stood in an alcove. On one wall was a built-in unit containing rows of hardcover books, a Sony tape deck, a cassette player, a VCR, and a twenty-seven-inch TV. I glanced back at the door. There were no signs of forced entry.

Rich reappeared with Phil. He was holding two evidence bags. He blew latent dust off his fingertips and said, "One half kilo of coke and a quarter ounce of smack. So which was his drug of choice?"

Phil said, "He dealt the coke and popped the smack."

"All right," Rich said. "Now figure this one. The coke was in the icebox. Not a single print on the wrapper."

Phil said, "It flew in there?"

We stared at each other. Then Phil shook his head and walked over to the entertainment unit.

He picked up a cassette tape and inserted it into the VCR. Then he stood back, raised an eyebrow, and grinned. On the monitor, a grainy black-and-white film began to roll.

We stood gazing at it. On the TV screen, a woman with long hair was lying on a wrought-iron bed, having intercourse with a man wearing a black hood. The woman's legs were wrapped around the guy's torso, and as she approached orgasm, the guy leaned back and produced a knife. He ran the knife across the woman's nipples and throat, then he suddenly reared back and plunged the knife into the woman's left breast. Blood flowed from the wound, and the woman appeared to experience orgasm as she went into her death throes.

Then the TV screen went blank.

Phil ejected the tape and said, "What we got here is one dead sicko."

He walked off to the kitchen, and I asked Rich how he knew Lister was making these. He beckoned me into a small alcove bedroom. It was set up as an editing room, and in the editing machine was some 16-mm film. Rich said it was the uncut version of what I'd just seen.

Rich said, "Every guy needs a hobby."

He and I then went into the bedroom, where Larsen was gazing at several framed photographs of women, silhouettes in black and white. They were artful, tasteful even. Larsen said they were all Lister's, all signed by him anyway. He had also found some folders containing Lister's income tax returns. They were lying on the bed next to several bank statements.

I glanced over Rich's shoulder as he looked at the tax returns. They indicated that Stephen Lister had claimed an income of slightly more than $180,000. Of this, about $140,000 was salary, the rest interest and dividends. The bank statements showed balances of more than half a million, split between three accounts. There was also a brokerage account maintained by the firm of Albert G. Moran Inc. containing shares worth upward of $300,000.

"Guy was a saver," Rich said.

He stepped back from the bed, then he moved over to a dresser and said there was one other thing he wanted to show me. From a drawer he took out a Walther P. 38 automatic.

"What did he need this for?"

He examined the weapon, then looked at me pointedly. "Didn't do him much good." He set the gun down on the dresser and added, "Careful, it's loaded."

We went back into the living room. Rich stood for a moment and looked around, then he said, "So he let the guy in, the guy backs him over here . . ."

From in front of the wall unit, Phil Gutierrez let out a sardonic cackle. "Listen to this . . ." He had taken down a high school yearbook and found Lister's picture. " '. . . Stephen R. Lister . . . dark horse, plays his cards close.' " He laughed again. "Someone had this guy's number way back when." He put the yearbook back. Then he stuck his hands in his pockets, grunted, and said, "Friggin' playboy."

I looked at my watch. It was a few minutes before ten. I told Rich I needed to get going if I was to write any kind of story. He said he'd ride down with me.

I said good-night to Phil. He told me I could buy him lunch any time I felt like it. Then Rich and I walked out to the lobby where one of the uniformed cops was holding the elevator. The guy released it, and Rich and I rode down.

After a couple of floors, I asked him, "So what do you make of it?"

Rich took his eyes off the floor indicator and said, "We found eight hundred in cash in his pocket." He took a piece of gum from a pack and offered me some, then he said, "I know . . . they may have missed it, but greedy fucks, right? They'd have looked around a bit."

"Unless he had a couple of units sitting out there . . ."

Rich stared at his shoes and said, "I doubt it."

"Why?"

"Because if a deal was going down, why didn't he have the gun with him?"

I caught a cab outside the building and rode down to midtown. It had been a while since I'd been in the newsroom on a Sunday night, and when I got off the elevator at the tenth floor, the shift of subeditors looked unfamiliar. I told Rudy Kenneally, the night editor, what to expect, then I walked back to the eight-by-eight partition that was my office and knocked out about fifteen hundreds words.

It was eleven-thirty by the time I'd finished, and when I came back to the newsroom, Kenneally was out to supper. I turned the story over to a subeditor, who read it, held his nose, and pronounced it "juicy." I told him it might warrant some extra play since it wasn't likely the other papers would have it.

Then before I left, I called Virginia and asked if she wanted me to stop by. She said yes, she needed to talk, and I felt I owed it to her after leaving her earlier.

When the cab dropped me at her place, she still looked pained. I fixed her a drink, and she asked if I'd been to Lister's place with the cops. I saw no point lying to her. She asked how it was, and I said it wasn't pretty. Then she asked me about the drugs, and I told her that wasn't the half of it. From the way it looked, I said, Lister had been trying his hand at making snuff films. Virginia stared at me blankly. Then she shook her head with a kind of weary resignation.

I wasn't sure what to make of her response. I told her the cops had found one finished film, and that Lister had set up a small editing room. But when she still didn't respond, I assumed she didn't want to know any more. After a while, she told me she had called Dick Bruton earlier. She said he was stunned, of course. She hadn't bothered calling Mitch again, or Rosenberg, because she didn't want to talk to anyone who might get any sort of satisfaction out of Lister's death. I asked her, "Was Lister a thorn in Jack's flesh?"

Virginia hesitated a moment, as if unsure whether to disclose anything. Then she nodded.

After fifteen minutes or so, I reminded her it was 1:30 in the morning. I suggested she get some sleep. I left her then and walked the half block to Columbus and waited for a cab, watching the street people sift through garbage outside the restaurants. Most people were already asleep behind the dull, unfocused drone of their air conditioners, and in the sudden letdown from the events of the evening, I felt depression set in.

The feeling persisted as I rode uptown. It began to lift once I got home—after I'd watched a half hour of late-night TV and nursed a strong drink. I'd learned long ago how to take the more brutal aspects of the city and convert them into grist for work, but no matter how much I reported about homicide, I never fooled myself. There was always a wall between me and what I witnessed, and despite what I wrote for dramatic effect, I never forgot that ignominious death fell far short of tragedy.

CHAPTER FIVE

"Kincaid!"

I was standing at the main desk in the newsroom the next morning when the familiar bellow rang out, and I turned to see Ted Cantor at his office door, making a sort of pawing motion to indicate he wanted to see me. I drained my coffee and headed over to him. When he'd finished his conversation with one of the editorial page editors, he turned to me and said, "Nice story." I thanked him and said it kind of fell into my lap.

"Didn't fall into their laps." He shoved the competition's edition at me. "Three paragraphs on page ten." Then he turned and marched into his office.

I followed him in and elaborated on what had happened, without mentioning, of course, that Virginia Danbury was trying to ease me into a contributor's slot at *City*. Cantor nodded slowly, and when I'd finished, he said, "Well, I'm glad someone around here hasn't forgotten he's a newsman."

This was not so much a compliment, as it was a swipe at other reporters on the staff. Two years ago, when the editorial board had decided to offer longer, softer stories to the growing suburban audience,

Cantor, then city editor, had been one of the last holdouts. To him, the diminished size of the news hole was almost a personal affront, and he reserved scorn for reporters who had pushed to be sent to features. I'd made it a point not to push. I figured I'd have a shot, between my court series and the award nomination, and sure enough, the offer came—from Jim Lennox, the editor in chief. I asked for a day or two to think about it, and later that day Cantor had come to me and said, "You'd better take it. You'll piss him off." Because of this, I'd maintained good relations with Cantor—which was just as well, since he was now managing editor.

He helped himself to coffee, then he swiveled in his chair, picked up the paper, and declared, "Some piece of work, this Lister."

I said, "He sure was."

I could see Cantor was interested, and I told him I'd like to follow up with a profile. I'd been looking for a way to get off the Koslo trial, and I figured here was my ticket. Cantor shrugged and said, "Fine by me. What do the cops think?"

I told him it looked like a drug hit, but the cops weren't assuming anything. I said, "Maybe I could go back to his school, talk to his friends."

Cantor eyed me closely. Then he said, "You mean like you did with that Amherst kid, the one who was dealing coke on the Lower East Side?"

I nodded. Cantor looked approving, and I thought, "So far, so good."

I told him the cops would be checking to see if Lister was wealthy going in or if the money in his bank accounts had come from dealing, and he said, "Well, if it turns out he was killed for some other reason, so much the better." Then he gestured expansively and said, "Sure, you can run with this—you can still keep an eye on Koslo."

I gave up. Cantor went off to his editorial meeting, and I went back to my cubicle to find a stack of messages waiting for me.

Among them was one from Henry Drake, and when I called him back, his secretary said, "Mr. Kincaid, ah yes . . . hold on a moment." I had the feeling this was one call she'd been told to put through, no matter what.

Then Henry came on the line, and without ceremony, he said, "Well, it's taken this place by storm, I can tell you."

I formed a mental picture of what the *City* offices must be like—the conversations going on behind closed doors, the morbid atmosphere of grief mingled with conspiracy. Henry seemed unaware how I came to be covering the story, and since he didn't ask, I didn't volunteer it, but when he finally gave me the opportunity to jump in, I put him on notice that I was writing a follow-up.

He said, "So is it question time?"

I asked if he'd mind.

"Shit, no . . . go ahead, so long as we're off the record . . ."

I didn't need to pump him. He was eager to talk. When I asked what Lister was like to work with, he told me Lister had been a divisive influence from day one, always arguing for "that look" for the magazine. I pointed out that the look had been successful, and Henry sniffed. "Sure it has. But we were making money before him."

I jotted down some notes. Then I asked him to elaborate on Lister's modus operandi. Henry laughed in response.

"What modus operandi? Mike . . . try dealing with a guy with his ego. We'd lose whole articles for some layout he'd convinced Dick was more important than the Bosch triptych. I tell you, I'm not one to speak ill of the dead, but I won't miss him."

He suggested that a few other people weren't shedding any tears either, and eventually I asked him if Lister had been instrumental in getting rid of people.

"A few."

"Anyone who might have put a bullet in him?"

Henry chuckled. "You think I'd give 'em up?" He told me Lister had always gotten more credit than he deserved. "It was *his* name that appeared in *W*, but he wasn't the only one who had input."

I jotted down a few more unflattering remarks—about Lister's pursuit of women in the art department—and as I was formulating another question, a copyboy appeared at my door and pointed to a phone on the desk outside my office. I put my hand over the receiver and asked, "Who?"

"A Detective Bianco."

I put Henry on hold. Earlier that morning, I'd called Rich and left a message asking him to keep me up-to-date. When I picked up, he said there were a couple of new details. Nothing earthshaking, but he suggested I meet him at the police garage on Twelfth Avenue around three.

I said I'd be there, then I got back on the phone with Henry and listened to him dish Lister for another half hour. The picture he was giving me was of a guy who had convinced his bosses he was indispensable. According to Henry, the chaos Lister generated was allowed to run unchecked because the end result was deemed worth it. "You had to see it to believe it—Bruton strolling the corridors with the blue lines under his arm, announcing to one and all that Stephen had pulled it off again, after everyone else had been busting their hump until midnight."

I said, "Sounds like an indictment of Bruton."

"It is," Henry said. "That about says it."

I thanked him and spent an hour typing up my notes.

Around two-fifteen, I grabbed a sandwich at Costello's and caught a cab over to the West Side. By three, I was standing outside the police garage near the piers on the West Side Highway, waiting for Rich. I'd been there ten minutes, watching a transatlantic liner tie up and thinking there wasn't much that was more graceful than an ocean liner, when a working girl sauntered by in hot pants and I decided maybe there was.

I remember the moment. The spasm of horniness. I'd been thinking of Ann Raymond off and on that morning, and seeing this girl's gentle sway brought her to mind again. At least it brought to mind that moment when she'd walked away from me at the *City* office party. I didn't have a phone number for her, but I figured Virginia could give it to me, then I decided no, I'd get it some other way. Virginia would only make a big deal out of it, and there was always the threat of her actually giving a dinner party.

In my reverie I was still gazing at the hooker and at that moment Rich's Caprice drew up, and Rich lowered the window and yelled, "Out trolling?" I grinned and got in, and we drove into the garage, past several dismantled cars to a loading bay at the far end of a ramp. Rich parked and looked at his watch, but he made no move to get out, and after a moment I said, "Are we waiting for someone?"

"Yeah, Phil."

"So what's new?"

"Couple more things since we last spoke."

He gave me a look that suggested that all would be made clear, and I knew well enough not to push him. I knew how methodical he was, and he'd never let me down before, and I had the kind of access to him that no other reporter in the city had.

After a while he asked, "So how's the world of features?"

I said right now I was enjoying being on a news story again.

Then he said, "You look beat. That because of last night, or you got a new love life?"

I said, "Funny you should mention . . ." and at that moment Phil Gutierrez pulled in in a gray Mercedes 560 SEL.

Phil got out, leaving the driver's door open. He greeted me with a nod and told Rich, "Take a look." Then he stuck his hands in his pockets and waited as Rich leaned in the car and glanced at the dashboard. Rich stepped back and said, "Okay." Then he turned to me and said, "Take a look. Tell me what the odometer says." I looked and saw it read 15,619 miles.

"Lister's car?" I asked.

Rich nodded, then he turned to Phil and said, "So it's a cheesy car—maybe the thing never worked."

"Bullshit. It works fine."

Phil took a service log from his briefcase and handed it to Rich. He said, "I just got done with the mechanic. He says Lister loved this fucking car . . . brought it in last Friday right on time." He indicated the top line of the log and said, "Fourteen thousand nine hundred and sixty-three miles." Then he jerked a thumb toward the Mercedes. "Now look at it."

Rich looked again at the odometer. Phil winked at me and said, "Still the same, Richie?"

Rich did his arithmetic in his head and concluded, "Six hundred and fifty-six additional miles."

"Six fifty-*three*—you gotta subtract three for my little jaunt." Phil stuck his hands in his pockets again and said, "He ran it up Saturday night, had to be."

I asked why.

"Because we know where he was most other times. We don't know where he was Saturday night—except we got this from under the driver's seat." He dug in his briecase again and produced a toll receipt for the Lincoln Tunnel dated Saturday. Then he said, "We know he didn't use his phone Saturday night."

"You got his MUD that quick?"

"Just Saturday's and Sunday's."

MUD stood for message unit details, the records of Lister's phone calls. Phil told me Larsen knew a woman at the phone company and that the woman had given them a quick read of Saturday's and Sunday's, more or less as a favor. Then he groused about how long it would take the phone company to supply the rest of the details before leaning in the car again and popping open the trunk. From it, he took out two models' portfolios, and a set of Jersey license plates. He laid these on a bench next to several transparent bags filled with hair and fiber vacuumed from the car.

"The plates were stolen Friday," he said. "What the hell did he need these for?"

Rich glanced at the plates, then he began checking out the photos of the models. After a moment Phil said, "The broads were with him at Nell's Friday night. That's a fancy club on Fourteenth."

Rich said, "I'm hip."

"They're screaming to get these back."

Phil waited until Rich finished his perusal of the models, then he said, "Larsen checked out the two calls he made Sunday. They were both to the art director at the magazine."

"Why'd he call in?"

"They was havin' a cover retouched, or something. One call at nine-twenty, the other at eleven forty-five, and we know he ate breakfast sometime in between."

Rich told me they'd found a credit card receipt in Lister's pocket from a restaurant on Columbus. The waiter had remembered Lister and said he ate alone and read the *Times*. Then he asked Phil, "Nobody claims to have seen him after that?"

"Not so far."

Rich nodded. Then he took a slow walk the length of the car and idly removed a lump of road tar from a tire. He wiped his hands on a rag, reached in the car, and opened the glove compartment. From it, he took a Mercedes manual, a Bic pen, a couple of candy wrappers, and two cassette tapes—Peter Gabriel and Hothouse Flowers. He studied the tapes for a moment, then he said, "Whatever happened to 'Lonely Teardrops'? It didn't get much better than that." He glanced at me, and I asked him if they'd found any driving gloves at the apartment.

Rich studied me a moment. Then he leveled a finger at me and said, "Gotcha. He comes home Sunday, dumps the flake in the icebox, he's still wearing the driving gloves. No prints on the wrapper. Nice try, Mike . . . only thing is . . . no, we didn't find no driving gloves."

He grinned and took a look under the car seats, and Phil said, "You won't find nothing, Rich. We vacuumed."

Rich closed the car door and said, "Okay, let's go over it again."

He started to run down what else they knew: Lister had been at Nell's until late Friday night. A neighbor had seen him leave his apartment Saturday morning around eleven. From another credit card receipt, they'd established that he'd eaten lunch that Saturday at the Russian Tea Room, but neither the maitre d' nor any waitress remembered him. The restaurant bill indicated he'd eaten with someone, but so far nobody knew who.

Phil flipped his notebook open and said, "And late Saturday afternoon, his agent called him at home . . ."

Rich lit a cigarette and said, "Fair enough."

Phil waited a moment, then he glanced at the car again and said, "So he didn't run up this kind of mileage driving around Manhattan. Where did he go Saturday night?"

"Washington, D.C.?" Rich suggested.

Neither Phil nor I answered, and after a moment, Phil went off to tell the mechanics to work up the car in case anything was hidden inside it. I asked Rich if there was anything he wanted me to omit from what I might write. He said there was nothing he could think of. He thought it might even be useful if I mentioned the mileage, in case Lister had visited a friend Saturday night. If it turned out he had, and the trip was unrelated to his death, it could save them some time. Then he said he planned to talk to people at *City Magazine* tomorrow.

I passed up his offer of a ride across town and used one of the mechanic's phones to call in for messages. There were half a dozen calls and two messages from Virginia Danbury, and when I called her back, she made a point of telling me she had called me several times. She sounded faintly irritated, and I assumed she was tired. Then she said she'd like to meet for a drink, and I agreed to meet her at the Montana Bar on Broadway.

When we hung up, I chatted with Phil for a while. He mentioned that Larsen had received a call from Lister's uncle, and that the uncle was arranging to collect his nephew's body. Then we wandered down to the far end of the garage where the mechanics were already taking apart the Mercedes. One of the mechanics slid out from under the car and told Phil that the car had weighed in exactly at its blue book weight. Phil said, "Take it apart anyway." He stood with his hands in his pockets as the mechanic slid back under the car, then he nudged a shoulder toward the car and said to me, "If I was the uncle, I'd be more interested in claiming this."

Around five, I left the garage and caught a cab uptown. I was at the bar a few minutes before Virginia, and when she came in, she said she would rather sit at a table. I wasn't sure if she was still upset, it was hard to tell, but in any event we headed for a far corner, and as soon as we sat down, the waiter came over and we ordered drinks. Once he went away, I said, "I guess you had a rough day"—something like that—and she said, "That's for damn sure." She didn't say anything else right away, and after a short silence I asked if she'd spoken to Mitch. She said he'd stopped by. I asked how that was.

"About what I expected."

She was looking at me in a deliberate sort of way.

I said, "How's Mitch's alibi?"

She didn't smile. She raised her shoulders a little and said, "He was out on Long Island—in his boat." Then she reached into her purse, took out a printed pamphlet, and handed it to me. "He asked me to give you this."

It was a guide to investments. Three weeks ago, I'd run into Mitch in a bar and had asked him for advice on setting up a college fund for Jackson—Mitch knew the world of finance as well as anyone. Virginia said, "He wants you to look this over and call him." Then she said, "I never got around to setting up your meeting with Jack—it wasn't the day for it."

I said I wasn't surprised. I told her there was no rush. And it wasn't until a minute later that I realized she hadn't intended the remark to be apologetic. In the meantime, the waiter brought our drinks, and when he went away, I told her I'd spent the afternoon with the cops and that I was following up on the story. She stared at me a moment, then she said in an injured way, "Are you telling me this is an official interview?"

I said it wasn't any kind of interview. But since we were friends, I just thought she ought to know. But she continued to stare at me, and eventually she said, "What good do you think you're doing yourself—writing about this?"

I said, "Come again."

"I thought you worked in features . . ."

"I do . . ."

But I could feel the temperature starting to plummet. And I began to realize what was nagging her. I said, "Hey, a story lands in your lap, you generally follow it."

"Is that so?"

We faced each other in silence. She was still looking at me critically.

"Look," I said after a moment. "I know you worked with this guy, and maybe he was your friend . . . but I can't help that."

This time she didn't respond, and again we faced each other in silence. And this time I waited, wondering if she'd back off.

But as the silence continued, I could see she wasn't about to, and I was starting to feel faintly irritated. I'd been in situations before when the job put me at odds with friends, but I'd assumed Virginia would

53

understand. After all, she was in the media business . . . she knew reporters had to step on toes from time to time.

Eventually she uttered a short sigh and said, "Do you really think nobody's going to notice?"

Maybe I was being naïve. I said, "Are you telling me you're bent out of shape about this?"

Virginia folded her arms. "Dick is . . . and I don't blame him. How would you react if someone embarrassed *your* magazine?"

The comment pissed me off. I took a sip of my drink. Then I said, "*I* didn't embarrass the magazine. Let's not confuse the issue here."

She didn't answer right away. She stared off at the bar for a moment, then she said, "Look, Mike—"

But I was hot now. I interrupted. "No, you look. I don't give a shit what Bruton thinks, and I don't really care for *your* take on this."

She stared at me a moment, then she said, "I'm just making you aware of the realities . . ."

"What realities?"

"The realities of interviewing at *City*. Dick has some say."

"Fuck Dick."

She sighed. "All right. If that's the way you want it . . ." She hesitated, then she said, "But since you ask . . . yes, it is a problem for me . . . on a personal level. That's why I wanted to see you. I didn't like what you wrote."

"Why not?"

"Because the man was murdered, after all . . ."

"For dealing drugs . . ."

"You don't know that! Who knows how long he'd had those drugs? . . . They could have been around . . . since . . . since the mid-eighties . . ."

I felt like I'd been blindsided. I said, "Are you kidding me? They find snuff films in his pad? Half a kilo of coke? What was he gonna do—blow half a kilo up his own nose?"

"I don't know!" Virginia's voice was rising. "He had a lot of art crowd friends. So he had a few drugs! So he played around, making some dirty movie . . . !"

I told her that was an understatement.

"Oh really? And you're Mr. Self-Righteous, who has to drag in all this. The man isn't entitled to a private life, because you've decided it's all fair game. No mention of his good points. None. The way you made it sound, he came off like some total creep! . . . Talk about trial by press . . . !"

She broke off, searching for words, and I suddenly got the picture. There was a difference in her mind between Stephen Lister and his art world circle, and some street dealer selling grams in the school yard. I said, "Are we excusing this guy because he was artistic?"

Virginia glared at me, then she said, "Maybe there's nothing to excuse him for. At least, you could have given him the benefit of the doubt."

I couldn't believe this. We were making an exception for this guy. Virginia glanced around the restaurant, and for the first time she seemed aware that her voice had risen. Then she ground out her cigarette and said, "So he got high once in a while? So what? Who knows what he might have been going through?"

I didn't answer for a while. I couldn't understand why she was taking this tack. Finally I said, "If you're bent on defending this guy, you're setting yourself up for a fall. In a couple of days, the cops'll know a lot more—"

She interrupted, "You don't know that. I spoke to a lot of people today who knew him better than I did, and they knew nothing about any dealing, or needle marks . . ."

"So he didn't go public . . ."

". . . including Ann."

I blinked. "Ann?"

"Ann Raymond . . . remember . . ."

I stared at her blankly. "*She* went out with him?"

"For a while, yes."

Virginia's tone was indignant. She was looking at me as if to ask, "Why should that surprise you?" It was the second bizarre turn in the conversation, and ultimately the more depressing one. I felt the air go out of me. I said, "Oh . . . that's nice."

She caught my drift. For a moment she maintained her look of disapproval, then her lip curled and she said, "You really are a self-righteous bastard, aren't you?" Without waiting for an answer, she went on, "This is a problem for you, isn't it?"

"What the fuck would you think?"

She looked at me with increasing scorn, then she said, "I don't believe this . . ."

She fell silent for a while, then she said, "Actually, self-righteous is an understatement. You paint everyone black because that's the way you want to see them."

I said the first thing that came into my head.

I said, "It doesn't strike me as so bizarre not to want to sleep with an AIDS risk."

In the silence that followed, I thought Virginia was going to walk out. Then she sighed, and gazed off coldly, and finally she said, "There're no shades of gray with you, are there?" I didn't answer, and she went on, "Ann says she never saw needle marks on his arm, but I don't suppose you'd be interested in knowing that."

"In court they'd call that hearsay."

"Don't give me that crap."

"It isn't crap."

"It's not even funny." She stared at me angrily, then she said, "It's a pity because she liked you. God knows why."

I felt a moment of conflict. But I was still reacting to Ann Raymond having dated this guy, and to Virginia's double standard. I told her she seemed to have one rule for the privileged, another for the lowlier classes, and after that conversation was difficult.

Finally, I reached for the tab. Virginia snatched it back and said she wasn't having this construed as an interview. She paid, and I let her, and we walked out, and as we stood outside on the sidewalk, I felt we should both take a step back, go back inside the bar, cool off and listen to the other's point of view at least. But when I made the first move, I got snubbed. Virginia stalked off and hailed a cab.

I let her go. Then I walked ten blocks to cool off before I got a cab.

I was still feeling blindsided. And despondent. And maybe a little vulnerable. And I knew why. Since my divorce, I'd lost a few friends, and I didn't want to lose any more, including this one. Maybe these losses had caused me to put a greater value on friendships, or maybe this was insecurity, or a protective self-interest, but either way—I found myself feeling a little fragile as I rode uptown.

At least for a while. Then, stubbornness and pride began to reassert itself, and I began to feel I had no reason to have to defend myself. And having shored myself up, I found myself making excuses for Virginia. She was still upset over Lister's death, and maybe she wasn't seeing clearly. She'd seen virtue in this guy, and maybe she didn't want to admit to a lack of judgment . . . Then, I thought, no, that wasn't it at all—this was an exercise in damage control. She and Bruton were trying to paper over who Lister was because, under the circumstances, what else could they do?

The cab dropped me on Broadway and I picked up some groceries, and when I got home, I tried to work, but I was still feeling irritable. It was hot, and the fan kept blowing my notes, and eventually I went out for a drink. When I got back, I wrote a brief follow-up story and phoned it in, and I didn't pull any punches, knowing that Dick Bruton would be poring over every line.

But when I'd finished, it was still only nine-thirty and I was restless. I took a shower and watched a ball game for a while, and at one point I thought about going out again. I even thought about calling a woman I'd dated a few months back, but I decided not to. I'd stopped seeing her abruptly, and I had a pretty fair idea of the reaction I'd get.

Eventually I went to my office, poured another drink, and sat at my desk. But evocations of loss seemed to be everywhere that night. Down on Riverside Drive, I could see a couple standing by a car, and even from my window, a hundred feet away, I could tell things weren't going well for them. They were thrashing something through. A couple of times the guy reached for the girl's hand, but each time she drew it back smartly, and finally I saw her shout something at him and walk off.

I came back into the living room and lay on the couch, and before I knew it, I was thinking about how it ended for Maggie and me. We'd been to a movie one night, and we were walking home, and I'd noticed she was quiet, but she could be that way at times. I tend to be quiet too after movies—I hate to go to some noisy bar and plunge into small talk. But that evening after the movie the silence between us grew longer, and by the time we got to the apartment I had the feeling something was going to be resolved one way or the other.

She was sitting on the sofa when it started. She said, "I can't go on like this."

I knew what she was feeling. I'd been feeling the same way for months. She'd tried, she said, but it wasn't working anymore, and as her words resounded, I got up and went to the window.

"What's wrong with us?" I said.

She didn't answer for a while, then she said, "We're very different. Sometimes I think we always were." I looked at her and felt pity for both of us. We were on the verge of being a family no longer.

"What about Jackson?" I said.

"Jackson will be okay. You know that."

There was another silence, then I said, "You're going back to California, and he's going to live with you? Is that it?"

"You don't really want him growing up here, do you?"

"Why not?" I snapped. "What's wrong with here?" It had been a major point of difference between us.

We went back and forth, covering the same ground, and about two hours later we reached a point where there was nothing more to say. We went to bed and lay in silence for a long time, then, at some point, we made love. Afterward, Maggie began to cry. She sat up and leaned forward, and I sat looking at the graceful arc of her back. After a while, she said, "It doesn't change things . . . we both want something different . . ."

A week later, she moved back to California. Jackson stayed with me until she found a place. Then he moved back with her. A month later, he told me on the phone, "Mom's dating a new guy," and over the next few months he let slip a few details, and eventually Maggie told me she was seeing someone. Six months later her new boyfriend moved in with her, and once I accepted this, things began to seem more defined.

Compared to most divorces, ours was easy. I agreed to pay support. She didn't ask for alimony. I slapped on my social grimace and ventured out into the world and tried to pretend the transition would be okay. It wasn't. I found I didn't want tenderness in relationships, nor anything conventional or romantic. What I wanted was distraction. And sex.

For a while I'd run around with an actress, but she seemed to have vanished into thin air, and lately I'd been searching for something, or rather someone, to fill the void. And for the past few days I'd thought Ann Raymond might fit the bill. I'd already conjured up erotic images of her, based on the few moments I'd spent with her. So she'd run with Lister and his crowd. I know this is perverse, but that interested me.

When I went to bed that night, I was feeling some irritation for having let my prudish side get the better of me, and for having said what I'd said about her to Virginia. Some part of me had meant it—still, as I dozed off that night, I was thinking that there was nothing to stop me from calling her—if I really wanted to kick up some dust, and see what she was about.

CHAPTER SIX

I DIDN'T CALL her, however. The next morning, caution got the better of me. I realized that if Virginia had been offended by what I'd written, Ann Raymond probably had been too. I called Virginia instead to see if I could smooth things over. Despite the previous evening, I thought we might be able to agree to differ. It didn't work out that way, and I guess what was in the paper that morning under my byline didn't help.

Virginia sounded sullen. I told her, under the circumstances, we should definitely forget about the *City* interview. She agreed, and when I added that I didn't want this to do permanent damage to our friendship, she sighed and said, "We'll just have to see." I saw no point going over the same ground again, and I suggested we both take a time-out for a week or so. She told me she had to take another call.

That morning I made some preliminary notes for the profile. Lister's demise, it seemed to me, was his failure to appreciate that other people were prepared to be more ruthless than he was. I figured it was only a matter of time before Rich could confirm that Lister was dealing, and when I called him later that morning he had some news: Lister had been making cash deposits every month for the past few years, in amounts of about eight or nine thousand dollars, a hair under the limit of ten thousand, which would require the bank to report such deposits.

"So he was dealing?" I said.

"Sure looks that way."

Rich then told me he'd met Lister's uncle the previous evening. "He was a nice old guy," he said. "Works for social security out in Hempstead." Rich chuckled. "He made a point of telling me not believe everything I read in the papers."

"You set him straight?"

"Hell no. Nice old guy like that. He told me he raised Lister after his folks died. Says he got him into photography. Says Lister was toting a camera around even as a kid."

He said he'd asked the uncle if he knew where Lister might have gone the Saturday night before he was killed, but that the uncle had claimed he hadn't spoken to Lister since Easter. Then he said, "Here's something though. I spoke to the bank manager this morning. He says Lister called him two weeks ago about a line of credit."

"What the hell would he want that for? He had a million liquid."

"A huge deal, maybe."

"Maybe."

I got the uncle's name from Rich and thought about calling him, but decided to hold off. And I was still working on my notes when Henry Drake called me. Word had traveled fast. Henry wanted to know why I'd backed out of the interview at *City*. I told him.

"Those shitheads . . ." Henry set about castigating Bruton and Virginia. He doubted Jack knew the real reason I'd backed out, but he planned to let him know. I said I'd sit this one out. Then Henry asked if I'd read Bruton's tribute to Lister. Apparently the competing paper had carried a quote of his that morning. I said I hadn't read it. "Pious son of a bitch. Make sure you don't miss it." Then Henry laughed, and after telling me Bruton was dismissing Lister's involvement in snuff films as some sort of obscure research, he said, "You really want to get Dick's goat, show up for the funeral Friday . . . It's in Glenville. We're all going. It's a command performance."

I wasn't sure if Henry meant it as a joke. But the more I thought about it off and on that week, the more I realized the funeral might not be a bad place to start. It might provide some color, a lead even. It might also give me some insight into Lister's past—a past he'd probably put behind him once he migrated the forty miles west to Manhattan.

I spent the next few days at the Koslo trial, then on Thursday I ran into Cantor in the newsroom. He asked what was going on with the case, and I told him I'd been keeping in touch with Bianco, but there were no major developments. Then I brought up the funeral. Cantor said, "Sure. Go." He was on his way to a meeting with Lennox, and I went to my office and called Henry and asked him what time the funeral was to take place.

He said, "You're really going?"

I said that's what I had in mind.

Henry pronounced the move "ballsy."

Glenville turned out to be a typical mid-Island town, about ten miles from the North Shore, with a well-kept main street, three sets of lights, a movie theater, and a library. On the drive in, I passed a well-tended golf course and a country club—there was money here, clearly. There was also a profusion of fake colonial signs, hinting the place had been around since the Revolutionary War, but despite these the town did not seem to have much to offer the casual visitor, and after I'd asked directions to the Episcopal church, I was kicking my heels with an hour to kill.

I crossed the main street to a deli and was ordering a sandwich when a voice behind me said, "Come to pay your respects, Mike?" I turned to face Mitch Danbury.

He was about the last person I expected to see. I said, "Not exactly," and I asked what he was doing here, and he quickly assured me this wasn't his idea.

He told the counterman to cancel the sandwich, then he steered me out of the place, insisting we find a bar, because no way was he sitting through this thing without a drink.

As we walked out, he said, "You think I'd choose to go to this guy's funeral?" He told me there'd been a concerted effort at the magazine to put on a show of support for Lister. Then he admitted he had been persuaded to attend by Virginia and Lisa.

I said, "Yeah, I heard about Lisa."

Mitch looked at me in a droll way as we walked to the nearest bar. We entered through a Western-style saloon door and took a table at a window open to the summer heat. Mitch seemed pleased to see me. We ordered drinks and sandwiches, and I noted he'd put on a few pounds since I'd last seen him. He grinned and said he'd earned it, then he asked me, "So, was Lister really into dealing and snuff films?"

I said it sure looked that way, and Mitch shook his head in disgust. Then he told me he'd heard all about my spat with Virginia.

I asked if she was still chewing on it.

"You know what she's like. She's got her head totally up her ass on this one."

I was glad someone at least was in my corner. I told him I hoped the thing would blow over, but he said, "Don't be so sure." Then he gave me a rundown of his recent problems with his sister.

First, he said, she seemed to have forgotten who she owed her job to. He felt this was partly his fault because a year or so after he'd raised the money for the magazine he'd taken a backseat. Stacovich was now the largest shareholder, and Stacovich wanted his own man— Bruton—as publisher. Mitch said he could understand Virginia wanting to get along with Bruton, but he felt she'd taken it too far. He said, "She backed Dick one hundred percent, and I warned her about Lister a couple of times, but she didn't listen."

He slathered his sandwich with mustard and went on, "You get a guy like him in the mix, it's bound to cause problems. I know he was a headache for Jack—I had a drink with Jack a couple of weeks ago, and all he did was bellyache about Lister." He chewed his sandwich for a moment, then he said, "For all his talent, you don't let a loose cannon like him roll around."

I said, "So your problems with him weren't only because of the summerhouse?"

"Oh that." Mitch wiped his mouth on a napkin. "Virginia told you about that, did she?" I nodded, and he said, "Well, it wasn't only that, but you could call it the capper."

He then launched into a long account of how Lister had been out to their house, and had taken pictures of the kids of some friends of his, ostensibly as a favor. The punch line was, Lister had then billed the couple for three hundred dollars.

I asked, "Did they like the pictures?"

Mitch scoffed and said, "He had a lot of class. Turning something like that into a business venture." He then told me that Lister had treated the place like a hotel, and that if he hadn't put his foot down, he'd have spent half the summer chauffeuring Lister's friends back and forth to the station. Then he asked me if there was anything new on the investigation front.

I said, "Not yet."

"So how many detectives do they assign to a case like this?"

"Three, so far."

"God, if I'm ever murdered, I hope the cops are so thorough."

Then he dropped the subject. He asked if I'd had a chance to look over the college fund forms yet, and I said I'd only glanced at them. He told me he could save me some time if I felt like swinging by his office next week, and we settled on a day. Then he checked his watch and said he'd better get over to the church. He'd agreed to meet Lisa before the thing started, and she'd been on his case lately about not showing up on time for things.

I said, "This sounds serious."

Mitch grinned but didn't offer any comment, and we were on our way out when I asked him how the *City* stock was holding up. It had taken a hit after what I wrote the previous Sunday night.

He grinned and said, "It's coming back—no thanks to you."

I wasn't sure how much he owned, but he grinned again and said, "Don't worry, Mike, I'm well diversified." Then he mentioned that he'd heard Bruton had been a buyer in recent weeks. He added with another grin, "Maybe that's why he's so pissed off at you."

I walked him back to his car and told him I planned to wait around until after the funeral started rather than risk any run-ins.

Mitch laughed, and I told him I'd been tossed out of a few formalities in my time, but never a funeral.

He drove off, and I walked back along the main street, where the poplars were hanging listless in the heat. My car was no longer in the shade, and I rolled the windows down and turned the air-conditioning on for a while, and when it was cool enough, I got in and rolled the windows back up and sat there, checking my watch a couple of times, and watching a couple of teens cruise the main street in a dragster. For some reason, I pictured Lister at nineteen, driving to the North Shore in a car like this, with some dewy-eyed little thing on his arm. I figured those were the continuities in his life—cars and women.

Around ten minutes to two, I took a swing by the church. A line of cars was already parked out front, and by the time I squared the block, the line had increased. I pulled up half a block away and sat with the car window down and watched tony models and art world people making their way in. A minute later, two cars pulled up in quick succession, and the contingents from *City Magazine* got out— Bruton and Virginia from one car, Jack Rosenberg, Henry, and Lisa Dennison from another. They congregated on the church steps, and I saw Mitch step out of the vestibule and join them. Eventually, they all trooped inside, and around five minutes after two, I decided that anyone who might recognize me was already in the church. I got out and walked up the church steps.

The service still hadn't started, and I heard the minister telling an older man in a dark suit that maybe he should wait another five minutes in case people from the city had been delayed by traffic. The older man nodded. He had a grave, hesitant face, and I guessed he might be Lister's uncle.

When he and the minister went inside, I moved over to a group of people who had been standing next to them. This was the smoking contingent, who were delaying going inside until the last minute. Most of them were in their thirties and they looked like locals, and I asked one man where the cemetery was, hoping to strike up a conversation. He gave me directions, but he wasn't forthcoming, and then he and his wife went inside the church.

I approached a sandy-haired fellow in a JC Penney suit and asked

him how far it was to the cemetery. He said, "About ten minutes."
Then he shook his head and said, "Tragic business." I agreed, and the
guy asked how I knew Stephen. I said he had illustrated an article of
mine, which at least was true. Then I asked him if he was an old
friend, and he said, yes, he and Stephen had gone to high school
together, and he wished Stephen had stayed in Glenville in view of
what had happened. Then he added, "Mind you, I guess you couldn't
expect that, not with his talent," and he was about to say something
else, but at that moment he was distracted by the arrival of a dignified
woman in her late fifties, who was with a younger man. My acquaintance said hello to the woman, and his manner was almost respectful.

I didn't catch the woman's name, but when she and her escort
went into the church, the guy turned to me and said in a reverent
tone, "Walt Palmer's widow."

"The congressman?"

He nodded.

There was no time for me to ask any more. The service was
starting. I moved inside with the stragglers and took a pew about six
rows from the back.

The organist began to play a sad stirring hymn, evoking in a
cicatrix of my memory the last time I'd heard it, at my father's funeral.
I joined in the chorus, getting along without a hymnbook, until a man
in front of me glanced around, saw I was without one, and handed
one to me. Ten rows forward, on the far side of the church, I could
see the City contingent. But nobody turned around, and I overcame
any lingering qualms about being invited to leave.

The choir was into its second hymn when I glanced around; and
when I saw what I saw, I did a double take. There was Ann Raymond—
three rows back, on the far side of the church—but it wasn't merely
the fact that she was standing there that I reacted to. It was what she
was wearing.

A slim-fitting black suit and a hat with a half veil, and the
effect was not only striking, it suggested some mischievous underwear
underneath. She looked like a movie mistress, determined to attend,
despite the family's objections.

For the moment, her head was down in her hymnbook. Then she

looked up, and I thought she'd noticed me, but with the veil it was hard to tell. A moment later, I stole another glance. This time she was staring off at the church wall, and I gazed at her freely, wondering what had prompted her to dress the part.

Then the hymn ended and we sat down. In the pulpit, the minister was saying, ". . . The circumstances of Stephen's death are tragic. But let us use these moments not to dwell on the pain his death has caused us. Let us remember he now resides in God's house. It was God who brought Stephen into this world, and to God he has returned . . ." I looked over at Ann Raymond and saw she was sitting motionless, her hands clasped in front of her, and as I continued to stare at her, her eyes veered toward me.

It was the briefest of contacts, but her mouth flickered slightly before she looked away. And as I faced the front again, I chuckled inwardly, wondering how she felt about being on the receiving end of an improper thought in church.

The minister ended his liturgy. He said we would now sing hymn number thirty-one. The congregation stood.

It was warm in the church. The man in front of me was mopping his brow. The last hymn seemed interminable, the last prayer mercifully brief, and when the service finally ended, I got up and headed outside, ahead of the pallbearers. I lit a cigarette and stood on the church steps, thinking I should probably stay out of trouble, go to my car, jot down a few notes, and then follow the cortege to the cemetery. But I'd barely taken a few puffs, when Ann Raymond came out.

We were alone on the church steps and she stared at me. Her veil was parted slightly, and she looked very pretty. I said, "Hi," and in response she continued to stare, then, as I took a step toward her, she shook her head in a resigned sort of way and said, "Don't get too near. I'm an AIDS risk, remember."

I felt my cheeks getting warm. She continued to stare at me, and I guess she waited long enough to see the full impact of her remark. Then she turned and marched off toward a black Saab, and as I watched her leave, I had the feeling she had thoroughly enjoyed the moment.

I continued to gaze after her as she drove away, feeling the sting of the rebuff and wanting to throttle Virginia. Then people began to emerge from the church, and I moved to one side of the church steps and stood there smarting. I lit another cigarette, and when I finally glanced back at the church steps, the *City* contingent had emerged, and when I next looked that way, Dick Bruton was striding toward me.

He started talking before he reached me.

"This is the height of bad taste. It's about as low as your reporting . . ."

At any other time, I might have come back at him, but just listening to this guy made me feel weary. I could see the rest of the *City* contingent staring at us, and finally I was aware Bruton had finished speaking and seemed to be waiting for my reaction. I said, "Is that on or off the record, Dick?" His jaw wavered a moment, then he strode away.

I decided to pass on the cemetery. I'd had enough for one day. I drove back to the bar where I'd had lunch with Mitch and ordered a straight scotch. Earlier, I'd figured I might stop by the local paper and see if they'd run any quotes from Lister's old school friends—friends I could follow up on—but I was no longer in the mood to have any doors slammed in my face.

I ordered a second scotch and began chatting with the bartender, and by the time he'd bought me a drink, and an hour had gone by, I was feeling less dejected. In fact, I was feeling a marked shift of mood. I was recovering from the feeling of being ganged up on, and before I knew it, I was getting fired up. It wasn't only the liquor. I have a slow burn, and sometimes it takes people messing with my head to get me fired up.

After three shots of booze, I was ready to return the favor. I knew I needed to talk to someone who'd known Lister intimately, and if that happened to coincide with another area of intrigue, so be it. I said good-bye to the bartender, and headed west on Route 25, and as I crossed the Throgs Neck Bridge late that afternoon and drove upstate, I made a solemn promise to myself that I wouldn't be deterred once the booze wore off.

In the morning I woke up with a headache, but the mountain air soon got rid of that, and I stuck to my resolve.

At nine-thirty, I made a call to information, then I checked a road map, and an hour later I was driving up a narrow lane between a stand of pines. After a mile, I slowed to check the names on mailboxes, and when I finally found the name I was looking for, I turned into a gravel driveway and parked the Buick next to a Georgian house about five miles east of the town of Rhinebeck.

It was a great-looking house, with a shingle roof and freshly painted shutters. A neat lawn and flowerbeds bordered one side of the property. I sat for a moment and admired the place, then as I was getting out of the car, I saw the front door opening, and Ann Raymond appeared, wearing jeans and a green sweater.

She stared at me in surprise, and I enjoyed the moment. It was worth showing up here just to see the look on her face, even if the direct approach didn't work. She recovered and folded her arms, and as I walked toward her, I didn't say anything until I was up close.

Then I said, "Remember me?"

"What are you doing here?"

She continued to stare at me, then she asked again what I was doing here. I said I was in the neighborhood.

She looked exasperated for a moment, as if trying to decide the best way to get rid of me. Then her attitude shifted and she said, "That's nice. Don't you believe in phones?"

I said I didn't have a phone.

"So what are you doing here?"

I told her I'd like to ask her a few questions. She blinked and gave me the exasperated look again, but I had the feeling we were already into the game.

"About what? Stephen?"

"Yes."

"Why on earth should I talk to you?"

"Well, we didn't have much time yesterday. You left kind of quick."

I could only guess at the extent of her involvement with Lister, but I'd decided the previous evening that if he had meant a great deal to her, she wouldn't waste much time telling me to get lost. But so far she hadn't, and so I took a chance and laid it on thick. I said I wanted someone to fill me in about what a wonderful guy he was because I'd had a hard time getting a positive point of view. For a moment, the remark threw her, then she said, "Really? I'm surprised, considering how many people came to his funeral."

She smiled, as if pleased with her smart comeback. But she still hadn't told me to get lost, and I had the feeling the longer this game went on, the better a shot I had. We continued to stare at each other, and finally I said, "Tell you what. Since I drove over here, why don't we go get a cup of coffee? Give you a chance to make up your mind if you want to talk or not."

She said, "I have all the coffee I need, right here, thanks."

I said, "That's fine. I'll have coffee here then."

We continued to face each other, and I just stood rock-still, like I was never going to budge, until eventually she planted her hands on her hips and said, "You have some nerve."

"I do, don't I?"

I was still counting on the hint of mutual attraction, but I wasn't making any bets.

Eventually she said, "What makes you think I have anything to say?"

"Anything nice, you mean?"

"Anything at all?"

I said I wouldn't know until we'd talked some.

She was silent for a moment, then she said, "You can be pretty offensive, you know that?"

"Yeah, I'm a little pushy."

"I'll say." She shook her head a little, then she said, "Why should I talk to you after what you wrote?"

"Like I said, I just figured you might have something positive to say."

"Like you really care?"

"Maybe I do. I'm not as closed-minded as some people might think."

71

She studied me closely, then she said, "Your stock's pretty low right now with some people we know in common. Doesn't that bother you?"

"Not much."

She studied me closely, then she surprised me. She laughed and said, "Well, that's one thing in your favor."

Her shoulders rose and fell in a short sigh, and I had the feeling she was wavering. Then she took a step to one side and leaned against the door, and eventually she said, "Here's the deal. You can come in, because I have a couple of questions to ask you. But I still don't know if I have anything to say. Is that understood?"

I said it was understood, and she eyed me cautiously, then she turned toward the door, and I followed her inside. We were over the first, and most difficult, hurdle.

She led me through a living room furnished with pine and antiques, and into a large country kitchen, where a computer stood on a table next to a vase of flowers. It was a warm room, not a showpiece but a room you could live in, work in. I glanced around, and after a moment or two I asked her how long she'd had the place.

"Couple of years."

I said it was nice, and she looked at me as she poured coffee as if to warn me not to get too personal. I asked her if she'd given up on the city to live here, and she said, "I still have a place in town, but I try to spend as little time there as possible." She handed me my coffee and said, "Well, I guess you might as well sit down."

I took a seat at the table, and she turned off the computer, and for a moment the only sound was the chatter of blue jays outside. We faced each other and I was very aware that I was alone with her in this house in the country, then she broke the silence, asking me how I'd found out where she lived. I said Virginia had told me a week ago—"in another context." I grinned. She didn't smile. She nodded slowly. Then she took a sip of her coffee and said, "I meant what I said, you know?"

"About what?"

"About asking you some questions."

I told her to fire away.

She stared out the window for a moment, then she sipped her coffee, set her cup down, gave me the deliberate look again, and finally asked, "Why did you make that nasty crack about me?"

I'd expected a question about what I'd written in the paper. Not this. And when I didn't answer right away, she tilted her head to one side and looked at me curiously, waiting. Finally, I said I hadn't intended for the remark to be passed on.

"That isn't what I asked. I'm curious about why you made it."

"I was arguing with Virginia at the time."

She raised her shoulders a bit wearily. Then, with a hint of impatience, she said, "You're still not answering my question. You said you didn't think it was smart to sleep with an AIDS risk—right?"

"That's close to it." I was feeling a little cornered.

"Okay, setting aside the presumption . . . what did you mean?"

I shrugged. "Isn't it obvious?"

"Not to me."

"Well . . . he had a couple of skin-pop marks on his arm . . ."

"A couple?"

I nodded.

"You're sure about that?"

"Yes." She didn't respond right away, and I went on, "I didn't mean anything by the remark. It came out in the middle of a fight with Virginia. I doubt he was the type to share his needles . . ."

"Never mind that. Didn't Virginia tell you the marks weren't there when I dated him?"

"Yes, she did."

"So why didn't you believe her about me?"

I didn't answer right away. I was about to say, "Well, I didn't know you," but that sounded trite, and before I could formulate a better response, she said, "At one time you were interested in me . . ."

The remark caught me off guard. She smiled slightly, then she said, "Didn't you trust yourself? Was that it?"

Her tone had changed. I wasn't sure if this was her game, her way of establishing control. Then she smiled again, and I felt something stir, and again I was aware that we were alone in this silent house in the country.

After a moment, I said, "Well, maybe not."

She was sitting six feet away, still studying me. Then she said, "That's really what I wanted to ask. You want to think about it . . . think about what it says about you?"

I shifted slightly and said, "Okay, I'll think about it."

"Good."

She seemed satisfied, having put me on the spot, and we were silent for a moment. Then I said, "You said there were a couple of questions?"

"Well yes. The other one ties in. If a reporter says he's interested in getting at the truth, why wouldn't he take the time to call me and ask me about something like that?"

Again, I was feeling cornered. I said, "You're right. My mistake. I should have."

"I think you should. Don't you find it interesting—if what you say is true—that this man recently started popping drugs?"

I said I guess so. And she didn't take her eyes off me. She just sat there looking at me, and I was feeling off-balance, and having a hard time deciding what to say next, and eventually, I said, "So how do you feel about talking?"

"Is that all you want?"

I was thrown. I didn't say anything.

She smiled, then she said, "I'm not really sure how honest a person you are."

"Why do you say that?"

"Because the way you were looking at me at that party, I definitely had the feeling you wanted to fuck me. And I just wondered why you're not the type to come right out and say it."

Her words resonated. I could feel the warmth on my cheeks. And several seconds rolled by, then I said, "I guess Lister was the type."

"Definitely . . . or have you changed your mind . . . because you found out I was involved with him?"

My mind was in a fog. I hadn't expected this. She had turned the tables on me, and all I could do was mumble something about finding her attractive, then suggest that maybe we ought to talk first. Then I realized immediately what I'd said.

"Oh . . ." She tilted her chin up and nodded with a kind of mock sagacity. "You're a talker, are you?" She reached for her coffee and said with a grin, "So you want to talk about Stephen?"

I felt like I was being backed into a corner and all the rounds were going to her. I'd recognized an edge to her when we'd first met, and Virginia had hinted she was a wild one, but nothing had prepared me for this.

She mused for a moment, then she said, "Actually, I guess I don't mind talking to you, so long as we're off the record. I really don't give a shit." She folded her arms. "Okay, we're off the record, ask away."

I didn't say anything for a moment, then she tilted her head to one side again and asked coyly, "Am I embarrassing you?"

"Not exactly."

"Liar."

She smiled. And with that smile, I recovered somewhat and said, "Okay, maybe you are."

"Good. I like honest men."

I suddenly felt that we'd passed beyond a certain point. Some promises were being made and I had the feeling they were going to be kept. Then she folded her arms again, and stared deliberately at me, and waited, and finally she said, "Go on. Ask." And for some idiotic reason I felt I had no choice but to ask questions.

I asked how long she'd dated Lister.

"Not long. Couple of months."

I took out a notepad, and she looked at me as if I'd performed a delicate operation. I asked if she minded.

"Uh-uh. I never use one myself."

"You'd sooner I didn't?"

"No. I write from impressions. But that's the way I am."

There was the hint of a putdown, but I let it go. I asked when she'd last seen Lister.

"About two weeks before he died."

"You were still dating him?"

"Not really. I ran into him at the City office." Her brow furrowed for a moment, then she said, "Actually, the word *date* isn't really accurate."

"Why not?"

"Well, it implies we had some future in mind, and it wasn't that way at all."

"So what was it?"

She laughed lightly, as if the answer should have been obvious. Then she said, "He was sexually interesting to me. And in other ways too."

She smiled again, and I was trying not to shift in my seat because behind the remarks was the hint that any moment she might suggest we go upstairs, and if she had, I doubted I'd have refused. For a second I flashed on an incident in a housing project in Queens some years ago, when I was interviewing a fifty-five-year-old woman who had witnessed a murder. In the middle of the interview, the woman had opened her blouse and invited me to do the interview in bed—at which point I fled. But I doubted I'd have been so quick to run from Ann Raymond.

I regrouped and said, "Did you know he was making snuff films?"

"No. As a matter of fact, I didn't. Mind you, I'm not too surprised."

"Would it have bothered you . . . if you'd known?"

Her nose wrinkled. "Maybe. I like most porno films, but I'm not into violence." She shrugged. "Hard to say." I didn't say anything, and eventually she said, "Don't take this the wrong way, but most people I meet are very literal-minded, and Stephen wasn't that way at all."

"And that interested you?"

She studied me closely again, then she said, "Is this about me, or him?"

She was astute all right. I conceded the point. Then she leaned back in her chair, gave me that look again, and said, "Is this getting you turned on, it's getting me turned on." Her grin turned sardonic, then she said, "Of course, we'd have to use rubbers, right?"

The game had come full circle, and I reacted to it with some annoyance. I said, "Was that the point of all this?"

"No . . . it was a joke . . . don't get angry." She grinned.

But I had the bit between my teeth now, and I felt free to ask anything I liked. I said, "Did you make him use a rubber?"

Her eyes narrowed slightly. Then she said, "Yes, as a matter of fact, since it seems to matter. He had a lot of girlfriends."

We lapsed into silence. I'd lost my train of thought, and I was still working back to it, and half wondering if this was all a joke on her part, then her expression became thoughtful and she said, "To be honest, I was surprised when I read what you wrote . . . about the drugs."

"Why?"

"Well, it was news to me."

"You never saw him do coke?"

"Nothing. Ever." She shook her head. "I'm not a drug person myself. I don't need drugs to get my kicks, so maybe that's why he never brought it up—but I was with him on a few occasions when he might have. You know, low lights, etc. . . . but he never did." She sipped her coffee again, then she shuddered slightly and said, "It feels quiet in here. Would you like some music?"

I said it was up to her, and she got up and moved over to a tape deck and flipped through a couple of tapes. She took her time, then she slipped a tape into the deck and the Gypsy Kings came over the speakers.

She turned to me, "This okay?"

I said it was fine, and she pirouetted once to the music, a quick, sexy twirl of her hips. For a moment, I thought she was going to ask me to dance. But she didn't. She sat down again and said, "Where were we?"

"Drugs."

"Oh right. No . . . to be honest, I don't think he ever mentioned drugs."

I waited to see if she had anything else to add, and when she didn't, I asked her, "Any idea why he might have been killed?"

"Not really . . ." She thought about this. "I mean, Stephen was bizarre . . . that's partly why I went out with him . . . but in all honesty . . . I think a lot of it was an act. Underneath it all, I think

77

he was actually a serious person. He just liked to act as if he was more weird than other people . . ."

"Weird in what way?"

"Well, like nothing could shock him."

"Was that why he liked you?"

She smiled and said, "No . . . I'm easily shocked."

I didn't belabor the point. I asked if she knew many of his friends.

"A few. He didn't really have close friends. It was mostly the party crowd."

I dawdled on my notepad, thinking what else to ask, and finally I said, "Why did it end for you two?"

"Well, it didn't really. He had lots of girlfriends . . . but he still called me. We just hadn't gotten together in a while."

I asked if she knew any of his other girlfriends, and she said no, and just then I heard a car pull up. She heard it too, and she didn't move for a moment, then she said, "Shit, I forgot. I promised someone I'd drive them over to Kingston this morning."

She still didn't move, and from the way she looked at me, I read that she meant to let me know that she was disappointed. I suddenly realized how far we'd come in a half hour.

Then she got up and looked out the window and gave me a rueful look again before she walked into the hallway. I heard her open the door, and I heard the cheerful voices of a man and a woman, whose lives clearly did not revolve around murder, drugs, or sex, and I could hear my interviewee making the swift transition to neighborliness. From the conversation I gathered the man was dropping off his wife. I heard him thank Ann, heard his footsteps on the gravel outside, then I heard the woman say from the hallway, "You've got company?"

Ann said, "It's okay."

The car started up outside. Then Ann walked in, followed by a woman of thirty whose right arm was in a cast. I got up, and Ann said, "Sarah Blatt—Mike Kincaid."

The woman smiled at me in a cheerful half-apologetic way, raised her arm, and said, "Water-skiing accident. This comes off today."

I said, "I'm just on my way."

Ann turned to her friend and said, "Give me a minute, Sarah," then she asked the woman if she could manage to help herself to coffee. The woman said, "I can wait," and she gave me a helpless smile again. Then I followed Ann outside.

We stood side by side on the front porch, and after a moment, she said, "Sorry about this."

I said, "Doesn't matter."

We both grinned, knowing that was a lie, and that a lot was going unsaid, and after a while she said, "I guess you're not so bad. Do you want to continue this?"

I nodded.

She half smiled, then she said, "I'm going to Boston tonight—I should be back Tuesday."

I said, "Suppose I call you Tuesday."

"All right."

She stuck out her hand and said, "Drive safely." Then she turned and headed back inside the house.

I watched her go, and as I drove off I decided there was one benefit to the sudden intrusion—maybe. I wasn't sure where the conversation might have led us that day, and maybe she was right, I didn't trust myself.

Horny or not, in a way I was glad of a free weekend to sort out what I'd just been through.

CHAPTER SEVEN

BUT SHE WAS on my mind constantly the rest of the day, and by the evening I was no longer fooling myself. It looked like this was my choice, and if it was to be, I knew I'd wind up in bed with her. Things hadn't worked out with any of the more conventional women I'd dated lately, and I'd decided, "So what if she'd dated Lister? He was dead, I wasn't." Right now she was what I needed. I wanted her hot little body. I wanted wild sex. It was really that simple.

I was willing to give her the benefit of the doubt about what she'd told me. She'd claimed she knew nothing about the snuff film interest, or the drugs, which seemed reasonable to me—after all, this guy had pulled the wool over Virginia's eyes. I figured her reasons for dating him were what she said. Sexual attraction. Why not—he was a good-looking guy. And if she had been attracted to him because he was bizarre, kinky even, then it would be pretty hypocritical of me to deny myself when I was attracted to her for the same reason.

I still thought off and on about the drugs—but again, I saw no reason not to believe her. She wasn't stupid—maybe his skin-popping was recent. And as she'd said, she'd made him use rubbers. As for other reservations, yes, I had a few, but they were overcome by reasons more compelling, and by Tuesday I was having a little difficulty concentrating.

I was still thinking about the drugs that morning when I brought her name up to Rich and Phil. I'd called Rich and told him I could use an update on the case, and when I brought her name up, we were in Rich's car in heavy traffic on Forty-second Street. Phil had said something about the coke in Lister's apartment being 80 percent pure. That's when I told them I'd interviewed an old girlfriend of Lister's, and that she claimed never to have seen him do drugs. Neither Rich nor Phil answered for a moment. They were watching some minor fracas on the sidewalk.

Then, as we drove on, Phil glanced around at me.

"So what's your point, Mike?"

"The point is, if he was into drugs, why didn't he want her to do a line or two with him?"

Phil stared at me a moment. Then he said, "Is she into drugs?"

"She says not."

"So maybe he kept it to himself. Either that, or she's lying."

I said, "I doubt she's lying."

Rich asked, "What's this woman's name again?"

"Ann Raymond."

Rich glanced across at Phil and said, "Check, see if she's on the list."

Phil took out his notebook and scanned it. He came across Ann's name. Someone had given it to them, as someone who might be able to help them—then Phil turned back to me as Rich pulled up at the Times Square light.

He said, "She thought he was clean as a whistle?"

"That's right."

Phil shrugged and said, "Well, she was wrong," and that put an end to the discussion.

Rich started to ask for suggestions about what to get his wife, Jeannie, for a tenth wedding anniversary gift. Phil wasn't much help. We had stopped opposite a porn store and Phil turned to me and cracked a smile. Eventually he directed Rich's attention to the store and said, "Maybe you can find something there." Rich dropped the subject, and two blocks later we pulled up outside the Midtown North Precinct.

Rich was checking the car windows because detectives' cars were no less vulnerable than any others on this block, and I was already out of the car when Phil suddenly exclaimed, "Son of a bitch!" He was standing at the passenger door, scraping the heel of his Thom McAn shoe on the curb. Then he raised it and showed me a wad of pink bubble gum neatly squashed into his nonslip treads. Rich came around the car, glanced at the shoe, and said, "You're lucky."

Phil didn't think so. He indicated the police building and said, "No way I'm tracking this in." Then he sat back in the car and rummaged in the glove compartment until he found something to suit his purpose—a screwdriver. He took off his shoe and proceeded to work the stuff out, and Rich stood watching him for a while, the smile fading from his lips as Phil began lobbing blobs of pink gum in the general direction of the open car door. Eventually Rich said, "This could take a while," and we both sat back in the car.

After a while Rich said to me, "I brought you up-to-date with the banker, right?" I nodded. Then he asked Phil, "How's Larsen making out with the MUD?"

"Couple of days, he says."

Phil grunted as he worked on the shoe. Then he said to Rich, "Did you tell Mike about the woman from Millbrook?"

Rich shook his head.

Phil turned around, grinning. He said, "We turned up some girl Lister got rough with at a party. Some student . . . she works part-time at a gallery that shows his photos." He slid the screwdriver into another tread and worked out a sticky strand, then he said, "He got in her pants, invited the guests to watch." He glanced at Rich, who had withheld comment, and said, "Well, she ain't no killer, but it says something about our guy."

Rich said, "Like we didn't know already."

He sat in silence as Phil aimed another blob of gum out the door. So did I. Ann Raymond lived only a few miles from Millbrook, and I couldn't help wondering if she'd been among the guests. Then Rich said, "I was thinking about what Mike said earlier."

Phil said, "About what?"

"About this girl never seeing him do drugs."

"What about it?"

"Well, maybe he just started using. Maybe that's why he got careless."

Phil shrugged and said, "Could be," and went back to working on his shoe.

Then Rich said, "Guy starts out dealing, then gets into the stuff."

Phil shrugged, and Rich was quiet for a moment, then he said, "It still bugs me that dope packet had no prints on it."

"Maybe he was wearin' gloves."

Phil seemed to dismiss this. Then he looked up and saw Rich was still thinking about it, and he said irritably, "It's gotta be the dope, Rich. Why else would he need the stolen plates?"

Rich had no answer, and after a moment he said, "Did you run his credit cards?"

Phil nodded. "All of 'em. Gas charges, restaurants. No pattern."

He shook his head and stuck his shoe back on. Then he indicated the station house and asked who we were meeting.

Rich said, "Oberman."

We walked into the precinct, past a screaming Dominican woman who was swearing out a complaint against a neighbor. Larsen was waiting in Rich's office, as was Oberman, a crime scene technician with rounded shoulders and a pasty face. Oberman brought a manila folder over to the desk and laid out several sheets of fingerprints and a number of plastic bags, sealed and dated. He said, "Not much." He handed Rich several sets of prints. Then he held up a plastic bag that appeared to contain nothing and said, "This might be the best thing you've got. You could call it fluff, but it's actually wool—navy wool— from the weave of a good blazer." He said they'd found it on Lister's shirt front. It didn't match any clothes of his.

Rich glanced at Phil. Oberman was already holding up a second bag. He said, "Car grease. From under his fingernails. He'd showered, he didn't get all this stuff out."

Phil said, "I told you . . . he switched the plates back."

Rich shrugged and said, "So?"

Phil seemed a bit deflated. Oberman kept going. He opened up a folder, handed a photo to Rich, and said, "What do you make of this?"

Rich stared at the picture. Phil and I moved around behind him and glanced over his shoulder. The photo was of a young woman with blonde hair. She was lying naked, facedown, in woods, among a scattering of leaves. But it was not a provocative pose. Far from it. There was nothing coy or revealing about the photo, and the girl's head was at a strange angle.

Rich asked, "Was this from his editing room?"

Larsen said, "Uh-uh."

Rich looked at the picture again, then he glanced at Oberman and said, "She looks dead."

Oberman said, "That's what I thought."

Rich turned to Larsen and asked, "Where did it come from?"

"File drawer in the bedroom . . . well, not exactly . . . we found it *behind* one of the drawers."

Phil said, "You think he was hiding it?"

Larsen shrugged, and Phil took the photo from Rich, and after studying it a moment, he said, "Could be something he used for the snuff. But you know what this looks like?"

Rich raised an eyebrow and said, "A crime scene photo?"

Phil nodded, then he looked at Larsen, and Larsen said, "I thought the same thing."

Rich turned to me and said, "Is this something he might have staged for the magazine?"

I said it was possible. Rich then handed the photo to Larsen and said, "Check, see if they ran anything like this. If not, send it around." Then he turned back to Oberman.

Oberman went over the prints, eliminating those of the super who'd found the body, and the neighbor who'd been with the super at the time. He said they'd run the rest of the prints in the computer, but nothing had turned up. Then he packed up his briefcase and left, and as he went out, the Chinese food Phil had ordered arrived.

Larsen began clearing aside papers on Rich's desk and handing out plastic forks. Rich ate sparingly. A couple of times he looked up to see Larsen spilling rice all over his desk. Finally Larsen demolished the last of the fortune cookies, then he took a stack of papers from his briefcase and said to Rich, "You wanna see some MUD? I got Saturday's and Sunday's."

Rich ground out his cigarette and said, "Sure."

Larsen ran down the row of digits. "Sunday. Nine-twenty, eleven forty-five—these ones were to the art director. Nothing in between. Nothing after that." He flipped the page and went on, "Saturday . . . nothing after six fifty-six P.M. . . . this last one was to a guy named Milo Stacovich. He owns stock in *City Magazine*."

"He's the largest stockholder," I said.

Rich grinned and said, "I knew we had Mike here for a reason." Then he asked Larsen, "What was that call about?"

"Still waiting . . . I got a call in to Stacovich."

He pointed to the next number and said, "Five-twelve, that's his agent . . ." He ran his finger up the page to a 516 area code. "This one's to an Isabel Palmer in Old Valley Shores. That's near Glenville. She's Congressman Palmer's widow."

I said, "She was at the funeral . . . with a young guy."

Larsen glanced up at me. "Hey, Mike, you been working overtime?" He turned to Rich. "The son, Brad, and Lister were in high school together, or so the mother says."

"Why'd he call her?" Rich asked.

"To get Brad's phone number."

Phil glanced at Rich, then he asked, "Where does Brad live?"

"East Side somewhere."

"So why'd he call the mother?"

Larsen shrugged. He didn't know, and I guess he hadn't asked. I turned away to conceal a smile. Rich wanted all the loose ends tied up before he dropped any lead. He was ever suspicious, and here was a murder victim who'd called an old friend's mother the day before he was killed.

Rich was still waiting. Then Phil said, "This guy, Brad. He didn't ever live in D.C. by any chance?"

Larsen shrugged. He didn't know. Eventually, he asked, "Why?"

" 'Cause that's about a five-hundred-mile round-trip, if you throw in a little driving around time at either end."

Rich was looking thoughtful. He and Phil were on the same page at least. Then Rich said, "He makes a call . . . to get a friend's phone number. Why doesn't he have the friend's number? Why doesn't he get it from directory?" Larsen shrugged, then Rich said, "A few hours later he makes a trip of five hundred miles?" He glanced at the MUD sheet and said, "Lister gets the phone number from the mother, but then he doesn't call the son . . . ."

Phil said, "Not from his own place anyway."

"Or maybe the phone wasn't answered."

Larsen scratched his head. Phil asked him, "Did you speak to the son?"

"Uh-uh."

"So maybe it wasn't to get a phone number . . . Maybe he and Brad were in business . . ."

Phil paused a moment. Then Rich said, "Couple of wiseasses doing deals? Could be Lister tries to reach Palmer at his mother's place. Maybe he spins her some crap about not having his phone number . . ."

The room was silent for a moment, then Phil said, "I like it."

Rich ground out his cigarette and said, "Fuck it. Let's talk to him."

Ten minutes later, I was about to leave and head on downtown to the Koslo trial. Then Larsen came in and announced, "Cooperative guy. He's coming over."

Rich looked surprised. "Who?"

"Brad Palmer." Larsen spread his hands wide and said, "It was easy for him. He was on his way back to Long Island with his mother."

Rich said, "We get the mother, too?"

Larsen nodded.

Rich looked irritated. "I gotta talk to him with his mother here?"

Larsen said, "What's the diff?"

Rich still looked irritated, and Larsen had the look of a man who could do nothing right. After a while he got up and walked out the office, and I asked Rich if he'd mind if I stuck around, see what came of this—I figured it was either that or be bored for the rest of the afternoon.

Rich said it was fine with him.

I made a couple of calls, then I ran into Larsen on the way to the men's room, and after listening to him grouse about Rich, I asked him if he could do me a favor. I said I could use a look over Lister's yearbook at some time so I could get the names of old classmates. Larsen said he wasn't sure if the yearbook was still at the apartment, or at the crime lab—he'd check.

He let me use his phone to make a few more calls, and when the Palmers showed up around two-thirty, he parked them in Rich's office while he and Rich ran the computer to see if Brad Palmer had an arrest record. Palmer didn't. While they were doing this, I walked by Rich's office a couple of times and got a glimpse of mother and son. Mrs. Palmer sat stiffly, looking as dignified as she had at the funeral. She was in her mid-fifties, a handsome woman with a full head of auburn hair. Her son, Brad, had her looks, but his face had a few lines, which made his preppy clothes seem somewhat incongruous. Eventually Rich and Larsen went into the office and closed the door, and that was the last I saw of the Palmers that day.

Phil insisted it didn't need three cops to be in on this, and he and I went out for coffee. We talked about the lousy trade the Mets had just made and didn't even discuss the case until we were on our way back. We were back to talking about the trade again as we came into the precinct, and as we approached Rich's office, the door was open and Rich was sitting glumly at his desk opposite Larsen. Phil said, "No Palmers?" And Rich said gruffly, "So much for that."

He told us what they'd learned.

Brad Palmer had never lived in Washington, D.C., not even when his father was in office. For the past seven years he'd been living in Connecticut. Two months ago he'd split with his wife—which is why he'd recently rented a place in town. He said he and Lister had been friends in high school, but he'd lost touch with Lister and hadn't seen him since their last high school reunion—four years ago. At least not until last month. At that time he'd run into Lister on Third

Avenue, and Lister had talked about getting together. Palmer's phone hadn't yet been installed in his new place, so he'd told Lister to call his mother to get the number.

Phil seemed disappointed. He said, "The mother knew Lister too?"

Rich nodded. "That's why she wanted to go to the funeral."

Phil picked at his teeth and removed a trace of lunch, then he asked, "Do we know for sure he never lived in D.C.?"

Rich shrugged. "Be easy enough to check."

Larsen said he'd check, but he wasn't planning on making it a priority. And when Rich shot him a look, he said, "Face it, Richie, we're pissing all over the place on this one."

Then he walked out the office, acting as if his time had been wasted, and when Phil had left too, Rich looked at me and said, "You know what? He's right."

I said it was worth the shot and offered to buy him a drink, but he declined, saying he had work to do.

I decided it was just as well. It was getting late in the day and I had a phone call to make.

CHAPTER EIGHT

WHEN I GOT home, I went to my office, stuck my notes in a drawer, and called Ann Raymond. She was back from Boston, and I asked her if she'd like to have dinner, and after a moment's pause, she said, "Yes . . . without the reporter's notepad."

I said, "Okay."

There was a brief pause, then she said, "Yes. That would be nice. When?"

"Soon."

"All right." She chuckled. "You want me to check my calendar, or should I just tell you I'm free all week."

"In that case, how's tonight?"

She made a little clicking noise with her tongue and asked, "I assume you're in town?"

I said I could drive up there.

"Uh-uh. I was planning to come into town tomorrow. I could come in tonight."

It was that straightforward. No games. She gave me the address of her place on the East Side and asked if I'd pick her up there at nine. She left the dinner reservations to me.

It was not yet six o'clock, but I spent a good portion of the next three hours getting ready—showering at length, shaving carefully, selecting a nice jacket—realizing as I went through these rituals that it had been a while since I'd done all this so conscientiously. Shortly before nine, I caught a cab over to the East Side. Her place in town was in a brownstone in the low Nineties, off Lexington, and after the cab dropped me, she buzzed me in and I climbed a couple of flights of stairs.

She was waiting at the apartment door, wearing a black dress. I said, "You look nice," which was an understatement. She looked great in black, and this outfit, like the one she'd worn at the funeral, hinted at silk and lace underneath. She said she was almost ready, and I followed her into the apartment.

It was a large one-bedroom, furnished, like her house, without enormous outlays of money, but the furniture was good, and she'd made the place seem even larger with a couple of well-placed mirrors. She poured me a drink, then she headed for the bedroom, and I caught a glimpse of a pile of clothes on the bed as she went in. Then the door closed, and five minutes later she emerged, having changed nothing, as far as I could see, and we went downstairs and caught a cab.

I'd made reservations at an Italian restaurant on Third Avenue, and when we were seated and had drinks in front of us, she said, "Well, it's been three days. What's new?"

I said not much. She sipped her wine, then she said, "I wasn't sure if I'd hear from you. I thought you might change your mind again."

"Not this time."

She grinned a slow, sexy grin, and without exactly switching gears, she said, "If you hadn't called me, I was going to call you."

I said I was flattered.

She grinned. "Nothing that forward . . . I was going to ask you not to tell Virginia that we'd talked."

I said there was not much chance of that. Virginia and I weren't talking. Then I realized she knew that. I called her bluff. I said, "You just needed a reason to call so I'd ask you out."

She backed up a tad and didn't respond. I told her I thought she wanted me to be honest.

"Only about some things."

I said I was still flattered, and she said, "You should be. You're a lucky guy."

She smiled, and there was no mistaking the innuendo.

The waiter arrived and we ordered dinner, and when he had left the table, she said, "Speaking of Virginia, I talked to her today. You're beyond reproach."

I said I couldn't help it if she was taking a hard line.

She agreed, and there was a short silence, then she said, "Actually, I tried to reason with her on your behalf—without telling her that we'd talked. It did no good."

I said, "You've changed your tune then since we last spoke."

She looked at me a bit surprised. "What do you mean?"

"Well, you weren't sure if I could be open-minded."

"I never said that. I wouldn't have talked to you if I didn't think so."

She was still looking at me, a bit surprised. I couldn't remember the exact course of the last conversation, and I decided it didn't matter. I was planning to let it go when she said, rather seriously, "Mike, I think you should know this. It bothers me that he wasn't what he pretended to be."

In a way, I was glad to hear this. I said, "Okay."

Then, after a moment, she said, "The evidence indicates he was selling, right? Drugs, I mean?"

I nodded, and she said, "Well, I'm a realist. I don't give a shit about films he was making, but I don't buy into drugs."

I nodded, and eventually I asked her, "Did you know he had a gun?"

She looked a bit scornful. "Oh that. Yes. So what? So do I."

I asked what type.

"Why?"

"Just asking."

"Bullshit." Then she said, "It's a shotgun. A Remington. I live alone in the country."

I felt a slight feeling of relief. Lister had been killed with a nine mil. Then she asked if I owned a gun. I told her no, and she reached across the table and touched my hand and said she assumed I was a bare-fists type of guy.

I demurred. Then she said, "Actually, Stephen seemed very proud of his gun. I thought he was acting like a little boy with it." She seemed pensive for a moment, then she said, "Do the police have any clues yet?"

I told her they had clues but they didn't add up to much. Then she sighed and said, "My fault. I brought this up. I didn't plan for you to interview me. Let's talk about something else."

"Fine with me."

I filled her glass, and she said, "What shall we talk about? Your past? You were married, right?—Virginia told me that."

"Anything but that."

"All right. But I don't want to talk about writing, that's boring. Let's talk about sex, I know you're interested in that." I shook my head, in blank amazement, then she tilted her head to one side and said, "You don't want to talk about sex?"

I said sex would be fine, and she said, "Good, because I've been trying to figure out what it is about you that attracts me."

Again, I demurred.

"I'm serious. You're okay-looking, but there's something, aside from the physical. It's hard for me to put a finger on it. You're not that complex . . ."

"Thanks."

"I wouldn't want you to be. Complex men are lousy lovers. They can't focus on anything that requires being single-minded."

She grinned, and I asked her, "Did that theory originate with you?"

"Theory?"

She grinned again, then she said, "I think I'm attracted to you because you want to be challenged. I think that's what you want."

Maybe she was right. There had been nothing challenging about my recent relationships, and certainly nothing challenging in the later years of my marriage. But I had a feeling this woman could keep me alert, keep me on my toes. Maybe she already had me reeling a little,

94

and her periodic, well-aimed darts were certainly having an impact. Yet strangely enough, I wasn't feeling defensive. I felt good. This was all new. And every libidinal urge I had was on the rampage.

Somehow we made it through dinner. And when she'd finished her coffee, she said, "So?"

I said, "So?"

She said, "Don't tell me you're not the first date type?"

"Maybe I don't see this as a first date."

She laughed sardonically, and in a mock wistful way she said, "Ah, you feel like you've known me forever." Then, in a more deliberate way, she leaned forward and whispered, "Good."

Then she took my hand, and leaned close to me, and whispered, "I've been horny since Saturday. I might have talked you into fucking me then if Sarah hadn't shown up."

What could I say? Eventually I said, "I might have put up a fight."

She grinned and rolled her hand across mine, and after a moment, she said, "Sure you would."

It was very exciting, and a little tense, sitting there waiting for the waiter to being the check. Finally he came by, and when I'd paid and picked up the receipt, she said, "Anyway, you're right. This doesn't feel like a first date."

Her hand was back in mine as we left. Outside, a warm breeze greeted us, and the hem of her dress fluttered. I hailed a cab and gave the driver her address, and in the dark cave of the cab she looked at me, teasing, and said, "Want to go out dancing?"

I said some other time.

She leaned back, and her hair brushed my cheek, and when I kissed her, she ran her tongue across my upper lip. My hands went under her dress, and we continued kissing until the cab dropped us. She climbed the brownstone steps ahead of me and rummaged for her key, and my arms went around her as I waited, and once we were inside we had a tough time negotiating the stairs.

Finally her apartment door closed, and we made it as far as the couch. Her dress rode up to her waist, and I caught a glimpse of red garters, then I looked up and saw her watching with an intense gaze as I entered her. It was ecstatic, spontaneous—in a word, perfect. Like making love for the first time, and to this day I still feel excitement when I think of it.

We removed the rest of our clothes and lay in the strewn pile and made love again. And afterward we lay studying each other. Then we went into the bedroom and talked for an hour or so, and when we eventually went at it again, she stared at me from a few inches above and said, "I guess we're going to do a lot of this."

I wanted to hear that. Something in me had come alive, and I felt that a steady diet of this could work wonders for me. It struck me that the odds had been against us, and when I told her so, she said, "That was a nice thing to say." Then she began to run her tongue down my chest, working slowly down to my navel, and then below. She said, "Relax. Don't think you're not going to come again, because you will." I lay there and submitted, and a few minutes later, she was looking into my eyes with a satisfied, mischievous grin.

She said, "Congratulations." Then she turned off the light and laughed in the dark. Finally, she fluffed her pillow and said, "Get some sleep. I want you to save your strength." But she was still wriggling her backside against me as I dozed off with my arms around her.

She stayed in town all week and we saw each other all but one night, and on Saturday we drove upstate together. We stopped off at her place so she could pick up her mail, then we drove on to my place. It rained on the drive up, but by the time we reached the cabin the skies had cleared and we could see the entire length of the Catskill range.

Ann got out of the car and stood with her hands on her hips, taking it all in, and after a moment she said, "I've got no complaints."

We went inside, and out to the porch, where we sat on the glider, not saying much. Finally we were in the country, with no distractions, and although we had managed to avoid the rest of the world for evenings at least during the week, somehow being in the country enhanced the feeling of being alone together. Eventually she said, "It's very private here."

"Just the deer and an occasional hoot owl."

96

"Like I said, very private . . ."

She was looking at me steadily, and we spent the next half hour in a kind of extended foreplay until I could stand it no longer. I pulled her up from the glider, and we went inside and went to bed, and when we next came up for air, it was already late afternoon.

She lay next to me after a nap, yawned lazily, and gazed out the window, then she said, "I like it here. I'd like to be here in the winter, I used to love the winter when I was a kid."

I lay back in the pillows, prepared to let her ramble on. But she didn't elaborate. Her thoughts seemed to have drifted, and after a while I asked her, "Where was that?"

"Where was what?"

"The winter. When you were a kid."

"Oh, Massachusetts."

"Your family still live there?"

"My father's dead. My mother's in a home for Alzheimer's patients over in Berkshire County."

I said, "Gee, I'm sorry."

"That's okay."

I couldn't think what to say for a moment. Then she asked me, "Are your parents still alive?"

I told her a little about my family, in a kind of reflective monologue. I brought up my father and told her about his and my many differences, and when I'd finished she asked me how I felt about my father now.

I said, "Okay, I guess."

Then there was that moment of contact again. We made love and drifted off to sleep again.

This time when we woke up, it was nearly dark. We thought about making dinner, but it seemed like too much trouble, and eventually we dressed and drove to a nearby restaurant. We stayed late and sat over brandies until after one, then we drove home and sat up even later on the porch, listening to a radio station from across the river in Woodstock.

Around three she went inside—to get a drink, she said. I sat staring at the night sky with its baskets of stars, hung bright that night without any moon. A song came on the radio from a few years back, a song I associated with a time when I was negotiating some rough seas, then I heard a rustle and turned, and Ann was standing at the door, wearing something silk.

She was in an entirely wanton mood, and I remember being suddenly aware that I wasn't on any rough seas at that moment. We went to bed, and afterward when she was asleep, I lay thinking about a lot of things. After a while I could hear her steady breathing. She was sound asleep, but I wasn't even tired, and rather than risk waking her, I got up and went out and sat on the porch again and stared at the sky . . . and this time as I sat there, I was thinking how the time can pass, how the years can go by in a strained marriage, and how you can easily forget what it is that makes you tick.

CHAPTER NINE

MONDAY CAME AROUND—a hazy, damp morning with a light mist hanging over the Hudson Valley. Doves cooed in the pines behind the cabin. As we walked outside with our coffee, the idea of playing hooky suggested itself. But the Koslo trial was still dogging me, and Ann had scheduled an interview with a professor at SUNY. She was reluctant to cancel at short notice. As she put it, "I get the feeling we'd still be facing this same decision tomorrow." I decided she was right. I should quit trying to persuade her. Around eight we started driving south.

I dropped her at her house in Dutchess County and drove on, thinking about our discussions over the weekend, about odd moments of laughter, bits of background she'd told me about herself. There had been moments when sex wasn't foremost in our thoughts, but it was never far away. I also had the feeling it never would be, as far as we were concerned, even though I'd approached Ann Raymond like a man wandering out of the desert.

Not surprisingly, the city seemed manageable that morning. I was the veritable "new man," with a lighter step, less burdened. Even the Monday rush hour didn't get to me—my attitude toward my fellow man's driving began to approach tolerance. When I reached Manhattan, I put the car in a lot on Second Avenue and walked the few blocks to the paper. I passed a florist and the scent of jasmine filled the air. Then I bought a pack of gum at the store in the lobby and rode upstairs to check my messages before going downtown.

Even the newsroom seemed bearable. The odor of human meanness, which I usually detected when I walked in, seemed less pungent that morning. I found time for coffee and pleasantries amid the clamor, and when I suggested to Art Gelber, the day editor, that I write a piece about Koslo's attorney, he seemed surprisingly receptive. Then Killion showed up from the trial to announce that the judge had called a recess to study a defense motion, and since this meant there was no reason for me to go downtown, the day seemed to be shaping up nicely. The serenity was not to last. As I was getting on the elevator to go to the library, I ran into Cantor.

Instead of his usual cheerless greeting, he grabbed my arm and told me to go wait in his office. Then he shuttled off along the corridor on some urgent errand, reading a batch of wire copy. I thought, "Shit, what's this about?"

I went to his office and sat and waited, and ten minutes later when he returned, he was with Joe Kendall, a reporter from the business section. He parked Kendall next to me, and after rummaging through some more wire copy, and making a quick call, he glanced up at Kendall as if to ask him what he was waiting for. Then he realized we were waiting for him, and he said gruffly, "All right, Joe. Go ahead."

Kendall scratched his earlobe and took a moment before saying anything. He was a soft-spoken guy who wore wire-rimmed glasses and herringbone jackets, which led a number of people to underestimate him. He seemed to be having trouble knowing where to begin. Then he told me, "Well, this concerns Stephen Lister."

I said, "Okay," and Cantor shot me a look that contained a hint of one-upmanship or reproach—I wasn't sure which. Then Kendall said, "I've turned up some details about his business dealings."

I said, "Okay," again, and once more I saw Cantor giving me that triumphant look, and I felt a slight unease. I knew Joe was a capable reporter, and his self-effacing manner belied the fact that at times he was a bulldog.

Joe went on, "I have a source who works for the Germond brothers. They publish a number of special-interest magazines—you know who they are, right?"

I nodded.

"Well, this source has come through for me before. And this weekend he called to tell me about a deal that was dead in the water, but he thought I ought to know about it anyway." Joe paused. "Apparently, Milo Stacovich was planning to buy the Germonds' stake in *City Magazine*. And his partner in the deal was to be . . . Stephen Lister . . ."

I sucked in my breath and I was aware that Cantor was studying me closely.

Joe went on, "From what this guy says, Stacovich had been active in the market for some time, and so had Lister, although I doubt he had Stacovich's resources. Apparently, Stacovich wanted a majority holding because he wanted to give Lister carte blanche to run the magazine."

I whistled softly, and Kendall said, "That's why it all fell apart when Lister died."

Cantor grunted and said, "When he was killed, you mean." He turned to me and said, "Well, Mike, how do you like them apples?"

I paid Joe his due. I said I was glad he was working for us. Cantor said, "Damn nice of you." Joe smiled.

Then I told them, "It fits. Lister was talking to Stacovich the night before he was killed. And a couple of weeks back he asked his banker about credit. To buy stock, I'd guess."

Joe Kendall looked at me thoughtfully, then he said, "Well, that's good to know, because I only have the one source on this."

We were silent for a moment. Then I asked Joe if Lister had been buying *City* stock through a broker named Moran. Joe nodded, and I said I remembered seeing Moran's brokerage statements in Lister's apartment, but there wasn't any *City* stock on the statements. Joe shrugged. He said if Lister had only been buying for the past month, the trades wouldn't have shown up on any statement yet.

I was still reacting to the news. So Lister had gotten to Stacovich and convinced him the magazine would fly higher if he got control. At least that's the way it sounded. But it still wasn't clear to me why Stacovich needed a majority holding to give his fair-haired boy the run of the magazine. After all, Dick Bruton was Stacovich's man, and as publisher, Bruton could do Stacovich's bidding. When I mentioned this to Joe, he said, "Maybe Stacovich expected opposition if he didn't have control."

"You mean from other shareholders?"

Joe nodded. "Or from the board. Maybe he wanted to give Bruton the shove, you never know."

I glanced at Cantor and saw he was taking all this in, then I remembered what Mitch had said: Bruton had been buying stock. I told Joe this and he didn't seem sure what to make of it. He said it was all interesting but he wasn't sure if it meant anything in terms of the murder.

I said, "Don't be so sure." And I immediately thought of several other people at City Magazine who would not have been too thrilled about Lister taking over, because in all probability they'd have been fired.

I looked over at Cantor, and he was still giving me his sour grin. Then he said, "All right, Joe, drop the other shoe."

Again, I felt a slight unease. Joe scratched his ear and thought for a moment, then he said, "Well, here's the really strange thing . . ." He paused. "Even though Stacovich and Lister were buying . . . and maybe, as you say, Bruton was too . . . the stock never went up all week . . . in fact, on the Thursday and Friday before he was killed, it went *down* . . ."

I stared at him blankly, then I said, "You mean someone was selling? Is that you're telling me?"

Cantor rolled his eyes. "That's generally the way markets work, Mike."

I told him it had been a while since I'd taken eco 1. Then I asked Joe, "Was it the Germonds?"

"Why would they sell? They're trying to get the best price possible from Stacovich . . ."

Again, Cantor rolled his eyes. He leaned forward and asked me, "Are we on the same page here?"

"Yes," I said irritably. I turned back to Joe, "So the stock was falling? It went down again the Monday after he was killed . . . after what I wrote. What's it done since?"

"Rebounded."

"So who was the seller?"

Joe laughed. "Well, that's what I'd like to know. I was about to look into it, but Ted thought we ought to talk first."

We all looked at each other. The implication was almost too absurd—that someone had actually sold, or shorted the stock, because they planned to drive the price down further by killing Stephen Lister.

Eventually Cantor said, "Hey, Mike, anything's possible."

I said, "I guess so."

We all sat in silence, then Cantor got up and poured himself some coffee. When he sat down again, he spread his fingers on the desk and said, "All right. Here's what I want you to do. Work on this together." He looked at me. "You know some stuff Joe doesn't, and it sounds like you can use a lesson or two in basic business. Besides, you each got connections and you can save each other some time. So check into this. Let's see what turns up."

Joe nodded. I looked at him and said it was fine by me.

Cantor said, "Okay. Get on it."

We walked out of Cantor's office, and I asked Joe where he'd like to start. He said Lister's broker, Moran, seemed like a good bet. I said fine, and we went back to Joe's cubicle, and I sat and waited while he got the number from directory.

It still seemed like a stretch to me that anyone would kill Lister to engineer a short-term profit in the market. I told Joe so, and his response was, "Damn. Kind of neat, if you ask me."

"Why not buy in, if everyone else was buying?"

Joe thought about this, then he said, "You're assuming the seller knew about the deal. What if someone was already on the short side, and this disrupted his plans?"

"You mean, the fact that Stacovich and Lister were buying?"

"Exactly."

He had a point, and I couldn't think of an immediate response, but I still didn't buy it. It just seemed too far-fetched. But what did interest me was the Stacovich-Lister agenda. I assumed they'd kept the deal as quiet as possible. But what if word had leaked out? From the Germonds' end? That could throw this case wide open. There were any number of people at the magazine who made no secret of hating Lister, whose jobs would have been imperiled if Lister had taken charge, but it also occurred to me that a few others who claimed to be admirers of his might have been pretty pissed off too if they'd found out what was really going on. Including Dick Bruton.

Joe got the number of Moran Inc. And dialed it. And I sat trying to decide where all the stuff I'd learned from Rich and Phil might fit in—the stolen plates, the drugs, the car mileage. None of it came together and I wondered if maybe it was all irrelevant, then I put it on the back burner as Joe got through to an Albert G. Moran.

He told Moran he needed to talk to him about Stephen Lister, and from Joe's response I could tell Moran was resisting. Joe then told the guy he was writing a front-page piece and that if it carried a "no comment" from Albert G. Moran, it would not look too good for Albert G. Moran.

I picked up the extension in time to hear Moran ask why he should give a fuck, but I could tell he was already backing down. Joe wasn't giving up anything until they could talk face-to-face, and finally Moran said, "Okay, be here at three," and he hung up.

Joe sat holding the phone and said, "This guy's a charmer." Then he hung up, and he and I grabbed a bite of lunch before taking the IRT downtown.

There were sweat patches in the armpits of the men in the trading room of Moran Inc., but in the corner office occupied by Albert G., the son of the founder, nobody was rushing about. Moran sat still as a statue, his hands resting on his ample belly, gazing at a computer screen. He hadn't moved from this position since Joe and I were shown in, and he had greeted us with a barely perceptible nod. I could understand why Lister had chosen this guy for his broker. He gave new meaning to the word *arrogance*.

Joe began asking questions, and Moran kept ducking them. Once in a while he would shift his hands to the desk and tap idly at the keyboard, then he would lean back in his chair again, stare at his screen, and answer Joe's questions with either a monosyllabic grunt or with a short evasive question of his own. For a while we went nowhere, then Joe finally got up, went to the window, and gazed down at Broad Street. Moran ignored him and continued to pay attention to his stock quotes.

Eventually Joe tried again. He scribbled some numbers on a piece of paper and set them down on the desk in front of Moran. Moran looked at him as if he were littering. Joe waited a moment, then he said, "These are the highs and lows for *City* stock for the week before last."

Moran said, "So . . . ?" It seemed to be his favorite word.

"Well, the stock never got above nine and a quarter all week."

"So?"

"Kind of strange, don't you think?"

Moran shrugged. "What's so strange about it?"

I could see Joe making the effort to be patient. He said, "The stock's thinly traded, and you've got Stacovich and Lister buying . . . but the price wasn't up. How come?"

Moran smiled slightly and said, "Ergo . . . ?"

Joe said, "Right. We'd like to know who."

They faced each other in silence a moment. Then Moran uttered a short laugh and said, "Damned if I know. My job was to buy."

It was bullshit, and he knew it. But he wasn't about to say any more, and when Joe looked at me and seemed about to lose it, I figured it was my moment to chime in. I said, "What I don't understand, Moran, is why you give a fuck."

His eyes swung around to me. Then he looked back at his screen. I figured this guy was no different from a lot of Wall Street guys who operated on the principle "the less said, the better"—at least until it came time to cover their asses. He had no reason to be concerned for himself—he was just keeping what went on in the club within the club.

Joe glanced at me, and I had the feeling he wanted me to keep going. I said, "Here's how it works, Moran. Joe writes his story, and I make sure the homicide detectives at Manhattan South see it, because crime's my beat and I know these guys. I tell 'em you've got something to hide, and two days from now they'll be running through here, slapping you with subpoenas and poring over your shit to see if it stinks. Now you really want that?"

Moran's mouth was open, and he was glaring at me, but he didn't reply, and I said fine and motioned Joe to the door. Then Moran said, "Wait a minute."

Joe half turned. I didn't. I took Joe's arm and steered him toward the door, saying, "Fuck him. Let him sweat it. We can get this from the exchange."

From behind me, Moran's voice boomed, "I said, hold on!"

This time I looked back. Moran was rising out of his seat, angry as hell. The slick veneer had disappeared.

"You think you can come in here and blackmail me?"

"Fuck you," I said. "You think we came down here to be dicked around?"

He was fuming. "What makes you think . . . ?"

"Give us the names," I snapped. "Or we're leaving."

His face went crimson. I caught most of the heat of his glare, then he seemed to recognize that he should opt for the path of least resistance. Slowly he settled back in his chair.

I looked at Joe and waited, and Moran gave me another baleful glare and still didn't say anything, so I said, "Come on, Moran, we haven't got all day."

Then, ignoring me, he turned to Joe, and said, "This off the record?"

Joe nodded.

Moran glared at us both this time, then he said, "I don't want the firm's name mentioned in this. Is that understood?"

Joe said, "Understood."

Moran turned to me and said, "That goes for you too?"

I said, "Count yourself lucky. Now give us the names."

Moran looked at me like he wanted to kill me. Then he took a breath and said, "The biggest sellers were O'Connell and Wischner."

Joe glanced at me, then in a level voice he asked Moran, "Were they selling throughout the week?"

"Thursday, Friday, I know for sure."

"Did they buy back in the following Tuesday?"

Moran smiled sourly. "I don't know. I wasn't trading then, since my client was dead. You'll have to ask them."

Joe said he planned to, and we walked out.

Once out in the lobby, I took a deep breath. Joe asked if I'd ever heard of O'Connell and Wischner, and I said, "Oh yeah." He looked at me with surprise.

I said they were a small firm. But the interesting thing was I'd met both partners once, a year ago, at a party in Long Island.

They were guests of Mitch Danbury.

An hour later, Joe and I were sitting in the fortieth-floor reception area of Danbury & Wolfe, waiting to talk to Mitch Danbury. We had caught a break, getting to see him right away without having to say why, because Mitch had postponed the appointment he and I had set up the previous week—the one at which we were supposed to talk about college funds. So he wasn't surprised to hear from me again.

I had planned to be up front when I'd called him from the lobby of Moran's building, but when he came on the line and I told him I needed to see him right away, he laughed and said, "The kid's growing up that fast, huh?" I said there was something else I needed to talk to him about, aside from the funds, but he didn't give me a chance to get into it. He said, "Mike, I'll be free in an hour. Let's talk when you get here." So I didn't feel too bad about blindsiding him.

Initially Joe and I had talked about whether Joe should go it alone with Mitch. Joe had asked, "How good a friend is he?" I said we were close enough for it to matter. Then we both agreed that we'd probably get to see Danbury faster if I played a role, and that was the deciding factor. We assumed, of course, that Mitch had to be the seller.

Joe turned to me as we sat in the reception. "So?" he said. "Any theories?"

I said I had one. "Danbury found out about the deal, and he was bailing out because he didn't want to be a minority shareholder in a company run by Lister."

Joe stared at me, then he asked, "Are you saying he didn't like Lister?"

"That's understating it." Joe looked at me in his studied way, and I said, "Forget it. He's not the type."

But Joe wasn't about to. He continued to stare at me, then he said, "He'd have been angry at being betrayed by Stacovich."

"I'm sure he was."

"If Stacovich did an end run on me like that, I'd be pretty incensed. Especially if I'd made him a pile of money." When I didn't reply, he asked, "All right, you don't buy it. So how do you want to play this?"

"This time you be the bad guy."

Joe said that was fine with him. Then the door opened and Joe started to get up, thinking the woman who had emerged was the receptionist. It wasn't. It was Lisa Dennison.

I saw Joe giving her the once over, and I can't say I blame him. She looked every bit as good as when I'd seen her at the *City* party. I heard Joe catch his breath, then he murmured, "Holy shit." I got to my feet. Lisa Dennison had recognized me and was on her way over.

"Mike . . . isn't it?"

I said she had a good memory. Then I introduced her to Joe. He couldn't take his eyes off her, and when he sat back down on the reception couch, his face was about three feet from her thighs. She stood there chatting to me.

"How's it going?" she inquired. "Well, actually, I know how it's going, Henry told me . . . so did Mitch."

Her eyes shifted toward Joe, then back to me, as if to communicate that she was aware she shouldn't say too much in front of a third party about my aborted go-round with *City*. I told her I couldn't expect to win any popularity contests.

"Well, not in some quarters. But it's hypocritical, that's the only word for it."

I nodded and asked if she had many free afternoons. She grinned and said she always took advantage of the slack day after deadlines. "Mitch and I are playing squash later down the street," she said. "But I generally take a lesson first."

Then she went on her way, and as she walked out, I looked at Joe, and he said, "Squash? With that?" He had deduced she was seeing Danbury, and he said he didn't feel too bad now about roughing him up. Then the door opened again, and Mitch's secretary appeared.

We were shown into an office with a magnificent view of New York harbor, and as we came in, Mitch was standing at his Chesterfield desk, looking as proud as J. P. Morgan himself. He was a bit surprised that I was with someone else, and I cut him off amid the cordialities. I told him right away that he hadn't given me the opportunity to explain things on the phone, so I needed to get something straight up front: Joe was from the paper too, and something had come up we needed to talk to him about. Mitch backed off a bit and said okay, slowly, maybe with some reservation, but he didn't seem too concerned. He motioned us to a couch and asked if we'd like something to drink. We both declined, and with that, I guess, our presence took on a slightly ominous note. Mitch reacted with a slow nod, then he buzzed his secretary and said he'd like some coffee. Then he tugged at his cuffs, took a seat opposite us, and indicated for us to fire away.

Joe was about to start in, but before he did, I interrupted again. I said in fairness that Mitch should know that even though he and I were well acquainted, I was here strictly on a professional basis. Joe nodded and glanced at Mitch and said, "Fair enough?"

Mitch gazed at me for a moment, then he chuckled and said to Joe, "Sounds like you're reading me my rights."

Joe didn't laugh. He said, "I guess what Mike means is this. We're on the record, until you say otherwise."

Mitch stared at Joe a moment. Then he said, "Or until I throw you out."

Again Joe didn't smile, and I found myself wishing he wouldn't

109

be so damn serious. I looked at Mitch and he winked at me. The guy had chutzpah—I'll say that for him—but I imagined Joe didn't find him too endearing, and I wasn't surprised when he led off by asking Mitch how much *City* stock he'd sold the previous week.

Mitch didn't blanch. He didn't visibly react in any way. He glanced at both of us in turn, and with a note of surprise in his voice, he said, "Is that what this is about?"

Joe said that's what he'd like to know, and he was looking as if he'd sit there all day waiting for an answer. Mitch looked at me and said, "Really?"

I told him we'd been looking into trading in *City* stock for the week before Stephen Lister died and that it was clear Mitch had been a heavy seller. This wasn't exactly true—all we knew was that Mitch's broker friends had been selling. But I figured if Mitch wasn't the principal, he would deny it right away. I reminded him again that we were on the record, and I was trying to keep my voice neutral.

Mitch stared at both of us a long time, then he said, "I see." Then there was a knock on his door and his secretary brought in his coffee. He indicated for her to set it on his desk, then when she left, he got up and wandered over to it. He stirred a sugar cube into the cup, then he brought the coffee back to his seat, and with a faint smile, he said, "You know, this sort of information generally stays between me and the IRS."

Joe said, "It's a publicly traded company." He smiled slightly but the threat was implicit. We could go about it the hard way if necessary. Still, Mitch didn't react in a negative way. In an even tone, he said, "I realize," then he added, "can I ask why this is so important?"

Joe glanced at me and I knew immediately what he was thinking. He didn't want to be the one to bring up Lister's deal because he was hoping Mitch would bring it up first. That way, even if he got nothing else, he could at least establish that Mitch knew about the deal.

I sensed Mitch realized this, and that he was playing it cute, and it occurred to me that he might be holding back because he was worried about a charge of insider trading. Then I thought, "No. How so?" He wasn't buying on the coattails of insider knowledge, envisioning a rise in the price—he was selling into strength.

I was aware of a long silence in the room. Nobody seemed to want to move off the dime, and so I said, "It's kind of a tangled web, Mitch, and there're a few reasons for us to play our cards close."

Mitch nodded. Then he said, "Okay, question. Since I know what you've been working on lately—I assume this concerns our late, unlamented friend, Mr. Lister?"

There was another silence. Then Joe said, "It may."

Mitch nodded again, then he looked at Joe and me in turn and finally said to me, "How would your colleague feel if I talked to you alone? Off the record?"

It was a masterstroke. He had put Joe on the spot, and Joe knew it. Joe took a breath, then he leaned forward and looked at me, and after a moment he said, "I'd be more comfortable if it was both of us, albeit *off* the record."

Before I could say anything, Mitch said, "Forget it. No dice."

Joe looked pissed, and out of loyalty to him I felt I had to call Mitch's bluff. I said, "Sorry, Mitch. I go with Joe on this one."

I moved, as if to get up from the couch, and Mitch quickly said, "Okay, how's this?" He turned to Joe and said, "Suppose I go *on* the record with Mike alone? How's that?"

Neither Joe nor I responded, then Mitch said to Joe in a kind of apologetic way, "It's nothing personal. I'd just feel more comfortable talking to Mike alone."

I glanced at Joe and read in his eyes that he didn't like this, but he could live with it. He knew my rep at the paper, and I figured he trusted me not to hold anything back from him. Still, this was a minor victory for Mitch, at least in setting the terms. And to take the edge off his victory, I said to him, "You realize Joe and I are colleagues? We share information?"

"That's fine. I'd just be more comfortable talking one-on-one."

Mitch sat and waited, and after a few moments Joe got up. He said pointedly, "Have fun." Then he left the room.

When he had gone, Mitch took a deep breath. He asked if I wanted a drink, and I felt at that moment it was important to decline. Mitch said, "Well, I could sure use one," and he got up and went to his liquor cabinet and poured himself a martini. He stirred it, and I sat there, watching him, and after a moment he looked up and said, "And I thought this was about college funds."

I didn't say anything, and he came back to his chair with his drink, then he said, "Okay, Lister." I didn't say anything, and Mitch gulped his martini and stared hard at me, then he said, "This has to do with Lister, right?" Again I didn't answer and he said, "Sure it does." Then he said, "Look, no hard feelings . . . I just hated to be put on the spot by your friend there. I didn't especially care for the guy."

Again I didn't say anything, and he continued to stare at me, then he nodded in a rueful way, and eventually he said, "Okay, where do you want me to start?"

"Wherever you like."

"How about with Stacovich?"

"That's fine."

"All right then. Let's talk about that son of a bitch."

I reminded him again that we were on the record, then he loosened his tie and just launched into it.

First, he described Stacovich as a hysteric who was always beefing about the way *City*'s stock was performing. Then he said, "Usually, that's as far as it gets—him beefing. But this time he didn't listen to me. Damn fool."

Then he told me that he knew Lister had been brown-nosing Stacovich, and that from what had happened he had to assume Lister had convinced Stacovich that the stock was never going any higher— "unless he was in charge, or the magazine got greater visibility, or some such crap." For a moment his face took on an angry look, then he said, "I'm guessing that's what happened. I haven't talked to Milo. But that son of a bitch knew the board would balk at putting Lister in charge because self-proclaimed geniuses don't have much of a track record running magazines."

I said, "So Stacovich went after the Germonds' shares to get control?"

Mitch nodded and said, "I guess," and I was quiet for a moment. Then I asked him, "So you did find out about the deal?"

"Why do you think I unloaded?"

I'd got that settled at least, and for the moment I held off asking the obvious question: How did he know? Instead, I said, "The day of the funeral we were talking. You said Dick Bruton had been buying stock. Did *he* know about the deal?"

Mitch reached for his drink and said, "I don't know. That was just something he told me, about a month back."

"Nothing since?"

"Uh-uh. Why?"

I said it didn't matter. Then I asked him, "So how did *you* know about the deal?"

Mitch reacted like I'd caught him off guard. He stared at his drink a moment, then he said, "Mike, I'd just as soon not get into that. It would involve betraying a confidence."

"All right. In that case, let's talk about what you did once you found out."

"What do you mean?"

"Well, how much did you cash in?"

Mitch looked kind of sullen. "Not everything. Most of it. You think I wanted to be part of Lister's show?"

We were silent for a moment. Then I asked him, "Did you buy back in Monday?"

"Jesus, Mike . . ."

"Did you?"

He hesitated, then he said, "Well, yes . . . I'd have been a damn fool not to."

"How much? All of it?"

"Well, a fair amount . . ."

"You realize the impression this could give?"

"What impression?"

He had to have thought about it. I asked him, only half joking, "Is your alibi solid?"

"Ferchrissakes, Mike . . . who cares if it's not?"

"You should. Is it?"

"Why should I care?" He laughed uproariously. "Like someone's going to suggest I killed the son of a bitch?"

"You were out on your boat . . . was anyone with you?"

He blinked and asked me, "How did you know that?"

"Virginia told me. Were you with anyone?"

"No . . ." He was still looking astonished that I knew where he'd been.

I said, "So, you don't have an alibi."

"Oh, don't be absurd . . ."

"I'm not being absurd. If Joe decides to write about the trading, and the cops come knocking at your door, you're gonna be answering some hard questions."

"Well, let 'em ask . . ."

He was defiant, but I could tell I'd gotten through to him. His actions with the stock would bear looking into, and I guessed some part of his stubborn self finally recognized this.

He said, "For God's sake, Mike, why would I kill him?"

"He teamed up with your pal Stacovich and tried to lock you into a shit situation. Besides, you hated him."

His jaw wavered. "Yes, but . . ."

He broke off, and I decided it was time to tell him I was reasonably confident he didn't do it.

"Thanks a lot."

"Yeah, but I know you, Mitch," I said. "The cops don't."

He didn't say anything, and I asked him if there was any way he could have run afoul of the SEC on this.

"Not that I can see . . . I hadn't really thought about it."

"Really?"

He didn't answer, and I tried again with my earlier question. I asked how he'd found out about the deal, but he still wasn't giving this to me, even though I'd softened him up. He said again, "It would involve betraying a confidence. I don't want to put someone's tit in the wringer if it isn't necessary."

I said it may be. He asked why.

"Well, for one thing, the cops might like to know who you got the information from because it could indicate whether the deal became known—at *City*."

He said, "Oh, I see." Then he shook his head and said he couldn't say any more.

About the only other thing he wanted to talk about was his boat trip, and I let him expound with his unease. He said he'd taken the boat out from Glen Cove around noon. When the weather had turned bad, he had made for the Connecticut shore. He claimed he had pulled in at a dock, near Greenwich, around three, to refuel. Then when the weather cleared, he headed back to Glen Cove, arriving around five. I asked if he'd kept the fuel receipt, and he said, "No, I paid cash."

"So nobody saw you all afternoon?"

"Well, what does that prove?"

"Nothing."

He took a breath and shook his head wearily, then he looked at me steadily and said, "You guys are something, how the hell did you get onto this anyway?"

I said that was something I couldn't tell him.

He was silent for a while, and I figured at the very least he was worried now that maybe the cops would see his actions in a dubious light. But then maybe I was wrong. A few minutes later, he looked at his watch and said, "Look, Mike, I'm sorry. We can pick this up some other time, but I've got to break it off right now. I've got a squash game."

It was around five when I left his office. Before I left he asked me if Joe or I would be writing about this, and I said I had to talk to Joe. Then he asked me if I planned on mentioning this to the detectives, since I was close to them. I said if I did, it might be the best thing I could do for him since I was probably the most credible character witness he'd got.

Finally, he asked me if I believed him, and I said, "To be honest, yes." Then I walked out.

The subway was crowded as I rode uptown. The air-conditioning wasn't working, and I was sweating by the time I left the car at midtown. I stopped for a beer before I went back to the paper, and when I got off the elevator, I went straight to Joe's cubicle and told him everything Mitch had told me.

He asked if I thought it was truth. I said yes. Then I spent an hour bringing him up to speed with all the other stuff I'd learned previously from Rich and Phil. I told him we should keep this other stuff in mind. Or at least try to see the new stuff in that context.

Joe said, "Maybe not."

I conceded he had a point. One part of it could all be irrelevant. I said, "I'd still like to know who tipped off Mitch about the deal."

Joe was quiet for a moment, then he said, "You think it might have been someone at *City?*"

I said I wouldn't discount it. I figured with all the stuff the cops had pointing to drugs, they wouldn't discount it either.

We were quiet again, then Joe said, "So do we lean on Danbury?"

"We could."

"Or you could mention this to your friends in homicide. Let them lean on him."

I said I'd think about it.

We talked this over and ultimately we decided that maybe we should run it by Cantor first, see which way he wanted to go with it. And as I was leaving Joe's office, he said, "Maybe the cops can look into Danbury's boat trip too."

Joe wasn't letting up on Mitch, and I told him he should forget it. My best argument was: "Lister didn't cost Mitch a dime. He came out ahead when he'd sold the stock."

Joe said, "Maybe it was a matter of pride."

Again, I told him to forget it.

When he and I were done, I called Ann. She had offered to make dinner that evening, and I called to see if the offer was still on. She said it sure was, and around seven I went home and changed and rested up for an hour before taking a cab over to her place.

When I arrived, her table was all set, and I could see she had gone to some effort, serving up linguine and mussels. I told her she was spoiling me, and when she asked what I usually ate, I said she'd prefer not to know. But over dinner I was aware that I wasn't being a great conversationalist. I had a lot on my mind, and I felt obligated to keep it to myself—that's the trouble with jobs where you have to maintain confidences, you end up holding inside more than you'd like to.

Finally she noted that I seemed quiet, and I apologized. I told her it had been that kind of a day. I said a few job-related details were still running through my mind. She grinned and asked, "Exciting stuff?"

"Not really."

"So what do I have to do to get your attention?"

I didn't answer directly, and after a moment she said, "I know," and she got up and headed for the bedroom. She stopped on the way and gave me a flash of thigh, and that was about all I needed to see. The sparks were lit, and for the next hour, she got my attention.

CHAPTER TEN

REPORTERS' SCHEDULES ARE rarely smooth. Joe and I arrived at the paper the next morning to learn that Cantor had taken off for Washington, for the American Newspaper Editors Convention. We decided it wasn't worth calling him there and that this could wait until he got back. I typed up a memo for him in the meantime, then I got a call from Larsen. He said he had Lister's yearbook, and if I still wanted to take a look at it, I should come by.

Around midmorning, I cabbed it over to the Midtown North Precinct and Xeroxed some names of the people in Lister's high school class. Rich wasn't around, which was probably just as well because I didn't want to get into the Mitch business with him until I'd talked to Cantor. When I got back to the paper, I made some calls to directory and managed to locate a handful of Lister's classmates who were still living in or near Glenville. Two were willing to talk to me. One guy went on at length about Lister's way with women. The other said he thought money had been very important to Lister, even in school.

I was in the middle of this when the day editor, Art Gelber, came back to my cubicle and asked what had happened to the profile I'd suggested on Koslo's attorney, Barry Colson. I told him something important had come up the day before, something Cantor had wanted

119

me to jump on. Art stood with his elbow propped against the cubicle door. He said, "Killion tells me Colson isn't planning on calling one defense witness. Maybe you ought to jump on that."

It sounded like I didn't have much choice. The piece was suddenly timely. I took the subway downtown, talked to Colson briefly, and spent the rest of the day at the courthouse, sitting through Danziger's summation.

In the morning Cantor was back, and Joe and I sat him down and brought him up-to-date on what we'd learned. When we'd finished, he sat and mused for a moment, then he asked Joe what he thought of this as a business story.

Joe said, "The deal that nearly was? Not much."

Cantor agreed. Then he looked at me and said, "But you think there might be a tie-in to the case if the deal leaked out?"

I said I wouldn't exclude it.

"Nor would I, but it could take time to flush out."

I agreed.

Again, Cantor sat and mused, and finally he said, "Okay, here's what we do. I like what we've got overall, and the way I see it, you've got lines to the cops, so if anything does come up later, you'll be the first to know. At least that's what I'm assuming . . ."

He raised an eyebrow to underscore the point. Then he said, "Two ways to go with this. Either we run it as a self-contained business story—and Joe doesn't think much of that. Or, we put it in your profile of Lister as a sidebar." I nodded, and he asked, "How close are you on the profile?"

I said I had enough to go with.

"Okay, write it up. We'll run it Sunday. Joe can do the sidebar."

Joe glanced at me and indicated this was fine with him. Then I brought up the issue of the Koslo trial, which was nearing conclusion, and asked Cantor if he still wanted me on that. He said, "Skip it today. Let Killion handle it." Then he said, "I'd like a piece on Colson the day the jury comes in."

I had a day's reprieve at least. I went back to my cubicle and settled down, doing what I liked to do best—writing a long piece. I worked hard, rounding out the details about Lister and the worlds he brushed against—and around three Joe came in with his sidebar, and we compared notes. The two pieces formed a rather neat portrait of greed and ambition.

I spent the late afternoon with the Sunday edition's editor, going over the piece. He liked it, and he had only a few minor suggestions, and when I was done with the revisions, I turned in the finished piece. Joe and I then went out and grabbed a bite to eat, and at one point during the meal he asked me where some of the juicier stuff in my story came from. I said, "Sources."

"They did you proud."

I said, "I guess so." It seemed inappropriate to tell him that I was about to go home and share a bed with one.

In the morning I made a point of being at the Koslo trial on time because I wanted to hear Colson's summation. His was more impassioned than Danziger's—defense summations generally are—and when Colson was through, it was eleven o'clock, and Judge Richardson called a short recess before instructing the jury.

I hung around during the recess, then I went back into court with Killion and listened as Judge Richardson laid out the fundamentals of the juror system, and the jurors' part in it:

"You are to decide this case solely on the evidence as you recall it. You are the sole judges of the weight of that evidence and the credibility of the witnesses. You may draw no inference whatever from the fact that the defendant did not take the stand. That is his right . . ."

I knew the liturgy by heart, and I seriously doubted the jury would come in that day. Even if they did, Killion was there to cover it, and if the jury convicted, as I suspected they would, I'd be writing a sidebar, at most, to Killion's story. I decided it was a day for taking lunch and lingering over a few drinks, and so around noon, I took the IRT uptown and shouldered my way through the bar crowd in Costello's.

Costello's is a reporters' bar, and as I was ordering a beer, an old friend squeezed in at the bar next me. His name was Giles Watt, and when he spotted me, his eyes bulged. "Jeezus H. Christ," he said. "It's the maven of mayhem."

Giles had worked at the paper with me until he quit to go to the competition. He was big guy in his mid-thirties, and some years ago he had spent time working for a wire service in London. As a result, his vocabulary was still sprinkled with the vernacular of the Anglo-Aussies he'd known on Fleet Street.

"Good to you see you, lad. You're looking chipper."

I told him it was the exemplary life I led.

"Me too." Giles patted his belly. "Ted keeping you on your toes, is he?"

I raised my glass.

Giles wiped the beer foam from his lips and confided, "The guy I'm working for right now makes Ted look sane. At least I'm on the national desk." He glanced at a menu and tossed it on the bar, then he said, "Mike, I don't know how you stood *Metro* all these years."

"There's wheat in the chaff," I said.

Giles ordered a cheeseburger, then he told me, "Anyway, I keep up. I read your stories on my old pal Steve Lister."

"*You* knew him?" I was genuinely shocked.

"Sure . . . kind of. He was part of a crowd I used to run with in the Hamptons."

"Jeez, I didn't know that. I wish I had, I'd have called you."

Giles quaffed his beer and said, "I nearly called *you*. 'Course, we're on opposite teams." Then he said, "I couldn't have given you much. Like I said, it was a while back."

"So what was he like?"

I was pumping him, hoping to extract something I could slot into the piece, even at this late date.

"Well, we weren't exactly running buddies. He was a friend of friends—you know the scene, find a big tent party in East Hampton and crash it. I'm talking a few years back."

"Was he at *City* then?"

"Maybe not . . ." Giles took another sip of his beer. "He was a little crazy. Who wasn't?"

"Was he into dope?"

Giles eyed me cautiously. Then he said, "I thought about that when I read your piece. Far as I recall, he wasn't. Mind you, he was never short of cash—I remember that—so maybe he was dealing even then."

He turned to greet another reporter who was meeting him for lunch. They asked me to join them, and I did, and the conversation turned to other subjects. I might have pushed Giles even more, but there really wasn't the opportunity, and the only other time the subject came up was when Giles's friend went to the men's room. Giles asked me, "So are you still on the Lister case, you devious bastard?"

I said I was baby-sitting it. Then Giles's friend returned, and the two of them left, and I figured I'd have one drink at the bar, then head back to the paper.

I had just ordered, and as I turned from the bar, I glanced back into the main room. There was Virginia Danbury eating lunch with a guy at a corner table. I figured the guy she was with must be a reporter she was courting because otherwise I'd never have expected to see her here. The Gloucester House, yes. Costello's, no. I wasn't sure if she'd seen me, but she gave no indication she had, and when her companion went to the men's room, I figured, "What the hell?" At least I'd sound her out.

I strolled over to her and she spotted me as I approached, and right away I knew this was a mistake. Still, I gave it a shot.

"Been a while," I said.

"Not long enough."

She glared at me, and I saw her hands tremble slightly. I got as far as saying, "Come on . . ." but she jumped all over me.

"That's exactly how I feel. So forget it."

There was a silence. Her eyes narrowed, then she averted her glance, looked down at her lap, smoothed her napkin, and when she looked up, she said, "Okay, Mike, thanks for stopping by. Now why don't you leave?"

Cold as ice.

I said, "I can understand you're pissed. But I was hoping you wouldn't take it this bad."

"How do you expect me to take it? You use every crumb of

information you can scrounge under the table to embarrass the magazine, and now you start on my family."

So Mitch had talked to her. Before I could say anything, she said, "Take a hike, Mike. I mean it."

"Why don't you take a minute to calm down?"

"Just go away!"

"Okay then."

I backed away. People's heads were turning. There was no point giving her a speech about a twelve-year friendship. I split, and as I walked back to the paper, wondering what Mitch might have told her, I figured this was one friendship I could write off for good.

I was still feeling a little shaky when I got back to my cubicle, and when I checked my messages, there was one from Rich Bianco. He was returning my call from late the previous afternoon—when I'd called to give him the gist of what would be running in the paper Sunday. He wasn't in when I called back, but he called me from his car a few minutes later, after calling in to pick up his messages. I said I had news for him. He said, "I got some for you too. You free right now?"

I said, "Sure," and he told me he was on his way downtown, and he'd pick me up if I could be in front of the building in ten minutes. I said I'd be there.

I made a quick call to Killion, but there was nothing going on downtown. The Koslo jury wasn't in, which didn't surprise me. So I took the elevator downstairs, and I was walking through the lobby when I saw Rich pull up. I got in the car and he made a U-turn and we headed west on Forty-second Street toward the precinct.

"So," he said. "Who goes first?"

I told him what Sunday's article contained, and I ran through the conversation with Mitch Danbury in detail, pointing out that I seriously doubted Mitch was involved.

Rich digested this, then he said, "But you're saying if he knew about the deal, there's a chance someone at *City* might have known about it?"

He understood what I meant, and I suggested he might want to lean on Danbury. Then I said, "My colleague thinks you should check his story too."

"About being out on his boat?"

I nodded, then Rich fell quiet. He seemed almost distracted. Then he said, "So where does this tie in to all the other stuff."

I said Kendall and I had talked about that. As far as we could tell, it didn't.

We crawled across the Times Square intersection, and Rich was quiet again, then he said, "Well, maybe what we got doesn't tie into much either, but it might tie into some stuff."

"What is it?"

"You'll see. It's really Larsen's baby."

"Come on. Give."

He grinned, and I backed off, realizing I was being impatient. Then he lit a cigarette at the next light, and after a moment, he said, "I'm trying to keep an open mind about a lot of this stuff on this case."

"You mean because it may not all tie in?"

He nodded and rolled the window down and said, "Sometimes it doesn't. You know that."

"So what's loose?"

"Whole lotta stuff. Plates, mileage, dope . . . any number of things. Take the woman he had lunch with at the Russian Tea Room. We still don't know who she is."

"She never came forward?"

"Uh-uh. Could be nothing, could be something. And every so often I remind myself that whoever killed him left eight hundred in cash in his pocket."

"Meaning you don't necessarily think it was a dope hit."

"Why didn't they turn him over, search his pad?"

He pulled up outside the precinct and said, "So there." Then he turned the ignition off.

On the way in he said, "Like I told you, this is Larsen's baby. I'll be curious to see what you make of it."

I said, "Fine," and we went into his office to find Larsen lounging in the chair with his feet on the desk and Phil studying the *Daily Racing Form*.

I could tell right away that Larsen was full of himself. He said, "Hey, Mike, how'd it go with the yearbook?"

I told him I'd turned up a couple of talkative folks. He asked what they'd said, but before I could answer, Rich said, "Read it in Sunday's paper, Ray—Mike already wrote *his* story."

Larsen said, "Oh yeah? He may want to rewrite it."

He glanced at Phil, and Phil tossed the *Daily Racing Form* aside and said, "Listen to this shit." Then he said, "Suppose we go through it without the fanfare, Ray."

I had the feeling Phil wasn't yet among the converted.

Larsen reacted defensively. He glanced at Rich and told Phil, "Fuck, I've been waiting for this guy." Then he laid out a stack of computerized MUD printouts on the desk.

Rich said he needed coffee first, and I noticed Larsen drumming his fingers on the desk while Rich was gone. Phil shook his head and picked up the paper again, then Rich walked back in, indicated the MUD, and asked, "How far do these go back?"

"Six months."

Larsen counted ten Xeroxed pages from the front of the inch-thick bundle, then he lowered the first page with its train of numbers onto the desk.

He said, "These are duplicates of Saturday's and Sunday's . . . we've been over these."

Rich said, "Okay," and parked himself in his desk seat.

He glanced at Larsen, and Larsen said, "Okay, Friday . . . he makes a one-minute call—"

Phil interrupted, "Let's get it straight here, Ray. When did the girl in the art department hear them arguing?"

Larsen glanced at his notebook and said, "Tuesday."

Phil nodded. Then he told Rich, "The gallery owner says Lister talked to her Monday. Okay?"

Rich nodded, and Phil seemed satisfied to have gotten this straight, whatever it was. Then he looked at me and said, "I hope you like pictures of naked ladies, Mike."

I said I generally did.

Phil chuckled and said, "Well, you'll like this one, believe me. We got thirty of 'em—series of photos called *Uptown Girl* . . ." As he started to reach into his briefcase, he said, "Here, check out this bush—"

But before he could get beyond that, Larsen interrupted, "Hey, Phil. Don't spoil it for him. Besides, Richie ain't even seen the MUD yet."

Phil rolled his eyes and said, "Okay."

Somewhat rebuffed, he sat down and cracked his knuckles, and Larsen turned to the MUD sheets again.

"Okay. Friday . . . Eight-fourteen P.M. . . . he makes a one-minute call."

Phil said, "You figure she hung up on him?"

Rich shrugged and said, "Or he got her machine."

Larsen said, "Whatever . . . Okay, Thursday . . . now it gets interesting." He flipped the page. "Thursday—one forty-five-minute call at eight-thirty. Another one for twenty minutes at ten oh-five."

Phil glanced at Larsen and said to Rich, "Ray thinks he was trying to let her down without a bump."

Larsen flipped to the next page: "Okay, Wednesday, nine oh-three. A call for one hour and twenty-five minutes . . ." His glance took in all of us. "Don't tell me these two had nothing to talk about. Okay . . ." He turned the page again. "Tuesday, no calls . . . that's the day they had their fight—the day she called him at the office." He flipped the page. "Monday . . . one call . . . nine twenty-one A.M. . . . half an hour, before he saw the gallery owner. Okay, Sunday . . . and this is interesting, too, because if you go aways back, these two talked a lot Sunday afternoons."

Rich said, "So what?"

Larsen said, "Well, it tells me Lister was home a lot on Sunday afternoons . . . so maybe she knew his habits."

Rich said, "How often did that happen?"

"Half a dozen times . . ."

I was still awaiting my opportunity to jump in. Then Phil turned to me and said, "You want dinner on us tonight, Mike?"

"Why?"

" 'Cause you're the one who first brought up her name."

I felt my face grow cold. I glanced at Phil and Larsen, then I walked around the desk and glanced at the MUD sheet. There was the 914 area code and the phone number—Ann's number.

I was vaguely aware of Rich saying, "Hey, Mike. What's up?"

And I think I said, "I just walked into a nightmare."

Half an hour later I was still sitting in the coffee shop across the street from the precinct, waiting for Rich. I'd told them all what was going on right after my remark about the nightmare, and an eerie silence had fallen on the room. Then Phil said, "Jesus Christ," and from the look on his face you'd have thought he'd been kicked in the gut.

As I recall it, they all then started to talk at once, and finally Rich said, "Mike, go sit in the coffee shop across the street and wait for me." I got up, and without another word I left the room. My head was spinning.

I sat in a corner, half aware of some argument in Greek going on between the countermen. I wasn't even sure how the cup of coffee got in front of me. And when I say I was in a nightmare, that was exactly how it felt. It was like being in an unclear state when you first wake up from a confusing dream and try to pull yourself out of it—only in this case the dream wouldn't let go. There was no wakefulness to grab on to, and I remained in the dream, steering blindly through it, vaguely aware that I was drinking foul-tasting coffee and staring out the window at the drifters on Forty-second Street. My brain was in a fog.

I don't know exactly when it began to clear, but after a while I was aware of some self-protective instinct rising up in me. Or maybe I was just coming out of shock. But slowly I began to realize that some mechanism had clicked in, and it was orienting me enough so that some perspective was returning. Then Rich and Phil walked in.

Rich sat down, gave my shoulder a squeeze, and said, "Hang in there, guy. We gotta talk this one through."

I mumbled something in response.

He said, "Crazy old world, right?"

He was doing his best to maintain a sense of humor, but it was a struggle. Then Phil said, "You look a little pale, Mike. You need some more time, or can you handle this?"

I said I was okay.

"You want a refill?" He glanced at my coffee cup, then called to the waiter, "Hey, Theo, get over here."

The waiter was preoccupied. Phil let out a long sigh, and for a while nobody spoke. Then Phil turned to Rich and said, "We gotta start somewhere. You wanna start from the top?"

Rich hesitated, then he reached into his briefcase, and I guessed what he was about to show me even before he took out the picture. He handed me an eight-by-ten glossy. It was a picture of Ann in a stylish point-toe ballet pose, only she wasn't wearing a stitch of clothing.

I handed the photo back to Rich. He glanced at Phil and put it away. When he next looked at me, his look was almost respectful, the look you'd expect from a guy who found a friend's embarrassment hard to take.

Eventually I cleared my throat and said, "All right. What's this all about?"

Rich glanced at Phil and in a dead level voice, he said, "Like Phil said, Mike, there's thirty more like this one. Some artsy series called *Uptown Girl*. Lister took 'em, but she didn't want 'em shown. At least that's what the gallery owner says."

Phil said, "Can't say I blame her."

I managed a faint grin and said, "No, you'd recognize her all right."

Phil seemed a bit cheered by my reaction. He said, "I guess you'd know, Mike." Then his smile tightened a bit and he said, "Mike, we gotta be a little careful here, you understand?"

I understood. I said I realized we were all on the spot, and they both nodded, but still nobody seemed to want to make a move. Then Rich said he needed to know if I intended to tell the lady she was under

129

investigation. I took a moment, then I nodded, and Rich glanced at Phil, who sighed and shook his head, then Rich said, "How serious is this, Mike?"

"It's fairly steady. This had kind of thrown me for a loop."

Rich flashed a quick grin. He was still trying to get a sense of where I stood, but there was no easy way to go about it. After a moment he said, "Hard to know where to begin."

I said it might help if he filled me in some.

I knew when I said this it would probably not get me very far, but I felt it was something I had to say.

Rich said, "I know, I know . . ." Then he glanced at Phil, and when he turned back to me, he said, "Look, Mike, I've known you a long time, and you've never fucked up. But this is a tough situation for Phil and me . . . we're way out on a limb here . . ."

I said I realized that. Then there was a long silence.

The waiter came by, finally, and we all ordered coffee, and when the waiter went away, Rich said, "Question, Mike. You sure you want to be taking her side?"

I said I wasn't necessarily. Then I said, "It's kind of hard to make an educated guess when you don't know all the facts."

There was another silence, then Phil said, "Yeah, but that's the problem, right?"

"You guys filling me in?"

"Sure. You understand why."

"Sure I do. If you've got a case, you don't want me blowing it."

There was a moment of strained silence, then Rich said, "I guess we're trying to anticipate a worst-case scenario, Mike, and that's no reflection on you."

I thought about this, then I said, "I guess if I went crazy, I could do a fair amount of damage."

Rich nodded slowly and said, "No kidding," and again I told him I understood. In their minds, there was always a possibility that I could start acting irrationally, and like Rich said, this was no reflection on me, at least as far as he and Phil were concerned. Cops understood loyalty, and how often it prevailed over judgment.

Rich said, "So where do we go from here?"

I didn't answer for a moment. I wasn't about to say I was capable of keeping an open mind. So I said simply, "I guess I don't expect to learn any more."

There was another silence, then I said, "All the same—unless you guys see it differently, I don't see how it would hurt to go over what you've already told me. It might even help."

"How so?" Rich said.

"Well, it ain't like I didn't hear it. And based on what I heard, I think you're way off base."

It was decision time for them. They could say no, just say, "Sorry, Mike—no can do." But as I waited, I saw Rich glance at Phil, then I saw him hold off saying anything because the waiter came by and refilled the coffee. Then the waiter went away, and Rich looked at Phil again, but Phil merely shrugged.

Finally Rich said, "Suppose we give Mike the benefit of the doubt here."

Phil sipped his coffee and said, "This is *your* call, amigo."

Rich snapped back, "Hey, he picked up what he heard listening to big-mouth Ray back there."

I could tell he was pissed at the whole situation. He had no real reason to be angry at Larsen. Meanwhile, Phil looked a bit chastened, and Rich was still fixing him with a glance. After a moment, Phil said, "You want my opinion? Okay. I don't think it's fair to him to ask him to keep this in bounds."

Rich uttered a snort, then he said, "Why don't you start with what you heard, Mike? That way, we're covered, kind of."

I glanced over at Phil again, assessing his reaction, and Phil nodded slowly. I guessed he was going with it.

I said, "All right—from the way it sounded, someone at *City* overheard her arguing with Lister. Then some gallery owner claims Lister planned to show the photos of her at an exhibit. Only she wasn't going for it. First question—did she sign a release?"

Phil and Rich exchanged looks, but neither answered, and I said, "Okay, I guess this is a one-way street. Point two: You figure she might have been pissed at him because he dumped her. Well, for what it's worth, that isn't my impression."

Rich stole a quick look at Phil, then he asked, "How so?"

"Far as I know, he didn't dump her. Second, I don't even think she was that involved. Third, and most important, I can't imagine her giving a shit, even if he showed the photos."

Phil looked at me in disbelief. He said, "We're talking about a professional lady here, Mike. She gives speeches at colleges."

"I still don't think she'd care, and that's the truth."

"So how come the gallery owner . . . ?"

He broke off, realizing he was about to say more than he intended. And after a short silence, I said, "I know you're looking at the phone calls too."

Rich said ominously, "And a couple of other things . . ."

I said, "Okay, I'm just giving you my opinion. That was the idea, right?"

Rich nodded, and I asked him, "How does this tie in with all the other stuff?" He didn't answer, and I really hadn't expected him to. After a while I said, "Doesn't sound to me like you're ready to hand her her head yet."

This was as far as we got. I realized I'd begun to sound a little aggressive, which was a mistake, and I saw Phil pull back within himself. He glanced at Rich and shook his head—a sort of warning—and Rich acknowledged with a nod, and I realized he agreed. It was too risky to go any further.

Rich lit a cigarette, then he juggled his lighter and looked at me steadily, and for the first time I saw just how hard this was for him. Some part of him wanted to believe for my sake that Ann Raymond wasn't involved, but like any cop, he wasn't about to ignore direction signs.

After a while he glanced at Phil and said with a faint smile, "I guess Mike doesn't think she did it."

Phil said, "I guess not."

Then Rich's expression grew serious and after a moment he said, "Mike, I'm gonna tell you something, and I know it probably won't do no good, but I'm gonna say it anyway. You've known this woman how long? Two, three weeks . . . ?" He let the question stand, then he drew on his cigarette and said, "Cool it."

I could think of no immediate response.

Phil said, "Do it, Mike."

Eventually I said, "I can't do that. I won't do anything stupid, but I can't do that."

Rich gazed at me closely, then he said, "So what are you gonna tell her?"

"I'm gonna tell her she's under investigation and that she should get an attorney." I saw Phil shake his head slowly, and I said, "Come on, Phil. We all gotta live with ourselves."

He didn't respond, and I said, "I think you'd do the same."

Phil said, "I wouldn't be stupid, Mike."

I grinned. I couldn't help it. I said, "Hey, Phil, I'm not planning on being stupid. I'm gonna try and approach this situation like a cop would."

Rich ground out his cigarette, and despite the awkwardness of the situation, he managed a smile. Eventually he said, "Maybe that's the smartest thing you've said tonight."

Phil said, "Unless he means he's gonna trip over his dick."

The joke didn't do much to offset the feeling of numbness that set in once I left them and caught a cab home. My thoughts were running off on tangents and I seemed to lose track of time—one minute I was sitting in a traffic jam at Lincoln Center, the next minute the cab was dropping me outside my building.

When I got in, I showered and changed and sat in my office a long time, staring the river and its pools of dappled light, and by seven that evening I'd come to terms with how I had to play this. I called Ann and asked how her day had gone—because I didn't want to spook her over the phone—and when she asked if I felt like going out to dinner, I said I had a few things I needed to talk to her about first, and that she should hold off making any reservations until I got over there.

I arrived around eight, and when she met me at the door, she was wearing jeans and a T-shirt, and she said she wasn't sure from the way I sounded on the phone if she should dress or not. I guess I'd be lying if I said I wasn't nervous. Certainly, as I looked at her, I felt a moment or two of hesitation. No matter what had gone on between us in the interim, I reminded myself that not so long ago she had dated a guy who'd been murdered, a guy who was into snuff films and drugs. And that no matter what she had said about knowing none of this, somewhere along the line she had posed nude for his camera.

But then I said to myself, "Why should that surprise me, knowing her?" And when some part of me processed this, and chilled out a little, I didn't waste much time. She fixed me a drink, then she sat down next to me, and right then and there I told her I had some bad news. She seemed a bit nervous, normally so, then I told her the police were investigating her in connection with Stephen Lister's death.

All the way home, earlier that evening, paranoia had built up in me on account of what Rich had implied in the coffee shop: that the cops were holding a few cards I didn't know about. And as I watched for Ann's reaction, I guess I was bearing this in mind. I know you can't always tell by reactions if people are lying or not—I guess that's why the polygraph business does okay—but at the moment Ann let go with a chuckle, as if this were a subtle joke that would be explained momentarily. I believed her totally.

For a moment, I was prepared to discount all the other stuff, the phone calls, the alleged argument, and the photos, and yet I remembered what I'd told Rich: I planned to approach this situation as a cop would.

Ann was staring at me and—or so it appeared to me—gradually realizing I was serious. I saw her mouth waver, and after a moment she said, "Mike, what's this all about?"

"Photos, among other things."

"Photos?"

"Photos of you, taken by him."

Again, her reaction was what I'd hoped for.

"Oh shit," she said, almost impatiently. "You've got to be kidding me."

"Uh-uh."

She floundered for a moment, then she said, "Okay, he took

134

some photos." Her glance met mine, and she reddened a bit as she began to get the picture. Then she asked, "Did you see them?"

"One."

I tried not to impart any overtone.

Ann looked at me a bit ruefully, then she said, "This is absurd."

"Not quite. Where were you that day?"

"What day?"

I looked at her, exasperated. "What day? The day he was killed."

"At home." She hesitated a moment. "Upstate. I was writing . . ."

"You were alone?"

"Yes."

"Did you call anyone?"

"I don't remember."

I nodded slowly. Then I told her about the phone calls and the argument. I said the cops were under the impression that she'd argued with Lister because he planned to exhibit the photos.

"That's ridiculous! I never argued with him!"

"Not in the art department? At the magazine?"

"No!"

"Well, someone says they heard you."

"They couldn't have! I mean, it never happened."

"Okay." I let her calm down a little, then I told her that apparently Lister had told some gallery owner that she didn't want the photos exhibited.

She gazed at me, her expression slack, then she said a bit feebly, "Well, he asked if he could show them. I said no."

"Did you sign a release?"

"Of course not! We just got a little wild one night, and he took them."

"Then he wanted to show them?"

"Well, not at the time. He brought it up about two months later. I said no."

I got up and poured us a couple more drinks, then when I sat down, I said, "So what did you talk about the week before he died? There were a lot of phone calls."

She looked at me, surprised that I knew so much. Then she said, "He wanted me to go away with him. He said he had the loan of a yacht in the Bahamas somewhere, and he had something to celebrate. I was busy, I didn't want to go."

"Did you argue about that?"

"Well, I was resisting. He kept calling me."

I stared at her steadily, then I said, "You never told me any of this."

Her expression changed, and I realized I'd gone too far. She was reacting as if I were accusing her. But it wasn't that. It was my jealous side coming to the fore, and some envy, albeit misplaced, emerging at the thought of her decorating Lister's yacht. I guess I was still reacting to the photos, although I had noted earlier that evening that I hadn't felt too much of a reaction to the thought of Lister's taking nude photos of her. Maybe I'd suppressed it. Or maybe I'd just come to accept the wild side of her—hell, it was what turned me on.

She was still looking at me critically. I apologized and said I hadn't meant to sound accusing. I'd just been blindsided all day.

Then she said, "What else is there?"

I told her that was all I knew right now, and it was all I was likely to know.

"What does that mean?"

"I'm off the case, off the story."

"Because of me?"

"Because of us, yes."

I'd tried to make this sound as if it were nobody's fault. But she didn't take it that way, and from the look she gave me, I had the feeling she was more concerned for me than for herself. I figured she still didn't get it. I told her, "This is serious, Ann. You're going to need a lawyer."

She stared at me in dismay, then she said, "Can't I just talk to the police? Can't you . . . ?"

"It doesn't work that way."

From her attitude I could tell she wanted to argue this, and my tone became a bit more forceful. I said, "Look, this is something I know a little about. Innocent or not, you get a lawyer when you talk to the cops."

She said, "Okay, okay." She seemed confused for a minute, then she was silent for a while, and finally, in a quieter voice, she said, "You don't have any doubts about this, do you?"

"Doubts about what?"

"That I . . . that this is absurd."

"No."

She was still staring at me. Then her face clouded and she said, "Mike, let me hear you say it. You don't think I killed him, do you? Why would I?"

"No, I don't think you killed him."

"No matter what the police may think?"

"No matter what they think."

But I was determined to hold some part of myself back. And throughout the evening I made the effort. I was still keeping in mind my promise to Rich. Even when she said she wasn't hungry, and I had to convince her that we should go out and grab a bite to eat; even when I was almost forcing food down her, because it was important that she eat since this was going to be a stressful time—still, some part of me was running a gut check. At the same time, I told her far more than I intended.

I told her about the story that was to run in Sunday's paper, and about Lister's financial dealings in the weeks before he was killed. And when I got to the punch line, she stared at me in astonishment and said, "You mean, he was going to be running the magazine?"

I nodded and told her I assumed this was what he felt like celebrating.

Then I tried to get her to recognize what it could mean if the deal had leaked out, but she was still reeling from the first revelation. She kept saying, "This is unreal!" Finally she asked me, "How do you know all this?" And I told her I couldn't tell her that. I didn't want to bring up Mitch Danbury's name. I said the important thing was, if the deal had leaked out, there was a chance someone at *City* might have known about it.

Then I had to get her to focus on her own situation again. I told her the police had alluded to some things about her that I wasn't privy to. I said she might be in for some surprises, and I asked her if she had any idea what these might be. She shook her head in a desperate way, and I told her she should be prepared for these anyway. Then I gave her the name of Aaron Hoffman, who was the best criminal defense attorney I knew, and I said she should call him in the morning, use my name, and retain him.

I guess that really threw a damper on the conversation. In any event, the silences grew longer and we both fell to brooding. Then the restaurant began to fill up, and it became difficult to talk because the tables were too close, and after one long awkward silence, we left rather than be forced to listen to the mundane banter at the next table.

We were standing on the sidewalk, waiting to cross Third Avenue. And I had slipped an arm around her and was watching for the light when I saw a tear streak her face. She wiped it away, then she saw no point in concealing what she was feeling, and she rested her head on my shoulder. She said quietly, "I'm shell-shocked." I said she had every right to be, and she managed a wan smile, and in that instant I realized something new had set in between us.

It wasn't just sex any longer. Some warmth had established itself, some deeper intimacy. And it seemed to carry over to our discussion in bed. At one point she asked me how I felt about the photos, and I said they didn't really bother me. She looked at me for a moment, then she said, "Are you sure?"

I said, "I guess not."

She sighed wearily, and she said she hoped I saw it that way because it was no big deal. Then she turned off the light and we lay in silence, and after a while she asked if I minded not making love that night. I said no, so long as it didn't become a habit.

She managed a laugh, and that was the first time she'd laughed all evening. Then she sighed again and rolled over and said, "God, I don't believe this. It's like a nightmare." I told her we'd find a way through it. Then I put my arms around her and held her close, because I figured she must be depressed as hell.

CHAPTER ELEVEN

RICH AND PHIL didn't waste any time. Around ten-thirty the next morning, Ann called me at the paper to say the cops had called her, and I was glad I'd told her what to do. The cops had asked if they could come by to talk to her, and she had said she was on the other line and would call them right back. Then she had called Hoffman, having called him once already to make an appointment, and this time she told him that her fears had just been confirmed. Ten minutes later, Phil got a call from Aaron Hoffman to say that if he had any questions to ask Ann Raymond about the murder of Stephen Lister, he could talk to her in the offices of Hoffman and Cline at two that afternoon.

There was little I could do to fill the hours until that meeting except kick my heels. The Koslo jury was still out, and I didn't want to be around courtrooms anyway. I hung around the newsroom for a while, then later that morning, Cantor stopped by my cubicle. He told me he'd read the Lister profile and liked it, and when he said this, it was hard for me to know where to put myself. The one consolation was the thing would run before Rich or Phil would be talking to any other reporters, so it wasn't likely the story would appear out-of-date, even if it was.

I didn't tell Cantor about the problem I faced. I figured if Rich and Phil did develop a case against Ann, it would have a rather substantial impact on my life anyway, so I'd cross that hurdle when I came to it. But I was already envisioning the scene—having to let Cantor know what had gone on and why I was off the story—and having him rip me apart, saying, "You fucked up, over a piece of tail, isn't that what you're telling me?" Or something like that. It wasn't a pleasant prospect.

Then later that afternoon, Ann called back. She sounded grim. I asked how it had gone, and she said, "Well, I'm glad the lawyer was there," which didn't bode well. Then she said, "Right now all I want to do is get out of town. Suppose we go upstate. I'd say let's go to your place, but to be honest, I feel a need to guard my own turf."

"Why?"

"Well, my City space has been violated."

I caught on. "A search warrant?"

"Yes . . ."

"What did they want?"

"A jacket. A blazer, actually. That's all, as far as I know."

I remembered. The fibers the crime scene technician had showed us that day in Rich's office—they were looking for a match.

Ann said she would really like to leave town as soon as possible, and I told her to go on ahead. I said I'd drive up later and meet her there. I figured I'd better stick around in case the Koslo jury came in. Then around four, I decided, "The hell with the Koslo jury." I had too much on my mind . . . Killion could handle it. I called Ann at her apartment, hoping she was still there, but I got her machine and I figured she had left already.

I left the paper around four-thirty, and as I drove upstate that Friday evening, I was thinking about a number of things. I had to believe that sooner or later something would leak out, and there was always a possibility that a story about Ann being questioned would appear somewhere. I figured I should call Rich on Monday and ask him to do me the favor at least of calling another reporter at the paper if something was about to break. I figured at that time I'd tell Cantor.

Then as I drove on, I found myself thinking how I might have reacted if the timing of events had been a little different. If this had come out two weeks earlier, after I'd first interviewed Ann, would I have asked her out? I doubted it, but as I thought about this, I realized I'd already shifted somewhat from my earlier resolve to look at everything as a cop might. I decided it wasn't easy to be Ann Raymond's lover and not be her advocate.

I still found myself wishing I knew all the details the cops had. But there was no way of getting these, and the one consolation from the entire episode was that at least I'd been up front with Rich and Phil. If their suspicions about Ann were lifted, I was reasonably confident at least I could get back in the game.

An hour later, I pulled up at her house, and ten minutes after I arrived, we were making out on a patch of lawn between hedgerows behind her house. It was a warm evening, and there were grass clippings in her hair, and an intensity in her eyes as she moved her body against mine, and I could feel the rhythm of her breathing getting louder from the exertion. There was an urgency to the sex—it was something we both needed after the tensions of the day, and we just went at it.

Afterward, she lay on her back, gazing at the sky, and eventually she said, "Remember what I said. About where I was, the day he was killed."

"You said you were here . . . alone."

"I know. But I remembered, I was at Bob and Sarah's until around one that day."

"Bob and Sarah?"

"You met Sarah—the lady with the broken arm."

"Oh right."

"Well, I had brunch with them that day. They live a couple of miles from here. What time was it he was killed?"

"Around two-thirty P.M."

Ann sat up and took a sip of her wine. Then, with a sudden gusto, she said, "Well, I'd have had to drive like hell to make it to the city, wouldn't I?"

I nodded and didn't say anything, and after a moment she sighed and said, "Of course, I guess you could always look at it the other way. I could have made it." She sighed again, "Shit, I still don't believe this . . ."

I told her not to get discouraged, and as the evening began to get cool, I suggested we go inside. I asked if she was ready to tell me now how things had gone with Hoffman and the cops—she had wanted to put off talking about it earlier. She said she was ready, then she got up, zipped up her jeans, and saluted in a mock military way. She flashed a grin and said, "I'm glad we did this. I just wanted to be sure we had our priorities straight."

When we went inside, she told me how things had gone with Hoffman. She said she had arrived at his office an hour before the cops, and that Hoffman had spent that hour with her going over ground rules. First, he had reminded her she hadn't been charged, and that she didn't have to say anything to the police, then or at any other time, if she didn't want to. However, he suggested that some degree of cooperation might be advisable, depending on what she told him— since there was no point antagonizing agents of the law unnecessarily.

Then he had asked her the crucial question—did she have an alibi? She told him what she had just told me, that she was at her house alone that afternoon but that she'd had brunch with friends earlier that day, until one. He had said "fine" and offered no further comment.

Then she said she ran down for Hoffman the information I had given her—about what the cops were working with. She explained the circumstances under which I'd learned it, and Hoffman had made some wry comment about how he'd always known I'd lean toward the defense one day. He had asked her a bit about her relationship with Lister, although he didn't get too specific, which she said surprised her. I said defense attorneys often didn't ask those kinds of questions, just as they generally didn't ask a client if he or she did it or not.

Ann seemed a bit perturbed by this. She sat in silence a moment, then she continued. "He said he thought we could talk to the cops.

But he was very insistent that if he told me not to answer a question, I was to shut up without asking why. And then the cops arrived."

I asked her how many were there, and she said two, and I asked her to describe them, just to make sure they were Rich and Phil. They were.

She said they gave Hoffman a copy of the search warrant, and he thanked them for it "kind of sarcastically." Then he told them that his client had agreed to be here, only to learn why they needed to speak to her about Stephen Lister. He had also pointed out that there might be any number of questions she chose not to answer, and that in fact he could not promise that she would say anything. But if they didn't like this, they could always go get an arrest warrant.

I said, "Scary stuff, huh?"

"Jesus, I'll say." She shuddered. Then she said the younger cop Bianco—had thanked her for taking the time to be there—"like I had a choice." I could see Rich saying it.

She said Bianco then had asked her about her relationship with Lister, and she had told him they went out for a while. "He says, 'Were you lovers, what?' I told him it was a sexual relationship. I said we weren't in love, or anything like that. So then he asks me how long it went on, and I said five months or so. And I guess the first time Aaron chimed in was when the other cop asked what Stephen and I were arguing about the week before he was killed."

She explained that Hoffman's hand had shot up in front of her like a semaphore signal, and that he had taken issue with the cops over the word *arguing*. Rich had asked him why he had a problem with that, and Hoffman had patiently explained that the word was a loaded one. "Every couple argues, Detective," he had said. "Friends argue. My wife and I argue. But it's a loaded word, and I can't let my client answer in view of what happened to Mr. Lister."

Rich had then asked her if she'd been in touch with Lister the week before he died. She told him there had been several phone conversations.

"Then he asked me if I'd had lunch with Stephen at the Russian Tea Room the Saturday before he died. I said no."

She asked me what that was about and I told her, then she thought for a moment before saying, "Oh yes. They asked who had called who that week. I told them Stephen had called me. Then they asked why he kept calling, and I told them he wanted me to go away with him. Then they got on to the photos."

"Did they show them to you?"

"Yes. One. Aaron looked at it first, it was kind of embarrassing . . . I said the photos were no big deal, but Aaron cut me off and I didn't get a chance to say how I felt about them."

She thought for a moment, then she said, "Let's see . . . they asked if I owned any weapons. I told them I had a shotgun, because I live alone in the country. They asked if I owned any other weapons. I said no. Then they asked where I was June tenth, the afternoon he was killed, and Aaron got kind of impatient and said, that maybe they should have asked that at the outset."

"And you told them what you just told me?"

"Yes. That I'd had brunch with my friends, Bob and Sarah Blatt until around one. Then I'd come back here and worked. They asked if I'd made any phone calls that afternoon, and I said I couldn't remember—it got a little rough then."

"Why?"

"Because they pressed the issue, and Aaron got kind of snippy. He told them to get my phone records if it was so important."

I said, "They will."

"That's what Aaron said. I wish I could remember if I did call anyone, but I'm pretty sure I didn't."

I was wondering how long it would take Rich and Phil to get her MUD. A couple of days, I guessed—they'd probably have the things by the middle of next week. Meanwhile, Ann was saying, "That was about it . . . except they showed me a picture of myself on the writer's page in *City Magazine*."

"Why?"

"I don't know. They asked who took it."

"Well, who did take it?"

"A friend of mine. About two years ago."

"Do you have the magazine here?"

"Somewhere."

She slid off the couch and dug in a pile of magazines on the credenza. She found the issue, then she flipped to the page and showed me the picture. I said, "It figures."

"What?"

"The cops were interested in a blazer, right?"

"Yes, they scraped half the pile off the thing."

"Look what you're wearing."

She said, "Oh," and looked puzzled. Then she said, "It's my speech-giving outfit. Why?"

I explained that the cops had found navy wool on Lister's body.

She stared at me, and after a moment she asked weakly, "So what does this mean?"

"Nothing," I said, not wanting to tell her about the forensic work that was probably going on with that fiber as we spoke. "Don't worry," I told her. "They're a long way from sending you up for life yet."

I was trying to be encouraging, but it was tough sledding, and when she got up wearily and started to make dinner, I felt I owed it to her to tell her what the cops were facing. While she cooked, I filled her in about Lister's activities in the days before he was killed. I mentioned the mileage and the stolen plates, both of which, I said, suggested a tie-in with the drugs found in refrigerator. I told her this would certainly be dogging the cops as they went about checking out her story.

She asked why.

"Well, take the worst case. Suppose you were indicted. The cops and the D.A. know that any good defense attorney would bring out this stuff on cross-examination. If only to confuse the issue."

She looked at me in a curious way, then she said, "You mean, assuming a defense attorney knew about it."

"I know about it. So will Aaron."

I grinned, and she looked at me gratefully. I was well aware that this had been on Rich's mind, too, the previous evening. He knew that if push came to shove, I might well give her attorney information that could hurt their case. Ann said, "I see," and she came around the kitchen counter and gave me a kiss. Then she went back to her cooking.

I pulled up a kitchen stool and said, "Let's talk some more about the photographs. What was Lister's attitude when he asked you if he could exhibit them?"

"Well, when I said no, he kind of made a joke about it. I never thought he'd offer them to any gallery."

She stirred the skillet and I thought for a moment. Then I said, "Didn't you tell me at one time that you'd run into him in the City office the week he was killed?"

"No. It was the week before that. That's when he asked me to go away with him. I didn't see him at all the week he was killed, so if anyone heard any conversation, it must have been over the phone."

"There was never a heated argument about you not going away with him?"

"Well, it was never heated on my end. I guess it was frustrating for him. I mean, he was pulling out all the stops . . ."

"But you never argued about the photos?"

She looked at me with a hint of impatience. Then she said, "Mike, I already told you—no."

She said I sounded like a cop just then, grilling her. I said I hadn't meant to. Then she looked up from the stove and asked, "Well, since you're good at being a cop, give me their side. Give me the scenario, according to them."

I said she didn't want to hear it. But she insisted. And in the face of her repeated demands, I gave in. Finally I said, "Okay, they're probably looking at it this way:

"She was involved, heavily involved. It was passionate enough that she didn't mind agreeing to some compromising photos. Then he dumped her, and he was running around with other women, and to add insult to injury, he was going to exhibit the photos, which led to arguments, because since she was a professional woman, the photos could hurt her. So there were a lot of phone calls back and forth . . ."

I broke off. Ann was staring at me. Then she said, "Go on."

I said, "Did you call him that week?"

"I can't remember. If I did, it wasn't that often."

I said okay, and after a moment she told me to keep going.

I said, "Well, I guess the way they're seeing it is this. Things reached a point where you felt trapped, powerless, humiliated. Which in the end gave way to rage. They know you own a shotgun, so you're familiar with weapons, and you don't have a solid alibi."

She was still staring at me, and I said, "Well, you wanted to know what they were thinking."

"I know. Go on."

She was still staring at me, and after a moment I said, "So maybe she goes to his apartment, makes one last try to get the photos back. He won't come across, or he laughs in her face, or, worse, he wants to humiliate her some more, maybe he even wants to fuck her since it's Sunday afternoon and he's bored and horny. And she blows up."

"And blows him away?"

"Or maybe she shows him the gun. He makes a grab for it. But right now, I can tell you this. No D.A. would even look at it."

"Why not?"

"Because it's nearly all supposition."

Her mood had been growing resigned as I ran through the scenario, but she seemed to take a little encouragement from my last remarks. Eventually, she said, "What if something else turns up?"

"My guess is, anything that turns up will be in your favor."

She adjusted the flame on the stove and began to stir again, and she was quiet for a while. Then she started to set the table, and when she moved the computer, a thought occurred to me. I said, "Did you work on the computer that afternoon?"

She nodded.

"Did you make back-up files that day?"

Her hand moved to her mouth in an involuntary way, then she said, "God, I never thought of that. For heaven's sake, those record the time, right?"

I nodded, and she turned down the stove and quickly plugged the computer in and turned it on. Then she squeezed my hand and hit the keys, and her files came up on the screen.

She fed in her back-up disk and changed drives, and her back-up files appeared along with their dates and times. Then she leaned forward to study them, but even from where I stood I could see there was nothing recorded for the day in question.

"Damn!" She thumped the table.

I said, "Never mind. It was worth a shot."

She turned off the computer and went back to the stove, and after a while, she turned to me and said, "Thanks for trying."

I told her not to get down, and I went over to her and put my arms around her and told her the food looked great. It did—pasta with sausage, peppers, and sun-dried tomatoes. She sprinkled Parmesan cheese on it and brought it over to the table, and the only other mention of the investigation over dinner was when she complained about what the cops had done to her blazer.

We managed to shift the conversation to other subjects, but it was hard going, and it wasn't until bedtime that the mood improved. And then only briefly. She had appeared at the bathroom door and she was smiling coyly as she got into bed, and then the phone rang.

At first she let it ring, and it stopped on the tenth ring. Then it rang again, almost immediately, and this time she said, "I'd better get it."

She leaned across me and picked up, and I heard the faint, excitable chatter of a woman's voice on the line. Ann sat up, cross-legged, and after a moment she glanced at me and lowered the phone a few inches so I could hear. I heard the woman on the line say, "Bob had no idea what it was about, so he decided to wait until I got back. I'm sorry to call so late."

Ann said, "That's all right."

She mouthed the name "Sarah Blatt" and I didn't hear what Sarah next said, but then Ann's face fell and she said, "Are you sure?"

There was more chatter from Sarah, and Ann continued to look despondent. Then she squirmed a little and said vaguely, "No, it's about this man who was murdered in New York."

She offered a brief explanation without saying she was under investigation, but apparently Sarah Blatt made some assumptions, and Ann tried to introduced a note of stoicism into her voice and said,

"Well, I shouldn't worry, Sarah. I gather they're talking to everyone who knew him."

But then she gave me a glum look, and when she hung up a few minutes later, she sank back on the pillows and said, "Shit."

I waited as she gazed at me. Then she said, "Bob Blatt told the cops I left around noon that day."

She rolled over on her stomach and propped her chin on her hands, and I stroked her hair for a moment. Then she said, "One o'clock would have been cutting it. Twelve would have given me plenty of time."

I said it still wasn't grounds for anything.

She smiled wanly, and then she rested her face on the pillow and looked at me steadily. Then, after a moment or two, her expression changed and in an angry voice she said, "You know, this is starting to piss me off. Here I am, in the middle of fucking you, and I've got to deal with this shit."

It was fighting talk, and we did make love after a while, but I could tell this was starting to get to her.

CHAPTER TWELVE

In the morning I was up before her and I was sitting on the patio when she came out. Saturday was the day she generally visited her mother, she said. She asked if I wanted to hang out here, or if I needed to drive over to my place. I said I had no reason to. I told her I didn't mind going with her.

She said that would be nice, and she went back upstairs to get dressed.

We left around ten, and on the short drive across the state line to Massachusetts, I asked her about her parents. She said her father had been a teacher. Her mother had worked for the phone company in her younger days. Then she said, "I'd just as soon you not come inside when I see my mother. I always end up fighting tears. Sometimes she doesn't even know who I am."

I said I understood.

But when we pulled up at the McArdle Nursing Home, a big, rambling place that looked like something out of Edith Wharton, her mother was sitting out on the porch. I glanced at Ann and she said, "Well, I guess you might as well meet her," and I said if she didn't want me to, I could take a walk. She said, "No, it's okay. Come say hello for a few minutes, then I'll sit with her a while."

We walked up some steps to the porch. Mrs. Raymond was in midconversation with another woman, but she broke off and smiled at us as we approached. She was in her late fifties. I didn't see the likeness to Ann at first glance, then when Ann sat down next to her mother, I saw certain similarities of expression—still, I decided Ann got most of her looks from her father. Ann introduced me, and Mrs. Raymond chatted about generalities, and for a minute or two she seemed almost normal. Then I realized the woman could have been talking to anyone about anything, and the full horror of Alzheimer's disease hit me. I felt something pitch in my stomach, and I felt for Ann as she brushed a lock of hair back from her mother's forehead.

After a while I left them alone and took a walk in the grounds, and about half an hour later, as I returned to the house, I saw Ann getting up off the porch. She went inside, and when she emerged a few minutes later, she beckoned to me. She kissed her mother good-bye, and Mrs. Raymond smiled pliantly, then Ann spoke to an administrator for a few minutes before finally joining me at the car. As we drove off, we were quiet, and I left Ann to her thoughts.

I guess about five minutes went by, then she said, "You seem quiet. Did this bother you?"

"No," I said. "I just figured you wanted some time—it's a wretched disease."

"I'm used to it. It's been three years. Sometimes it's better than others . . . today wasn't too bad."

"She knew you?"

"Some of the time, maybe. You talk to her about certain things . . . some things come back."

She asked if she could have a cigarette, and I lit her one and handed it to her. She took only a couple of puffs, then tossed the cigarette away, and after staring at the road for a while, she said, "You seem kind of sullen, are you?"

"No."

I wasn't sure why she was even asking. I figured the visit had upset her. Then she said, "Are you sure? You're not thinking of yourself in relation to me?"

"What do you mean?"

She didn't say anything for a moment. She adjusted the air-conditioning, then the rearview mirror, and after another glance at me, she said, "Well, I wondered if all this was bothering you."

"All what?"

"Being off the story. Having your relationship with the cops go sour. Having to explain things to your boss. That's not bothering you?"

I said, "It's not bothering me right now. That's not why I'm quiet."

"But it has bothered you off and on?"

"I'm not blaming you, if that's what you're asking."

She glanced over at me, and after a moment she said, "I think you'd have reason to be a little resentful."

"Why?"

"Well, you've been close to this guy, Bianco, for years. He's a good source. And your boss may be on your case. You can't exactly say I've been perfect for you."

She seemed to want to make an issue of it, and I was feeling a little annoyed.

I said, "I figure you're as good as it gets."

"Why, because we fuck so well?"

I told her to pull the car over, and she looked at me with concern that she might have pissed me off. Then she found a convenient spot on a grass verge, parked, and turned off the engine. I waited until she looked over at me, then I said, "Are we testing the waters here, or what?"

"Maybe I'm concerned about you."

"Why?"

"Because you've made some sacrifices. People don't always want to admit when they're resentful."

"I'm not resentful."

She didn't respond, and I told her I thought it was classy of her to be thinking about me, given the pressure she was under. She smiled faintly and said she didn't want to see me lose my job over this, and

I told her I might get reamed, but there wasn't much chance of that. Then I told her I had the feeling things would get back on track with Rich Bianco once this was cleared up.

She said, "You think things are going to be cleared up?"

I nodded.

"I'm not so sure."

I ran a finger down her cheek and told her again not to get down. I said I was with her on this. She smiled faintly and kissed me once, then she sat staring through the windshield, and after a moment she sighed and said, "Over some nudie photos. Give me a break."

She shook her head and looked scornful for a moment, then she said, "It's not like I was the only naked woman he ever photographed."

"That's for sure." Then I said, "By the way, the cops found a photo in his pad of a girl who looked dead. It looked like a crime scene photo . . . did he ever show it to you?"

She was staring at me.

"Dead?"

"That's how she looked . . ."

She shook her head slightly, as if to clear her thoughts, then she said, "Mike, there's something I didn't tell you. And I think it's time I did." She reached for another cigarette, then she said, "I lied to you. I saw the tape."

"What?"

It was my turn to stare at her. I felt my mouth getting a little dry.

"I saw the snuff film," she said, "I lied because I didn't want you to think I . . ." She broke off and lowered her eyes. Then she said, ". . . for obvious reasons . . ."

I was still staring at her. "Jeezus Christ," I said, after a while.

Part of me understood. Part of me was pissed. I took a breath. "All right," I said. "Let's hear all of it." My voice sounded as if it contained lead.

She looked up at me. Then she said, "He knew some people who were into heavy-duty pornography . . . he used to talk to them about making snuff films—fake ones."

She was still looking at me, and then I heard my reporter's voice speaking. I said, "We're talking here about a guy who was murdered. Someone gets killed, there's generally a reason." Then I said, "If he ran with some bad company, who knows?"

I stared off at the fields. The thought occurred to me that he might have been trafficking in this stuff, aside from the drugs. After a moment, I asked her, "Did you know these people? His snuff film crowd?"

Her mouth twitched in a kind of self-deprecating way, and after a moment she said, "I met them . . . a couple of times."

"Nice company?"

"Don't rub it in. I told you he was weird . . ."

"How about you?"

She said wearily, "Okay, I'm a voyeur as well as an exhibitionist."

"Don't get defensive."

She flexed her shoulders, and I said, "You didn't tell the cops this?"

"Of course not."

"Well, there might come a time when you want to lay this on Aaron at least."

"Why? Aren't I into this enough as it is?"

I told her she was missing the point. Lister had some weird friends. Into snuff films? There could have been a money dispute. The point was, he ran with weirdness.

She was looking at me doubtfully, and eventually she said, "So did I, I guess."

"But it's one more reason why this guy might have been killed. Every little bit helps."

We were silent a moment, then I asked her, "Do you know these people?"

"I know where they hang out."

"Where?"

"Clubs downtown. I met the woman he used for the film . . . Beth somebody . . . she has a group of friends."

The worm was really gnawing at me now. She was silent for a moment, then she said, "This scares you, doesn't it? About me."

I didn't answer, and she looked away. After a moment, she said, "Some of it was research. At least that's how I justified it. I'm not as weird as it seems."

Maybe not. But I was thinking maybe *I* was crazy. Maybe she was dangerous, and I should heed some inner voice and bail. But at the same time I was seeing images—Lister borrowing a girl from some freaky art crowd, making his movie, dabbling. I wondered, did they turn the tables on him? Pull a little stunt of their own? Show him something for real? Maybe they filmed it.

Then the worm began to gnaw again. I turned to Ann and said, "It's Saturday. You feel like going into town?"

She looked at me in surprise, and I said, "Why not? We can go slumming it."

"Are you crazy?"

"No. Let's see if we can find these people."

She stared at me, and eventually she said, "Why, Mike? Tell me why."

"Hey, why not?"

After a moment she said, "No way." I figured she didn't get it.

I said, "Fine. I can go alone. I've seen the movie. Just tell me where the woman hangs out."

Ann didn't say anything. She started the car abruptly and drove off, and after a mile or so of silence, she glanced over at me and said, "Why do you want to do this?"

I said it didn't matter. I'd already changed my mind. Then, after another silence, she said, "No, on second thought, let's do it." And I decided maybe she did get it.

I said okay. And I was angry at myself for having started this. I knew why I'd brought it up, and I wished I hadn't, but it was like I needed to know. Just what were her limits? It was like wanting to find out about the parts of her I felt she was keeping from me, or at least see if they really were so dark. I felt if I faced them maybe I could come to terms with them. It was something like that. Or maybe it was just perversity.

I remember the rest of the day as weird. We didn't talk much, and we spent most of it in her garden—with me reading the paper and her puttering about—the two of us acting like any suburban couple. A number of times I was ready to tell her I'd changed my mind, but some obstinacy prevented me.

The dice were cast. Around nine we set off for the city, and as we drove, I could feel the worm getting the better of me, and there was not much I could do about it. About halfway to town she pulled off the road into a Howard Johnson's parking lot. She asked me if I'd like to drive, and I said, "Sure," and we got out to switch seats. Then, as we walked around the car, she stopped me. She said, "Why are you mad at me?"

I said I wasn't. She insisted I was.

"Is it because I lied, or because I was closer to Stephen's weirdness than you'd like me to be?"

I said it wasn't that she'd lied.

Her brow furrowed and she said, "Isn't that a dichotomy? You like the fact that I'm a little wild."

I said maybe it was. It was hard to explain.

She sighed and said, "Look, Mike, I can't deny I went out with the guy."

I said I knew that.

She rocked on the balls of her feet, and I planted a heel on the rear fender, and we faced each other in silence. Then she said, "Maybe you are more complex than I thought."

I didn't say anything, and after a moment she said, "For God's sake, let's not fight over this. If it turns out I'm too weird for you, you can always tell me to get lost." She eyed me steadily, then she nodded toward the HoJo and said, "I want some coffee. How about you?"

I said okay, and she said she'd get it, and she headed off across the parking lot.

I thought about what she'd said. Why was I getting bent out of shape? It didn't really make sense. I figured she could be one way with one guy, another way with another. This wasn't necessarily a condemnation of her. I could be different with different women.

She emerged a few minutes later, carrying the Styrofoam cups, and by then I'd already decided to make amends. I said, "You're right. Some mood got to me."

She smiled and handed me my coffee. Then she said, "Are we better now?"

I grinned, and we got back in the car, and I drove on.

An hour later, we were at my place on Riverside, and she was rummaging through a closet, complaining, "Mike! Don't you have any clothes? Everything's gray or blue . . ." She was scouring through a rack of half a dozen jackets, with a look of disapproval. Then she asked, "Don't you own anything black?"

I said, "That's your department."

She shook her head and told me I was hopeless. Finally, she found an old denim jacket on the floor and said, "Here, wear this, and some boots. These are weird places."

I groused as I dressed. She watched me, sitting on the edge of the bed in her tight black pipe-stem jeans and a heavy leather jacket, and for a second I flashed on her dressing for a night with Lister. It was weird how it kept coming up, how her past intrigued me one moment and depressed me the next.

We left the apartment around eleven and drove downtown. The first club she wanted to try was on East Sixth Street. She said it had been a sex club back in the mid-eighties. We turned off Avenue A and pulled up outside it, and after ten minutes of watching the crowd come and go, I said, "Okay, let's go take a look."

We went in. It wasn't what I'd call a heavy scene, a few S&M freaks, a lot of gawkers. We took a table and ordered drinks, and Ann checked out the place from time to time, but she didn't see Lister's friends, not that I cared that much by then if she did, and by one-thirty I was bored. The only moment worthy of note was when a skinny woman in a sleeveless shirt and a push-up bra asked me to take her photo. She posed next to her boyfriend and I snapped the shutter, and for some reason the woman felt like telling me she was scouting movie locations.

CITY OF LIES

We left then and drove across town to a place Ann said was a different scene entirely. It was in the West Village near the river, and as we pulled up outside it, I saw there were no windows to this place, just a door with a guy standing sentry, deciding who went in and who did not. Ann told me they didn't really care for gawkers here. She said the guy at the door had given her and Lister a hard time the night they'd arranged to meet the "Beth woman" and her friends here.

I had parked on the far side of the street about forty feet from the place. Ann said, "You want to try?"

I didn't answer right away. I was watching a guy and a woman coming out. The woman was young, white, and skinny, with her hair in dreadlocks. The guy was wearing a leather vest and oil-stained jeans. He was about six three, with a hatchet face and a bandanna tied around his forehead. He picked up the girl and dumped her on the rear seat of his Harley, then he started the bike. It had hot cams, no front fender, and a suicide clutch, and I could see this guy one night with his scalp hanging down his arm.

I said, "Ready," and we got out, and to my surprise, the guy at the door merely scowled and stepped back. Inside, the place stank of sweat and beer, and God knows what else, and I felt my stomach flutter a little as the clientele stared at us. A lot of heavy-leather types, biker jackets, studs, a few women. I checked out the group at the first table, then I caught a glimpse of something going on in the back of the room, saw some bare reddish flesh, crotch high, and heard a groan or two above the voices, which fell progressively silent as we walked farther in. I stared at the faces, checking out the women, and I saw one guy raise a beer bottle and chug on it, and I flashed on a night in New Paltz when I was about nineteen and wound up in the middle of a brawl. I remembered a beer bottle splitting along its seam as a guy tried to knock its end off to get a jagged edge for a weapon.

Maybe thirty seconds so far, but it felt like an eternity. Every eye in the place was on us—mean fucking eyes. I admired Lister for having the balls to come to this place, not to mention Ann.

I stood at the door to a back room and stared at a guy sitting with a woman in a tank top. He was a big stud with a hawkish nose and a nasty frown, and he saw me look at his girl who had long hair, like the girl in the movie. It wasn't her, and I couldn't see any other women. I turned Ann around, and we walked out, and I told the guy at the door, "Some other time."

Ann was holding her breath when we got back to the car.

I said, "Peachy in there, right?"

She managed a quick smile, then we drove off, and as we crossed Fourteenth Street, she said, "There's one other place we could try. It's a diner on Twelfth."

I said, "Fine."

She sighed and said, "I still don't know why we're doing this."

"You know."

"Seriously."

"Seriously?" I lit a cigarette. "If we see the woman, I'd like to rattle her cage."

We drove ten blocks uptown and pulled into the diner parking lot on Twelfth. The diner was filled with a loud assorted crowd you'd expect on a Saturday night, and we had been sitting in a booth for ten minutes, talking about something else entirely, when Ann fell silent. She leaned toward me and pointed out the window into the parking lot. A cab had pulled in and a woman and two guys were getting out. The woman closed the cab door and turned to face the diner, and I recognized her as the woman on the film.

I glanced across at Ann.

She had been looking a little pale in the harsh diner light, but now she looked paler. I asked if these people would recognize her, and she said maybe.

I watched them come in and occupy a booth at the far end of the room. They seemed ordinary enough—a few hints of their inclinations in what they wore, nothing too obvious. One of the guys was older, probably near forty—I decided he was the brains of the outfit.

He was the one who eventually got up to go to the men's room, and on his way by, he glanced at Ann and recognized her. He said, "Hi . . . Ann, isn't it?"

Ann said yes and snapped her fingers, like she couldn't remember the guy's name. The guy said, "Fritz."

I told him to sit down, and he slid in across from me, next to

Ann. Then I indicated the people across the room, and said, "You're all Stephen's friends?"

The guy smiled at Ann and nodded. Then he said, "How is Stephen?" Like he never read a paper. I couldn't tell if it was an act or not.

Ann started to explain what had happened, and I interrupted. I pointed across the room abruptly and said, "Your lady friend . . . what's her name?"

"Beth . . ."

"Right. I recognized her. I saw her on the grab frame we took off the snuff film at the police lab."

The guy stared at me. Then he looked at Ann and got up without a word.

On the way out, Ann was blabbering. She asked what the hell that had accomplished, aside from scaring her to death.

I said, "Nothing. I didn't get a read." And as we got in the car, I told her to chill out.

It had been my turn to stunt a little.

We got in the car and drove uptown, and she was silent for a long time. Then she began to laugh a little. I found myself smiling too, and despite the absurdity of the evening, I was already feeling that I'd resolved some inner conflict in regard her.

I have no idea if the incident the next night was mere coincidence. Ann said she had no idea either. She didn't know if Lister had told these people anything about her. But around eleven-thirty P.M. that Sunday evening, we were lying in bed, not yet asleep, when there was the sound of a car engine, and the glare of headlights illuminated the bedroom.

Ann sat up. Nervous.

I hauled myself out of bed, tugged on my pants, and went to the window. The car was about ten yards from the house, its headlights beaming. I couldn't make out the model or the plate number with the headlight glare. But the car just sat there. And nobody got out.

Ann moved in back of me and said, "Who is it?"

I said I didn't know.

She said, "Don't go out there," and I knew what she was thinking. She was thinking about the people from the night before.

I said I didn't plan to. But I went downstairs. Then I heard her coming down the stairs after me. And as I stood in the living room, the car started to back up slowly, and I decided it could easily have been some innocent soul looking for a neighbor's house. Or even a cop assigned by the county police to keep an eye on Ann.

I turned, and she was standing behind me, and in her hand she was holding her shotgun. When the car had gone, she ejected the cartridge and looked at me with some relief, and it was the image of her expertise as she handled that gun that stayed with me, long after the car finally took off into the night.

CHAPTER THIRTEEN

ANN STAYED IN the country Monday. I came into town with the intention of first talking to Rich, then dealing with Cantor. My story on Lister had run the day before, and there was some fallout from that—a number of irate messages, and a call from Henry Drake—but before I could get to these, I got word from Killion that the Koslo jury was coming in. I put off everything else and headed down to the courthouse.

It turned out Killion had jumped the gun. By noon nothing had happened, and when I heard from a court officer that the jury had gone to lunch, I put my own early-warning system in place and took Killion out to an Italian restaurant on Mulberry Street. Throughout the meal, he was on edge. He was new to this and almost panic-stricken about being caught off guard, and when he kept glancing at his watch, I told him to cool it—there wasn't a judge in New York who wouldn't allow half an hour for the evening news TV crews to assemble.

When we got back to court, I took the court officer aside and thanked him again in the best New York way, with a ten-dollar bill. More often than not, court officers know what is going on in jury rooms, and eventually this guy confided what was worth knowing.

There was a single juror holdout. I let Killion in on the secret, and he stared at me as if I had violated the sanctity of the jury room. I told him that when he was working the court beat, he was expected to put in for "tips," and I could see he was starting to understand.

I hung out with him the rest of the day—as a show of support—but still nothing happened, and around five I called Ann, and she asked if I'd spoken to Rich Bianco. I said, "Not yet," and I told her I was waiting on the Koslo verdict. I said I'd make of point of calling Rich tomorrow. She said by tomorrow she'd probably be talking to herself and so she planned to come into town Wednesday. She asked if we could get together for dinner that evening, and I said, "Of course."

I did nothing that evening except lie around and think about what I should say to the people I had to talk to. But when I called Rich in the morning, he was out, and when I got to the paper, Cantor wasn't to be found, and rather than sit around and kick my heels all day, I went down to the courthouse again. My timing was good. As I was walking in, I saw the first signs of a flurry, and when I ran into Killion, he exclaimed, "Mike. It's happening!" We took our seats in the press row, and I found myself envying his youthful enthusiasm.

I looked over at Koslo. He was one smart scumsucker in his immaculate blue suit and white shirt—a cool customer. He continued chatting to his attorney as Judge Richardson walked in and told the bailiff to bring in the jury. The packed courtroom grew tense.

There is nothing like a jury verdict. Especially in a homicide case. Very little in fiction or drama can compare. The defendant's fate is already sealed, and it will be revealed momentarily, and yet for the next few minutes the tension is almost unbearable as everyone in the room searches the jurors' faces for clues.

Richardson waited for the spectator mumbles to reach an acceptable level. Then he turned to the jury.

"Juror Foreperson—has the jury has reached a verdict?"

"Yes, Your Honor."

As Richardson picked up a sheet of paper, there was no other sound in the courtroom.

"The charge of murder in the first degree. How do you find the defendant?"

"Guilty."

The sound in the courtroom was like air being let out of a balloon. I looked at Koslo. His face showed no emotion. The judge polled the jurors individually. All said guilty. Danziger looked triumphant. This was a sweet moment for him.

When the judge had set a date for sentencing, I followed Danziger out to the hallway. Other reporters were trying to corner him, and eventually he invited the press en masse to his office where he would say a few words. Killion and I went upstairs and listened to him make a brief statement to the effect that the jury had spoken. And as we walked out, Killion was telling me that Danziger had done one hell of a job.

"He did okay," I said.

I wasn't feeling much enthusiasm for prosecutors at that moment, but in any event we talked for a while about Danziger's political ambitions, then I went back to the pressroom and wrote a brief story about Colson's questionable strategy in not calling a single defense witness. I called it: "Nobody Sang for the Mob Boss," and when I'd filled eight pages or so, I faxed the story in to the paper and took the IRT uptown.

My story was already edited by the time I got there, and I was on my way to my cubicle to call Rich Bianco when I ran into Cantor. He said, "Hey, Mike. They finally got the S.O.B., huh?" He told me he'd just read my piece.

I don't know what it was about his demeanor at that moment, but he seemed in a better mood than I'd seen him in for a while, and I decided to hell with talking to Rich first, this was as good a moment as any. I told Cantor I needed a few minutes in his office, and I guess he caught my sense of urgency because for once he didn't make me wait. He said, "Sure."

We walked to his office in silence, and as soon as I closed the door, I leveled with him. I said, "I'm off the Lister story. I've gotten involved with a woman Lister dated, and now she's under investigation."

"Jeezus." Cantor reacted without evidence of ire. But then his eyes narrowed a little, and he said, "You're taking yourself off the story? . . . Is that what you're telling me?"

"Not exactly."

I told him the detectives knew about it, and it wasn't a matter of choice.

"Your friend Bianco?"

I nodded.

"Is he pissed?"

I said I didn't think so. But we had talked it over, and there was nothing else to do.

Cantor stared at me a moment, then he scratched his chin. I was already feeling some surprise that he hadn't erupted.

He didn't seem to know what to say, then he scratched his chin again, and after a while he said evenly, "You know, Mike, I've been thinking about talking to you for some time. Are you unhappy at the paper?"

I tried making a joke of it. "Not any more than usual—why?"

He didn't laugh. "All right," he said after a moment. "I'll put my cards on the table. When a guy's talking to a magazine about going to work for them, I kind of assume he's not too thrilled about sticking around."

He'd caught me totally off guard, but maybe I should have expected this. Cantor had a long reach in this town.

I said, "You know, huh?"

I sensed he was almost embarrassed for me.

"You want to talk about it, Mike?"

"All right." I took a moment. "I was sniffing around a bit. They tapped me. We had a brief dance—nothing came of it."

"Because of this Lister business?"

He was better informed than I thought. I said, "You running a spy ring, as well as a paper, Ted?"

The remark came close to being an insult, but for some reason it amused him. Then he said, "Well, was it the Lister business?"

166

"Yeah. That's why they cooled on me."

Cantor sneered a little. Then he said, "I love it. Pity it didn't set your head straight." I didn't say anything, and he said, "So I'd be interested in knowing why."

"Why I was talking to them?"

He nodded.

"I felt I could write some richer stuff."

He nodded slowly, then he said, "Well, I guess that's understandable. I had a feeling you were champing at the bit."

I didn't say anything, and after a moment he said, "I nearly said something to you at the time. But I wasn't sure it would do any good." Then he said, "So how do you feel about it now?"

"I dunno." I was still surprised there'd been no theatrics. I said, "I guess I'm still sorting out a few things."

His eyes narrowed again, and he said, "Sounds like it." Then he said, "You know, you're well liked here, Mike. And you've got a fair amount of leeway. I'm not saying you can't ask for more, but this place has been pretty good to you."

I said I realized that.

Then he said, "Well, here's how I feel about it . . . I think you should take a week off and think about it."

I stared at him blankly. Then, without a trace of malice, he said, "I'm serious. It's been a couple of years since you took any time off, and when a guy's working day and night, he tends to get his head stuck up his ass. So take a week off and decide whether you want to work here or not. And if you don't that's fine. But at least we'll both know where we stand . . ."

I figured he was being about as fair as I had a right to expect. I said, "Well, I'm pretty sure I still want to work here . . . but I'll take the week."

"Good . . . and while you're taking the time, give some thought to this other business."

I wasn't sure what to say. I said, "Okay," but he was still staring at me, and after a while he said, "Or doesn't that bother you?"

"'Course it bothers me."

His mouth twisted a little, then he said, "Maybe it's none of my business, but I've known a few guys who got divorced, and sometimes guys in your shoes aren't playing with a full deck."

I felt myself starting to react, and I thought, "Shut up. You're lucky you're not getting reamed."

But I guess he thought I objected, because in an almost apologetic tone, he said, "All I'm saying is, you may not be thinking too clearly."

I said I could see how someone might question my judgment.

He shrugged. "Well, she went out with this guy, right?"

"She sure did."

"And I guess it was more than a couple of lunches since the cops are looking at her?"

I nodded, and he got up and poured himself some coffee, then he said, "But you don't think she's involved?"

"That's right."

"Well, I guess you know what you're doing." He sipped his coffee. "Either that, or she's one great piece of ass."

The remark rattled me, and made me think. Hearing him say it so bluntly. I didn't say anything. And eventually Cantor said, "Okay, I'll get someone to take over for you. Can you grease the wheels with Bianco?"

"If he's receptive."

"Okay, do it. Let me know when you're taking off."

I went back to my cubicle, feeling I'd gotten off lightly considering I was guilty on two counts. And yet the feeling persisted that I'd blotted my copybook and dropped several points in his estimation. I was also thinking that maybe I'd have preferred an explosion rather than any amount of consideration. I sat thinking about this, and about what Cantor had said about Ann, which was still echoing, and I thought it might not be a bad idea to take a short vacation. Then I thought shit no, I'd come this far, and I felt a loyalty to her now. I could just as easily spend some time upstate.

I was also a little pissed off that someone had dropped the dime on me about my conversations with City, and since I'd never returned Henry Drake's call from the previous day, I called him and tried to suss out who it might have been. Henry, of course, didn't want to talk about this. He wanted to talk about my story which had run Sunday. He said he'd been stunned to learn of Lister's deal. And he understood the allusions I'd made about the deal possibly having leaked out to someone at *City*—I'd only alluded to this in the story because I couldn't really hit it head-on. He said Virginia had egg all over her face because of what Mitch had been up to.

It occurred to me to ask what Bruton's reaction had been. Henry laughed aloud. He said Bruton was walking around like a man who'd been sentenced to be shot and didn't know how to earn a reprieve.

"You mean Stacovich planned to get rid of him?"

"It sure looks that way."

I asked if he was sure Bruton didn't know about the deal.

"No way. I saw his face Monday."

He was still joking about people on the staff being suspects, and when I finally steered him back to what Cantor had learned, he laughed again and said, "You're surprised?"

I said, "I guess I shouldn't be."

Then he said that the police were still putting in periodic appearances at the magazine, and I wasn't sure what to make of that. And when I finally realized I wasn't going to learn who my malefactor had been, I cut the conversation short.

It was getting late, and I was feeling uneasy that Rich had still not called me back. I'd begun to wonder if he'd worked himself into a snit in the past few days.

I called again but he was still out, and I left another message and a half hour later he did call back. He said, "Sorry. I got busy. I was gonna call you."

Which was nice to hear.

Then he waited for me to talk, and I asked if there was anything new he could tell me, adding that I'd understand if he couldn't. He said, "You know how it is," and so I asked him how he'd feel about working with another reporter at the paper.

He was silent for a moment, then he said, "You wanna talk in person . . . go have a drink?"

I said, "Yeah, why not?"

"Okay." Then he said, "I got a crazy evening here. Meet me tomorrow morning somewhere, we can have breakfast."

I said that would be fine.

"You'll be at your place in the morning?"

"Yeah."

"Okay, I'll call you there."

I started to tell him I'd make a point of staying away from any other reporter he might work with, but he cut me off. He said, "Relax, Mike. I'd sooner do this one-on-one." Then he said, "I see they finally nailed that bastard, Koslo."

"Yeah."

He chuckled. "I told you crime doesn't pay."

—— CHAPTER FOURTEEN ——

AROUND NINE-THIRTY THE next morning, I was sitting on a Hudson River pier, a block west of the Midtown North Precinct, waiting for Rich. When he'd called earlier that morning, he'd said he would rather meet somewhere other than the precinct, and he suggested the coffee shop across the street. I said I didn't have fond memories of that place, and so we settled for breakfast outdoors on the pier.

For the past ten minutes I'd been watching the Circle Line boats come and go and recalling the two occasions in my life when I'd actually taken one. The first time was with my parents when I was about nine years old—we'd made a day trip into the city, a major concession on my father's part. The second time was with Maggie soon after we arrived in the city from California. And as I sat on the pier, I was thinking it seemed to be my fate to be attached to people who wanted nothing more to do with New York than be tourists.

At least until Ann. Then I started thinking that maybe Ann didn't have much fondness for the city either.

I'd been thinking off and on about my conversation with Cantor, and about staying at the paper, and I had started to think that even if Ann wasn't indicted, this episode could still cause her a lot of pain and embarrassment. And I wondered what her reaction might be, and whether she'd still want to remain in New York. I wasn't sure if I still cared about New York as I once did, and I figured that if things stayed on track with us, and I imagined they would, we might be better off seeking some tranquillity somewhere else. I guess I was just examining options—sometimes it takes a crisis to make you do that. Then I saw Rich's car pull up at the end of the pier.

He got out and strolled toward me, carrying a brown bag, and as he sat down on the rotting railroad tie next to me, he seemed to be in a fairly subdued mood. He said, "I got two bacon 'n' eggs on rolls, coupla doughnuts, coffee—take your pick."

"You went all out."

"My treat." He glanced out at the water and said, "See this spot. A broad in a dress jumped in here one night, only *she* was a *he* by the time they finished her out at Thirtieth Street."

I said, "It's miracle water."

Rich grinned and handed me my coffee. The story wasn't a bad icebreaker. Then he said, "So was Aaron Hoffman your idea?"

"My *choice*."

"I figured."

He chuckled and shook his head slightly, then he chewed his doughnut, and I asked him what was so funny.

He hesitated, then he said, "I'd like you to have been there. I'd like you to have seen Hoffman's face when we handed him that photo." He was still chuckling, and I didn't think the remark was so funny. He went on, "First decent-looking client he's probably ever had, and he gets to see her in the buff."

I was still staring at him. Then he said, "Not funny, huh? Well, it's kind of funny from where I'm sitting because I've got news for you." He swilled his coffee. "Your little lady's off the hook."

"What?"

"Just what I said."

It took a moment for this to sink in.

"You're serious?"

"Oh yeah."

He wasn't kidding. And I felt a kind of warmth spreading through me. It was like all my nerves suddenly relaxed. Something just welled up inside me and made every muscle go limp—and after a moment I had to get up and take a couple of steps to make sure the system was still intact. There were so many thoughts hammering through my brain I couldn't organize them.

I heard myself say, "How come?"

Rich dug in his jacket pocket and handed me a single MUD sheet. It was from Ann's phone in Rhinebeck, and it was dated June 10—the Sunday Lister was killed. There was one call at 9:17 A.M., a local one—and another at 1:48 P.M., to a 413 area code—western Massachusetts.

I was astonished. I said, "She made a call?"

"That's right. And we know for sure it was her."

I was staring at him. I still didn't know what to say. Then he told me, "I didn't get confirmation until late last night. I'd have called you then, but I figured you needed your beauty sleep."

"So who did she call?"

"An administrator at some clinic where they keep her mother. The administrator remembers speaking to her. She says she called to remind them not to let her mother outside when the grass was being cut. Her mother gets hay fever."

"She forgot about this?"

"Hey—little thing like that?" Rich shrugged. "Can you remember who you called three weeks ago?" He wiped away the sugar from a doughnut. "So, unless she had a chopper standing by, no way she made it to the city by two-thirty."

I was still reeling from the news. How the hell could she forget? I said to Rich, "Does she know yet?"

"Uh-uh. I tried calling her . . . both numbers . . . but I got her machine. I didn't leave a message."

"She's driving into town this morning."

Rich grinned. "Well, I guess you can tell her yourself."

It was unbelievable. Fantastic news. I was starting to feel cocky. Rich looked at me kind of sheepishly, then he said, "Face it, Mike. We got tunnel vision on this one."

I could afford to be charitable. I said, "I guess so."

Rich made a little gesture of admission, and I asked him, "So what else was there . . . that made you so gung ho?"

"You really wanna know?"

"Yeah."

He took another sip of his coffee, then he said, "Well, I dunno if it was any one thing . . . you know about the phone calls, the gallery owner, the photos. This woman in the art department had a story for us. She says she picked up a phone one day, realized Lister was on the line, and when she heard him arguing with a woman, she listened in. She says she knew it was Ann Raymond because she recognized the voice—she helped illustrate the piece she'd written. She says she knew she'd been seeing Lister . . ." Rich tossed away his coffee dregs. "She heard your lady say stuff like 'You really don't want me,' and 'What's so important about this?' and she heard Lister saying it was real important to him."

"And you took it to mean the photos?"

"Sure."

"She says he was pressuring her to take a trip."

Rich shrugged. "I know, she told us. It makes sense in that context, but at the time . . ."

He reached over and took a sip of my coffee, then he said, "So there was that. Then there was what you said, interestingly. That factored into it. You said she claimed she'd never seen him do dope . . . remember? So we figured maybe this was part of the whole picture. She'd been looking at this guy one way, then she found out he was something else. And in the meantime he got her bare-assed and took the pics, then he told her he planned to show them, and that really ticked her off . . ."

Rich was counting the points off on his fingers.

"So then she goes to the funeral, right? All decked out. What does that tell you? Maybe she's in mourning on account of what she did . . . I mean, women do strange things . . ."

He paused. Then he said, "We figured, since there was a lot of chitchat between them, that maybe he took a drive up there Saturday night, which might explain some of the mileage. Phil's idea was that maybe the dope deal went down Friday after Nell's . . . at least that's what we were thinking—"

I interrupted. "You're assuming there *was* a dope deal."

"Right. Assuming there was . . ." He paused again. "Let's see . . . what else? We checked DMV. She got a couple of speeding tickets the past three months, one just a month ago . . . so we figured that she might be a little hysterical. And we knew she had a shotgun, so she knew her way around guns. Oh yeah . . . and Phil figured she could have been the one he had lunch with at the Russian Tea Room that Saturday."

"She says she wasn't."

"I guess not." He grinned and said, "Don't worry, Mike. She doesn't have to prove it."

He was silent for a moment, then he said, "I saw the rest of her MUD for that week. She called him once. He was the one calling her." He indicated the MUD sheet for Sunday, which I was still holding, and said, "So part of the theory went up in smoke, even without this."

I returned the MUD sheet to him, and he said, "So, Mike, you in a mood to laugh a little?"

"Jeezus, I'll say."

"You wanna try calling her?"

I looked at my watch. It was ten o'clock. I said she was probably still driving in.

He grinned. "Then you got some time. I'm on my way over to Lister's place for a final look-see before we give the place back to the landlord. You wanna come?"

I figured this was his way of telling me we were back on track. I asked if we were.

"No reason not to be. You were straight with us. I talked to Phil. He's cool about it."

I said I was glad to hear it. I told him I'd wished I'd known a day earlier so I could have avoided leveling with my boss.

Rich grinned. "Timing's everything, Mike. So you coming, or what?"

"Maybe I oughta leave a message."

"Ferchrissakes, we'll be an hour . . . tell her in person. She don't look like the suicidal type, and I ain't gonna keep you from that hot bod."

I told him he was pushing it.

I was still feeling the surge of relief as we drove uptown. And it wasn't for a while that I was aware that Rich was silent. When I asked him why, he said, "No reason. Just thinking." I told him again what a relief it was, just to get a conversation going.

Eventually he asked me how it had been the past few days. I said it had been rough on both of us. He said, "I'll bet." Then he said, "Last week I had my doubts about you, you know? . . . Getting involved with a woman who'd been seeing him. But I gotta say, when I met her at Hoffman's, I kind of liked her."

I said, "Don't get ideas."

He glanced over at me and grinned. "You know what I mean. She seemed okay. She's cute as hell, don't get me wrong." After a moment, he added, "I still can't see her with this guy."

I said it puzzled me too sometimes.

"Hey, it happens."

He made the turn off the West Side Highway on to Seventy-ninth Street, then he said, "I met one of Jeannie's old beaux once. Biggest asshole I ever met in my life. This thing with you and her set me thinking about it."

We drove in silence then until we parked outside Lister's apartment building. I was feeling relaxed, but at the same time I couldn't wait to get over to Ann's place and let her know the news. About the last place I wanted to be was at Lister's pad, but I figured what the hell. We probably wouldn't be long, and as far as I knew, Ann planned to be around her apartment most of the day. Besides, I had to realize I was back on the story again.

Rich had a key to the main door of Lister's building, and when we went in there was a new notice posted on the wall in the lobby. I stood reading it as we waited for the elevator.

"To all tenants," it read. "There was a murder in this building Sunday, June 10. The tenant in 7B, Mr. Lister, was shot and killed.

176

The police think he may have been shot by an intruder. Therefore, DO NOT, repeat NOT, buzz in people you don't know." It was signed: "The Management."

The elevator arrived, and Richie and I rode up to the seventh floor. When we opened the apartment up, there was still a faint stench in the air. We stepped inside and turned on the lights, and the place seemed sparser than when I'd last seen it. There was still tape on the floor where the body had lain, but the rug was gone.

"Anything in particular you're looking for?" I asked.

He sighed. "Same thing I've been looking for all along. Something we might have overlooked."

He started to look around, and I went into the bathroom to take a leak. The place was grimy after three weeks of disuse. Rich came in and rooted around in the medicine cabinet. It contained nothing of significance. We went back into the living room, then into the kitchen, and Rich groped around in the backs of cabinets. He said people often hid things for safekeeping and forgot about them. Then he told me he'd never known an apartment yet that had been thoroughly searched. A car was one thing—you could break a car down—but you couldn't break down an apartment.

I shuffled back and forth as Rich went through the bedroom dressers and closets, but about all he collected for his trouble were dust balls. And when he was done and came out and took a seat in the living room, he seemed despondent. I said, "We all done?"

"I guess."

Then he said, "I still feel like I'm chasing my tail on this one. We've got a lot of stuff, but it don't lead anywhere . . ." He broke off and glanced around the apartment, then he asked, "What does your gut tell you?"

"Nothing much."

Then I told him I'd met the woman from the snuff film.

"Really?" Rich's attention perked up.

I told him of Ann's admission and what it had led to Saturday night. I even told him about the car showing up at her place Sunday evening. I said, "I guess you might want to check these people out."

Rich mused for a moment, then he said, "Interesting." He lit a cigarette and added, "By the way, when we get down to the car, remind me to show you something."

"Okay."

Then he said, "Incidentally, I spoke to your pal Danbury. I dunno what to make of where he says he went that day. He had to know it was gonna rain . . . and he's a boat guy? Don't tell me he doesn't check the weather?"

"Did you find out how he knew about Lister's deal?"

Rich smiled. "From a broker who works for Albert G. Moran."

"You're kidding me?"

"Uh-uh. We talked to the guy. Scared him half to death. He's a squash court pal of Danbury's."

"Shit," I said. "There goes that theory."

"Yeah, I was a little disappointed." Rich ground out his cigarette and asked, "You still don't think it could have been Danbury?"

"Why? He'd risk it all, to kill Lister?"

Rich nodded slowly. "I guess not." Then he got up and started turning off lights.

When we were outside, I said, "What's the thing you wanted to show me?"

"Oh yeah. This is interesting. If you're free tomorrow, and you wanna take a drive, let me know."

We got in the car, and he took a manila envelope from the glove compartment, and handed it to me. Inside were two pictures, one of a teenage girl in tennis whites, the other the photo I'd seen before, of the girl lying facedown in leaves in the woods. I assumed it was the photo they'd found in Lister's file, but when I looked at Rich, he said, "Uh-uh."

"What?"

"This one's from a real case file."

"What?" I was astonished.

"The girl is dead. Fifteen years dead. That's her by the way . . . in the other picture . . . this isn't anything he staged."

My mouth flapped. I stared at the new photo and asked him, "So where did this come from?"

"Glenville, Long Island." He started the car. "Next time you wanna bitch about computers, remember . . . couple of years back we could never have matched this."

"So who is she?"

"Her name's Melissa Townley." He shoved the car in drive and pulled out. "She was strangled, July 26, 1975, near Glenville. Case is still open."

I was still staring at him, and he said, "Now you're gonna ask me what the fuck he was doing with a photo like this?"

"Right."

"Beats me." Rich stopped at the light at Central Park West, then he said, "You're doin' what I did. Getting all intrigued."

"Well shit . . ."

"Remember what the uncle said? How Lister was toting that camera around even as a kid?"

I thought for a minute, then I said, "How old would Lister have been when the girl was killed?"

"Seventeen . . ." The light changed and Rich made a left, then he said, "I did just what you're doing—asked myself what the fuck was he doing with this? I'm thinking maybe he worked a summer job at a local paper. Or maybe he had a relative on the force, and he swiped it. Then, I'm saying, 'So why's he still hanging on to this?' Then I start thinking, maybe this isn't from the files, maybe he took the photo after he killed her—we know he's interested in snuff films . . ."

Rich grinned and waved the photo, then he said, "Only thing is, this isn't my case."

"Jeezus, though . . ."

"I know. That's why I say, you wanna drive out tomorrow and take a look at the rest of these. See if his is an official police photo, and if he swiped it . . . 'cause if not, maybe he did off the girl . . . either way, it's a nice story for you."

I agreed it was. Then I said, "You don't think there's a connection between the two cases, do you?"

Rich grinned and said, "I wondered when you'd work around to that. You mean, a belated revenge?"

I nodded.

"I already checked. The Townley parents are dead. And the girl was an only child. So I guess not."

"What about a boyfriend?"

"I doubt it. There might be something in the file."

I was silent awhile, then I said, "But if not, it's square one."

Rich shrugged, then he said, "I try not to see it that way. We know he was into dope. We know he had money socked away. But, yeah, for all we know, it could have been personal. He could have taken pictures of some guy's wife, for all we know."

I was silent for a moment, then I said, "Someone at *City* could still have known about his deal, even if Danbury didn't find out about it that way."

Rich smiled briefly. "You still like that one, huh? Okay, there's that too."

"You have a problem with that?"

"No. 'Course not." Then he said, "I read your story closely. Nice piece."

"Thanks."

He pulled up outside Ann's apartment building and said, "So, you feel like taking a drive tomorrow?"

"Sure."

He glanced toward the apartment and said, "I guess you two have got some celebrating to do."

"I guess so."

"Well, forget this shit for a while. You want me to call you here or at your place."

"Make it my place."

"You're sure?"

"Yeah. You get her on the phone, she's liable to ask you for a new jacket."

Rich grinned. Then he said, "That was the one thing that matched."

I guess I looked a bit startled.

Then he grinned again and said, "Don't sweat it. They use that wool in about forty percent of decent blazers."

CHAPTER FIFTEEN

I GENERALLY APPROACH life with the attitude that it's best not to get too high about the highs. It's been my experience that life will break off a wicked curveball when you least expect it. But having boasted of my moderation, I will admit there were springs in my step as I bounded up the steps to Ann's apartment that day.

She was home, and she met me at the landing, asking, "Mike, what are you doing . . . what's going on . . . ?"

I pulled her inside and gave her the news, and as the realization hit home, I watched her go through the sea change.

Half an hour later, she was still sitting on the edge of the couch, shaking her head, and saying over and over, "I can't believe it." She said she remembered making the call, but she could have sworn she'd made it Saturday after she got back from the clinic. Then she got up and went to the window, and after a moment she said, "Everything that happens, I'm going to write down from now on. I mean it. Everything."

She sat down again, and I told her what Rich had said, 'Who would remember making a casual call three weeks ago?' Ann was still shaking her head, then she asked what else Rich had to say. I laid out what had led the cops to focus on her, and at one point she interrupted to ask who it was at *City* who claimed to have heard her arguing with Lister. I said I didn't know the woman's name, but she was in the art department.

Ann seemed resentful. "Bitch. I hate people like that."

Then she asked me how things stood with Rich, and I said, "We're fine. He just dropped me over here."

I took her hand—after all, it had been half an hour since I arrived—and after a while she caught on. She grinned as she stood up, and she said, "I'm a bit giddy, I hope I can do this." I led her into the bedroom, and afterward as we lay there, hearing the blare of a TV from a neighbor's apartment, Ann suddenly started to laugh. She hugged me close, and after a few moments she exclaimed, "God, it feels so good!"

Like it had just dawned on her.

She flopped back on the pillows and lay with her arms behind her head, and after a while she laughed again and said it took something like this to make you fully appreciate things.

Then she said, "Last night, I had this dream . . . I was in a long line, and I was being singled out for blame. It was on a campus somewhere, and everyone knew it was me." She stopped short. "I can't explain . . . it was awful." Then she turned her head slightly and smiled at me. "You've no idea how this feels."

I said I had some idea. I'd been living it.

"You did, didn't you?" Her look grew more intense, then a tear filled her eye, and she said, "You were my friend, Mike." Then she wiped away her tear and said, "I really love you."

It was the first time she'd ever said it, and I said the same thing, and we both lay there a long time, and I guess we were both a bit embarrassed by the admission. It was the second time in a week I felt the relationship had taken a stride forward, but this time there was no reason for me to be holding anything back. We lay back in bed and made love again, and since neither of us had anything urgent on our agendas, we stayed there most of the day.

Around five, I called Cantor and brought him up-to-date. He sounded pleased for me, but he was in the middle of some minor crisis as usual, and after making a joke about this being a good reason for me not to show my face at the paper, he said, "I meant what I said. Take some time off."

I told him I planned to. And when I hung up, Ann asked where I felt like going to celebrate. I told her I didn't care, and she made a reservation, and a few hours later we were sitting in a good Italian restaurant in the Village.

She was wearing black pumps, silk pants and a mauve jacket, and I'd been enjoying looking at her as she got ready at the apartment. I listened to her talk about how all this would eliminate a lot of superficial bullshit from her life because the past few weeks she had put everything into perspective.

She said, "Being condemned focuses the mind, wonderfully." Then she added, "I plan to slow down a little, that's for sure."

I told her what Cantor had told me to do: take some time off. And she glanced up from her salad and said, "You should." Then she asked, "What would you like to do?" And before I could answer, she went on, "In fact . . . let's talk about your dreams, Mike. I never really know what's going on in your head—all that crime lore stored up in there."

I said I still had a few dreams.

"Like what?"

"Oh, places I'd like to go."

"Okay, where would you like to go?" She tapped her plate with her fork, demanding an answer.

"Egypt."

"Egypt?"

"Yes."

"Why?"

I said I liked the Nile landscape.

She said, "It's flat." Then she laughed and said, "Really? Are you serious? You'd like to go to Egypt?"

"It's not anything urgent . . . I wouldn't mind."

"Well, let's go together then."

"Sure."

"Then fuck it, let's go."

I suggested maybe we go somewhere she'd like to go. But she insisted. "No, let's go to Egypt, I've never been there."

She raised her wineglass, and we both got fairly drunk after that, and at one juncture I felt like telling her how much I'd grown to care for her since I first sat down in her kitchen in Rhinebeck. But it didn't seem necessary. And whatever I said, I felt, would come out sounding trite. There was really no point trying to describe or analyze what was occurring. We both knew it, or so it seemed to me, and so I told her how my attitude toward the city had changed since that morning. I said I felt New York had dished out all it could, and that we'd both taken it and survived, and she sat looking at me, a little drunk and amused. Maybe I should have told her what I was really feeling—but I'm not good at that stuff, I never was, and I guess I felt that telling her I loved her had been enough for one day.

In the morning I was up early and took a cab back to my place. I'd told Ann I had an appointment with Rich Bianco, but I didn't get into where we were going. I figured the less I talked about the case, the quicker she'd be able to put aside what she'd been through.

Around nine-fifteen, Rich called from his car phone to say he was on his way uptown. He picked me up outside my building, and we headed out to Long Island across the Triborough Bridge. He asked how my evening had gone, and when I ignored some of his innuendos, he made a few cracks. But I did tell him about our impromptu plan to go see the Pyramids, and he said, "Well, that's a little farther than Jeannie and I are going."

I glanced over at him, and he said, "It's our wedding anniversary."

"Oh right."

He dug in his pocket and showed me an emerald ring he'd bought her, then he told me he'd rented the same room at the hotel in Bermuda where he and Jeannie had spent their honeymoon. I told him he was a hopeless romantic and asked when he was taking off, and he said Friday evening. Then we got into talking about Lister again, and the photo of the dead teenager, Melissa Townley.

Rich said he'd spoken to the local police chief the previous afternoon—a guy named Hagstrom. "He got pretty excited about maybe closing the books on this one." Then he said, "By the way, I told him you were a whiz on photos, so act authoritative."

I said, "No problem," then he told me Hagstrom had checked out the girl and learned she'd gone to Glenville High when Lister was there. He said Hagstrom had also checked and learned that Lister had never had a job at the local paper. I said, "That's good to know," and Rich agreed it was, but he wasn't losing sight of the fact that he was investigating Lister's murder, and that the Townley case was a sidelight. He was silent for a while, and I dug in the glove compartment and took out the photos. I said, "She was a pretty kid." Rich agreed she was, and as we drove on, I found myself speculating about how good Lister might have become at concealing the worst aspects of his personality.

But the trip turned out to be a bust. The meeting with Hagstrom did not produce anything clear-cut. The chief had no personal knowledge of the case—he had been appointed chief only two years ago after moving to the area from Suffolk County. Another man had been in charge for five years before him. Rich asked who the chief was at the time of the murder, and Hagstrom said, "That would be Chief Bushong. He died a few years back."

Rich digested this, then he took out Lister's photo from his briefcase and set it on the desk next to the half dozen photos Hagstrom was spreading out from the case file. We all gazed at the pictures for a few moments, then Hagstrom said, "Not much to choose."

Rich was still studying them. All the photos of the girl's body had been shot from different angles. The photographer, whoever he was, had been conscientious. But there were no names or dates or markings on the case file photos, just as there weren't on Lister's, and when Rich picked up a couple of pictures and compared the stock, they were all standard eight-by-ten glossy. Chief Hagstrom rubbed his neck, disappointed. "Well," he said, "I guess this doesn't clear up anything."

Rich said, "Take a look, Mike," and while I looked, Rich asked Hagstrom for a magnifying glass. And after Hagstrom found one, each of us took turns inspecting Lister's photo and a sample of the others. Rich said he'd like to take one photo with him for the lab, but based on what he could see, there was no way of knowing if Lister had taken the picture independently or if he had somehow obtained it from this file.

Rich then dug out the phone number of Lister's uncle and called him to double-check if Lister had ever worked at any Long Island paper in any capacity. The uncle said not as far as he knew. Hagstrom then called in an older officer and asked him if anyone named Stephen Lister had ever worked at the station, as a janitor or anything like that, and the older officer said no. He knew the name, Lister. He'd also read about Lister's murder in the local paper. And he vaguely remembered Lister as a kid. But as far as he could recall, Lister had never been in the station, not even for a traffic ticket.

"No relative on the force?" Rich asked.

The older officer shook his head. "Not as far as I know."

"You remember the Townley case?"

"Oh sure."

Rich then introduced himself, and the older officer said his name was Dominic Cioffi. He and Rich then briefly compared ancestries, and I admired the way Rich went about downplaying his status as a big-city cop in front of these guys, acting like one of them. Then Cioffi said, "Yeah, I remember the case. We only had one killing before that, and I remember how this one drove Carl crazy."

"The chief at the time," Hagstrom inserted.

"Sure," Cioffi insisted. "Drove him nuts. We thought we had the guy for a while. A music tutor, he was."

"A music tutor?"

"Yeah. This girl's. She lived over in the Shores. He gave her lessons."

Hagstrom interjected that the Shores was the wealthier part of the community.

Then Rich asked, "So what happened to the tutor?"

Cioffi shrugged. "We never could prove anything."

"And you don't remember Stephen Lister's name ever being connected to the case?"

186

Cioffi shook his head. He said he was sure it wasn't. Hagstrom then indicated the case file and said, "It isn't in here either. I read through the whole thing last night."

Rich looked at me and said, "Bummer, huh?"

Ten minutes later we were on our way back to the city, and after a long silence Rich said, "So what did we expect? Everything about this case is inconclusive . . . why should this be any different?"

I said, "Would have been nice though."

"Sure would."

I said, "Nice story, too. Open with a murder fifteen years ago. Implicate Lister, and write about poetic justice."

Rich lit a cigarette and said, "You want my opinion? He ripped off the damn picture."

I said I'd been looking at it that way too. I didn't figure Lister for a killer.

"Because your lady went out with him?"

"Maybe it's that, but he just didn't seem like the type."

We drove on in silence and eventually Rich said he was glad he was taking a few days off. He said he could use a break from this case. I asked him if Phil would still be working on it.

"Oh sure."

He said when he'd left that morning, Phil and Larsen were starting to go through Lister's MUD for the past six months.

"How many calls are there?"

Rich grinned.

"Two thousand two hundred and forty-seven. I'm gonna think of those poor bastards when I'm sunning myself in Bermuda."

CHAPTER SIXTEEN

I DON'T KNOW what it was that jogged my mind the following Monday afternoon, but I remember when it happened. I was thinking of calling Phil, since Rich was away, just to check in. Then I thought of him burrowing through those MUD sheets, and I decided this probably wasn't the most auspicious time. I had this image of him and Larsen going over all those numbers, grousing about how this was probably a wild-goose chase, and yet having to do it in case Lister had made a call a few months back that might give them a lead. Then I thought: The fact that nothing had cropped up in the recent MUD suggested that Lister might have used public phones for whatever he was up to—if anything.

So those were my thoughts . . . and at that moment Ann called. She said there was a good restaurant that had just opened up near her place in the country and she wouldn't mind eating there that coming weekend. I said that was fine with me. Then she said, "Well, if we're going to do it, I need to make reservations now, because it's hard to get in . . ."

And at that moment, a bell went off.

When I got off the phone with Ann, I sat thinking. It wasn't what was *in* the MUD we should have been thinking of. It was what should have been there, but wasn't. Like a call to a restaurant for a lunch reservation . . . to a place where you would need a reservation for a busy Saturday lunchtime. Where was Lister's call to the Russian Tea Room for his lunch reservation that Saturday? That wasn't in his MUD. During a Saturday lunchtime the place would be crowded . . . and Lister didn't strike me as the type who would just show up without one, especially since he was planning on lunching with someone . . .

So there was a definite possibility that whoever he'd eaten with had made the reservation.

My first thought was to call Phil. Then I remembered feeling a moment of regret that Rich was not around because Rich would get it right away, and I wasn't sure Phil would. I could see Phil raising objections. I could hear him saying, "Okay, two things. First, whose name are we looking for? Second, we don't know if the lunch is connected to anything, right?"

I could hear myself saying, "But it might be." And again, I could hear Phil saying, "Okay, whose name?"

And as I sat at my desk, I reminded myself that, as Rich had once said, it might be significant that nobody had ever come forward to say they'd had lunch with Lister that day.

A couple of times I picked up the phone to call Phil. And both times I set the phone down. I decided maybe I didn't need anyone for this. I looked at my watch. It was three-fifteen. Not a bad time. I took a cab over to Central Park and sat on the grass for half an hour, working out a few things.

Then around four, I walked down Seventh Avenue and along West Fifty-seventh Street and entered the plush, raffish restaurant. I took the unhurried maître d' aside and told him it was important I speak to him alone. He wasn't busy, and I guess his thought was that I was a customer with some minor grievance, but one who didn't want a scene. He was agreeable, and we walked back to the empty end of the restaurant.

I knew the cops must have spoken to him about Lister having eaten there, and that the date, Saturday, June 9, would probably ring a bell. So I figured I couldn't stray too far from the mark. I told him

I'd just gotten back to town from vacation and that my wife, having read up on the murder of Stephen Lister, had reminded me that we'd eaten there one day early in June, and that we'd seen Stephen Lister eating there with a certain person. I said from the stories I'd read, I gathered the police were interested in talking to anyone who might have seen who Lister was lunching with on June 9—but before going to the police with this, and perhaps involving some innocent party, I wanted to be sure that June 9 was in fact the day we had lunched there.

I told the maître d' this in deadly earnest, and he faced me no less seriously, then I asked him, "Do you still have the reservations lists?" He said, "Of course. They're in the book at the front of the restaurant."

I held my breath as we walked over there. The restaurant was quiet, and we sat down with the book at the nearest table. The maître d' moistened his finger delicately and flipped back through the pages to June 9. I told him I couldn't remember whether we'd eaten there at noon or one, which I figured would give me a fair amount of latitude. He asked my name, and I said, "Danziger," giving him the first name I could think of in case this act of subterfuge ever came back to haunt me, then I added quickly, "The reservation could have been in the names of one of the ladies we had lunch with . . . my wife wasn't sure."

"And their names?"

"One's Carmichael. That's her maiden name . . . the other is Rothstein."

I was tap dancing, making it up as I went along, but it had the desired effect. He turned the book toward me and let me do the work.

I started to run my finger down the names, not sure what I was looking for, and thinking that maybe I should have called Phil. At least he would be able to cross-reference with the names from Lister's MUD. And it was hard to read the names, because the maître d' had put a pencil line through them once people had showed up for lunch.

I went through the noon list and was starting on the 12:30s when the coat check woman asked to speak to the maître d'. He got up and left the table. I figured she'd bought me a few extra minutes, and I went back through the noons again to make sure my initial read hadn't been too cursory. Nothing rang any bells, then I moved on through the 12:30s, and 12:45s, puzzling over a couple of names that were virtually unreadable. Over my shoulder, I could hear the coat check woman arguing some point of etiquette with the maître d', then I turned to the 1:00 P.M.s.

I was three names into these when my blood jumped. At first I couldn't believe it. My first thought was "coincidence?"

I even read through a dozen more names before my eye traveled back up the page and my finger settled on the name again.

Dennison.

"Did you find it?" The maître d' was suddenly at my shoulder.

I told him no, with a vehemence he mistook for relief. "It must have been another day."

He said, "We can go back and check those if you'd like."

I said there was no reason to. I felt I'd fulfilled my civic duty. He smiled a tight smile and said he understood. Then I thanked him for his patience and walked out into the hot summer evening.

You may recall me mentioning at the start of this story the many occasions I could have pulled back and not been involved in these events? This was one such opportunity. But reporting is a complex business. It presents a lot of situations in which the correct ethical course is unclear. And in retrospect, I still have a hard time deciding whether or not I had an obligation at that point to turn over what I'd learned to Phil Gutierrez—in Rich's absence.

I know reporters who would argue that I didn't have an obligation. They would argue that the situation wasn't compelling enough, and that a reporter's first responsibility is to get the story. After all, this wasn't a case in which someone had confessed a crime to me. Nor had I obtained knowledge of any crime—after all, it is no crime for a woman to have lunch with a man. Still, it seemed to me, even at the time, that I might have come across a detail pertaining to a crime, a detail that might be relevant. And if Rich had been in town, I still think I'd have shared the information with him.

But he wasn't. He was in Bermuda. And I didn't have the same kind of working relationship with Phil that I had with Rich Bianco. With Rich, I had a history of holding off on stories. Our deal was that if I held off and adhered to his agenda, I'd always get the story first. I didn't have this arrangement with Phil—indeed, I wasn't even sure if there might be some lingering doubts on his part about me because of the business with Ann—I hadn't spoken to him since she'd been cleared. And there was something else, too, and ultimately I guess it was the deciding factor: I'd come across this detail on my own . . . because of my own initiative . . . and I guess in some way I wanted to reward that initiative.

It did occur to me too that acting on my own at this stage didn't preclude filling in Rich at some point later. I guess I had this in mind all along, even as I took the next step.

It crossed my mind briefly to call Lisa Dennison and tell her I wanted to meet with her, but I was sure if I did, I'd get a cool response. She would have read my story in the paper the previous Sunday, with its details about Mitch's shenanigans, and I decided that no matter how friendly she might have been to me at our last meeting, she would now view me as an adversary.

Despite what I'd learned in the past few minutes, I envisioned her standing by Mitch. I figured she might be critical of him, but I was betting she'd stick by him. And for this reason I doubted she'd agree to talk with me unless I could show her I was holding some cards.

The best way to do that was to not give her much choice. I needed a face-to-face.

Around eight that evening, after I'd gotten her number from information, I took a cab downtown. She lived in SoHo on Wooster Street in a loft conversion. I had no way of knowing if she was home, but it was eight-thirty on a Monday evening, and when I rang her buzzer she answered.

"Yes?"

"Lisa," I said. "It's Mike Kincaid."

The intercom fell silent. I rang the buzzer again. This time she said, "I can't hear. Who is this?"

I figured she was a little nervous.

"Mike Kincaid!"

"What are you doing here?"

"I need to talk to you. It's important."

This time the intercom did not click off. It hummed for a few seconds, then she buzzed me in. And I was a little surprised that she hadn't made more of a fight of it.

When I got off the elevator, she was waiting on the landing outside her loft, looking very attractive in jeans and a man's shirt, but looking at me in a sort of irritated way.

She said, "What are doing here?"

I said, "Do you mind if we talk inside?" And as I drew level with her, I did my best to give her the impression this was a fait accompli, and that there was no way we were not going to have a conversation. She hesitated, and when I held out a hand toward the apartment door, she looked at me with some resentment. Then she turned and headed inside, and I walked in after her and headed straight for the sofa.

She stood next to the coffee table looking at me in a curious, puzzled way. Then she said, "If this is about Mitch, I don't have anything to say . . ."

"It's not about Mitch."

She gave me her puzzled look again, and eventually she asked, "So what is it about?"

I said, "It's about Stephen Lister."

I saw her mouth make an involuntary twitch, but she was still affecting the puzzled look. And I knew right then that if I was going to cut through a lot of bullshit, I'd have to take a flyer. I said, "I know you were fucking him, and I just wondered why you never told the police that."

The color drained from her cheeks, and for a moment she was like a different person. Then the color returned and her face lit up crimson.

"How dare you? How dare you say that? That's an outright lie!"

"No, it's not." I kept my voice level. "And the real question is, why didn't you tell the cops?"

194

"There's nothing to tell! How dare you come in here, making things up like this!"

But I already knew, just by the vehemence of the reaction. I'd hit the nail on the head. She tried to back off and act as if this were some stupid joke that she couldn't understand, but the retreat came too late, and I guess she knew she'd already tipped her hand. Still, she gave it a whirl, trying to cover.

"Do you think this is funny? Or do you get off on this?" When I didn't answer right away, she said, "I heard about what you did with Mitch!"

I said, "Let's leave Mitch out of this. The question is, do you want to talk or not?"

I knew I had to move it along, keep her off-balance. It's always a tough role, harder still when you know you're bullying, but it's part of the job.

She was staring at me. Then she said, "Get out of here! What I do with my personal life is none of your business."

I didn't move. I said, "You're denying it then?"

"What? . . ." She groped for words. "Of course, I'm denying it. I just told you! Now get out of here!"

"All right," I said. "I'll go to the cops with this. But I think you'd be a lot better off talking to me."

"What?"

She looked startled, and unnerved, and I gave her a few moments to think about this. I deliberately hadn't mentioned the Russian Tea Room lunch yet because I didn't want her to suspect this was all I had. Besides, it had served its purpose. Now I had to see where it led.

I said, "Come on, Lisa. I turn this over to the cops, and they'll be knocking at your door for months."

"You can't prove anything!"

It was an abrupt, inadvertent response. Almost as good as an admission. I said, "Yes, I can. And there's a lot we need to discuss. And if you're smart, you'll give some thought to the ground rules— unless you killed him—in which case I'd suggest you say nothing until you've talked to a lawyer."

Her mouth flapped.

She said, "What?" Then she laughed sarcastically and said, "*I* killed him?" She was doing her best to cover her nervousness.

I didn't say anything for a while. And eventually she said, "What makes you think this is even important?"

Again, I didn't say anything. I just looked at her and shrugged, and she gazed back at me for a while, then she laughed lightly and said, "I know nothing."

I lit a cigarette and waited. I'd have waited all night if I had to—hell, she was easy on the eye. She repeated what she'd just said—that she knew nothing. Then she said again, "And who I see socially is none of your business, or the cops' business, for that matter." But this time she didn't deny that she'd been seeing him, and I made a point of not responding to what she had said. Silence was a tactic I'd learned long ago when I'd first gone to work at the paper.

I'd done an interview once with a veteran reporter, and after the interview he had told me, "Mike, you gotta learn to shut up once in a while . . ." I'd looked at him in surprise, and he'd said, "Don't you talk when they're supposed to be talking—even if you feel like a jerk when nobody's saying anything. 'Cause that's when they'll tell you what they didn't intend to tell you." It was a piece of advice I'd not forgotten.

Eventually Lisa sighed and shook her head as the silence continued. Then she said, "What do you expect me to say?"

I said, "I'd like you to fill me in about you and Lister. And tell me anything that might pertain to why he was killed . . ."

"I told you, I know nothing about that."

"All right, then talk about you and him."

"Why the hell should I?"

"I already told you why."

She looked at me in a curious, almost frustrated way, then she stared at her feet, and finally she said, "Okay, I knew the guy, obviously. So what if I did?"

"Fine. Go on." I figured the admission was complete now.

"You still haven't told me why you'd go to the cops."

"That's right. It all depends on what you tell me."

She was still staring at me defiantly, then she surprised me. She said, "Are we off the record here?"

"No."

This shook her. She said, "Why not?"

"Because I can't guarantee this won't wind up with the cops. It depends on what you say . . ."

Her nervousness increased. "I don't understand . . . you just said . . ."

"All I can say is I don't want to see you get hurt unnecessarily . . . or anyone else . . ."

She looked at me steadily, and I think maybe she believed me. Then she sighed, and after a moment she said, "I think certain people have been hurt enough already."

I said, "Okay." Not really meaning anything.

Then she said, "You want a drink or something?"

Did she think she could charm me? I said, "Not right now."

"Well, I do."

She got up, went to the refrigerator, and poured herself a glass of wine.

She glanced at me once from the kitchen, then she came back to the living area and took a seat across from me and didn't say anything for a long time.

After a while, she took a sip of her wine. Then in a flat voice she said, "I still don't see the importance of this."

I said, "You and Lister were having an affair . . ."

She rolled her eyes, and I waited. Then she said, "We went out about dozen times . . . but it was a while ago . . . about a year ago."

"Did you sleep with him?"

"Yes." Her tone was flat.

"And was it still going on?"

"Not for me . . ." She was more emphatic. "I stopped it when I started seeing Mitch."

"How did Lister take that?"

She looked at me cautiously, then she said, "Not too well." She

197

took another sip of wine and didn't elaborate for a moment, then she said, "I guess he didn't take it too well," and there was a hint of understatement in the way she said this.

I waited a moment, then I asked her, "Did Mitch know you went out with him?"

"No!" This time she was emphatic. "And I'd prefer he didn't know, especially after what came out about Stephen." I nodded and she said, "Do you think you can be discreet about that at least?"

I didn't answer her directly. I said, "How do you know Mitch didn't know?"

"He didn't . . . I mean, I'm sure he didn't."

"Why? Was this thing with Lister a secret?"

"Well, we weren't public about it, if that's what you mean."

I raised an eyebrow and said, "You didn't want anyone at the magazine to know, and neither did he?"

"That's about it."

"Conflicting agendas? Between art and editorial?"

Her mouth turned down, and she said, "Very funny."

I could understand why they'd want to keep it quiet, then I asked her, "So what was he like when it ended?"

"It was awkward."

"Because you were still working in the same place . . . ?"

"Well yes . . . of course."

"Was he pressuring you?"

"Sometimes."

"Did he ever threaten to tell Mitch?"

She looked at me, startled, getting a hint, perhaps, of where I was headed. Then she said, "No, he never did that."

I was about to ask something else, then I saw that she was about to go on. I checked myself, and she said, "He knew if he'd done that, I'd have been furious."

I read between the lines. If he'd ever blown their secret, she'd have gotten angry. It meant only one thing. It was still going on. That was her hold over him. I gazed at her and realized I was looking at someone who knew a thing or two about manipulation.

Then I said, "You *were* still fucking him."

"No!"

"Yes, you were." I started to lose patience.

She said, "I was seeing Mitch! Stephen was seeing other women!"

"Bullshit . . . what was it, a once-in-a-while thing?"

She didn't answer, and I said, "You better tell me, Lisa, and you know why." Then she lowered her eyes and remained silent for a minute, then finally she looked up at me, and she nodded. She said, "How did you find out about this?"

I said, "I can't answer that just yet . . . maybe not at all . . . How do you think I found out?"

"That isn't really fair."

"Sure it is."

We faced each other in silence for a moment, and then she told me again I wasn't being fair. She looked at me wearily and said, "It couldn't have been anything found at his place because I'm sure I'd have heard about it from the police."

I said, "You're right about that."

"So how did you find out?"

I said maybe I'd tell her later. Then I asked her, "What did you do the Friday before he was killed? After that party at the Stanhope Foundation?"

She hesitated a moment, then she said, "I went to dinner with Mitch."

"Did you spend the night with him?"

"No . . ."

"Why not?"

She hesitated. "It's kind of personal."

I waited, and after a moment she rolled her eyes and said, "It was that time of the month. I had cramps. I wanted to go home."

"So what did you do the next day?"

She stared at me for a moment, then she said, "I stayed in town, did some shopping."

"That's all?"

I was giving her a fair chance.

"Pretty much."

"Is everything else you've told me a lie?"

199

My attitude had hardened and I saw her jaw fall. Then, before she could say anything, I asked her, "Do you think there's a chance Mitch did it?"

She was still reeling from being called a liar. But she responded to what I'd just asked her.

"No, of course not. That's ridiculous . . ."

"Bullshit. You think he might have."

"I do not . . . !"

"You do. That's why you're scared. That's why you've been sitting on this. Why do you think it might have been Mitch? Because you think he might have found out?"

"This is crazy . . . !"

"You were still seeing Lister, and you think Mitch found out. You think he might have done it, but you can't quite believe it."

"No! How can you say that?"

I said, "All right, you wanna keep lying to me. Talk to the cops."

I got up abruptly, and there was panic in her eyes.

"Okay, okay . . . I wasn't sure . . ." She broke off and floundered for a moment, then she said, "Can't you see, I didn't want to even think about it. I didn't want any of this to come out . . . I didn't want anyone to know . . ."

"That you were still seeing Lister?"

"It wasn't like that. I only saw him twice."

"Why?"

"I don't know." She was having a hard time explaining. Then she exclaimed, "He remembered my birthday!" She faced me, looking humiliated. "He sent me some jewelry! I know this sounds dumb, but Mitch forgot my birthday, and Stephen could be very nice sometimes . . . I let him take me out to dinner . . ."

"And you spent the night together?"

"Yes . . ." There was anguish in her voice. "I guess I was resentful . . ." She sat down slowly on the couch, then she said, "I told him this didn't change anything, but I guess I encouraged him."

I stared at her a moment while she calmed down, then I sat down again and asked her, "So he started asking you out again?"

"Yes."

200

"Did you go?"

"No . . . not until that Saturday. We had lunch. I wanted to make it clear to him that it was over."

"Where did you have lunch?"

"At the Russian Tea Room."

She spoke with a sadness, and I sat watching her, feeling a little sorry for her, but glad at least that we were finally on track. Then she said, "I know what you're thinking, but I'm certain Mitch knew none of this, and I don't believe Stephen ever told him."

"You don't think he might have let Mitch know, after you pulled the plug on him that Saturday?"

"No . . ."

"Why not?"

"Because I didn't pull the plug. I mean, I told him how I felt, but he seemed to have other things on his mind . . . he was kind of distracted . . . it was like I never got through to him." She dabbed at her eyes with a tissue, then she went on, "He just sort of patted my hand and said, 'How about going away?' Like he wasn't really listening, or he couldn't believe I was serious about Mitch. Either that, or he thought I'd give in."

I figured this was true. The guy hadn't talked Ann into going away, so he was hitting on his old flame.

I asked her, "Did he mention anything that day about his deal to get control of *City*?"

"No. Not directly."

"What do you mean, not directly?"

She hesitated, then she said, "Well, I had a feeling something was going on. He was pretty smug throughout the lunch. He kept telling me how a lot of things were going to change. Then at one point I got up to go to the ladies' room, and when I came out, he was on the phone outside. He was in the middle of some negotiation . . . I guess it was about the deal . . . I assumed it was . . . after I read what you wrote."

"Was he talking to Stacovich?"

"No, someone called Palmer."

I felt a sudden ringing in my ears.

Then she said, "I heard him saying something like 'Look, Palmer, get this straight . . .' Then I walked by him, and he came back to the table, and he was just as smug as before . . ."

I guess it took a while before she faced me directly and she noticed that my attitude had changed. The first clue I had that I was a little white was when she leaned forward and aimed a look of concern my way and said, "Are you all right?"

I told her I was fine. I said I hadn't eaten all day. Then I asked her to elaborate on Lister's attitude on the phone, and she said, "He was being pretty tough."

"Threatening?"

"I guess so . . ."

That was all I asked her. She kept telling me she was convinced Mitch knew nothing.

Finally, I said, "You know what? I believe you."

She looked at me in surprise, and she asked why.

I said I couldn't go into that. And I spent the next ten minutes or so convincing her that neither she, nor Mitch, had anything to fear from me.

—— CHAPTER SEVENTEEN ——

IT WAS COOL and pleasant as I drove out to Long Island early the next morning, but there was little breeze, and the mist over the East River hinted at a hot and humid day to come. I rolled the car windows down and the air fanned through the Buick, and as my thoughts spun along to the sound of the tires, I can honestly say that at no point that morning did I question the wisdom of what I was doing. I had the bull by the horns and I wasn't about to let go.

My thoughts were still racing as I drove by a sign for Old Valley Shores on the way into Glenville. I'd done some homework the night before, looking over a road map of Long Island, and since it was still early and I had some extra time, I made the turn and drove for about two miles along this road until I saw a sign for Old Valley Shores Estates. I followed this sign and drove for a mile alongside a stone wall until I pulled up at the Old Valley Shores Estates entrance. This was where the Townleys had lived, and where Mrs. Palmer still lived. It looked as if it had been a gated community at one time, but it no longer was.

I drove in, passing houses that all ran a million and up, but after glancing at the names on a few dozen mailboxes, I still hadn't found the Palmer place. Finally I drove back to the main road and turned back the way I'd come. About half a mile along this road was a service station, and when I pulled in, the guy who walked out to my car looked as if he'd worked at the place for about twenty years. I asked him directions to Old Valley Shores Estates, and when he started to tell me, I let him talk. Then, as he replaced my gas cap, I asked him if he knew where the Palmer place was.

"Through the main entrance. Take the third lane on the right. It's the last place on the right. Yellow house."

"Big place, is it?"

"Best view on the estates."

I handed him my credit card and followed him into the office.

He wrote out my receipt and I said, "How's Mrs. Palmer to deal with?"

"She's okay." He handed me my card. "I never cared for Walt, or his politics."

I said I didn't either, and he took me for a fellow Democrat.

I knew a little about Walter Palmer, but I'd made a point of reading up on him the night before. He'd made money in real estate in the sixties, and he'd represented this district for sixteen years. He'd been a powerhouse in the Nixon and Ford administrations at one time, and he'd once come within a vote or two of being party whip. His obit said he'd died in office.

I thanked the station attendant for his help. Then I checked my watch and decided I'd come back to Old Valley Shores Estates later to take a look at the Palmer place. In the meantime, I drove back to Glenville, and by nine-fifteen I was parked outside the public library, waiting for it to open.

I read the paper in the car, but I couldn't concentrate that morning, and after a while I found myself reading the same sentence over and over. Finally, I put the paper away and got out and crossed Main Street to a deli, where I bought some coffee and a bagel, realizing as I ate, that this was the first food I'd put in my stomach since lunch the previous day. Then shortly after nine-thirty, the library opened. It wasn't any grand place, just your typical small-town library. I glanced through a few local phone books in the reference section, then I walked over to the librarian, a woman of thirty-five, with light brown hair and round glasses.

I asked her if she kept back issues of the *Glenville Gazette*, and she said yes, she had all this year's.

"And before that?"

She said everything before that was on microfilm, and I asked her how far those went back.

"To January 1968. But a few years might be missing. Which year were you looking for?"

"Nineteen seventy-five."

"Oh, I think we have all those . . ."

We were interrupted by an elderly woman whose seniority gave her a certain privilege. She inquired about a new Gothic novel, and I found myself forming a mental picture of Virginia Danbury in thirty years. Virginia had been on my mind off and on all morning. I imagined if I nailed this down, she'd be one of several people who would be forced to admit that I was right. I guess there was some part of me that wanted to "show 'em."

The librarian was being really nice to the elderly woman. She winked at me and checked her files, then she said, "We don't have it yet, Mrs. Simmons, but I'll make sure to order it today."

The old woman walked off, and the librarian smiled at me and said, "I'll get those microfilms for you."

We walked over to a file drawer, and she took out the films. Then she showed me to an alcove where the microfilm machine was housed, and I went to work.

I ran the film forward to the last week of July 1975, but the paper was published on a Friday, and because Melissa Townley's body had been discovered the day the paper went to press, the first details about the case were sketchy. On the front page of the July 28 edition was a story that stated that the body of the girl had been discovered at seven-thirty in the morning, July 27, on a vacant lot in the estates, by one Vernon Sherman, who had been walking his dog. The police had no comment, beyond noting that the girl had been strangled following a struggle. The community was described as shocked and outraged.

I ran the microfilm forward to the next week. This time, half the front page was devoted to the murder. There was a picture of Melissa Townley, smiling a cheerful schoolgirl's smile, and another one of several classmates grieving at her funeral. I started to read.

The story led off by saying that the police were still struggling to piece together Melissa Townley's movements from the time she left her home around four P.M. on Wednesday, July 26, until she was killed—according to the coroner's estimate—around six P.M. that evening. The girl apparently had taken a piano lesson at three that afternoon—I assumed this was how the music teacher figured into it— and she had then told her parents she was going to visit a girl friend who lived a mile away. She had not shown up at the girl friend's house, nor had she taken her bike as she usually did, which led the police to think that she might have had a rendezvous. Still, the police chief, Carl Bushong, had refused to speculate about whether Melissa Townley knew her assailant, nor would he give any indication about possible leads.

The story stated that county authorities were assisting in the investigation, and that the police were continuing to interview Melissa Townley's school friends. The story then carried expressions of remorse and tributes from various classmates.

From a Janice Gilbert: "I can't believe this happened, I'm in a state of shock."

From a Robbie Davola: "Melissa was about the last person you'd expect this to happen to."

And lo and behold . . . a name jumped out at me. There was a tribute from one Stephen Lister. He was quoted as saying: "Melissa was the kindest person you'd ever want to meet."

A current of excitement ran through me as I read this. Not only had Lister had the photo in his possession, he had known her. And although it was only a detail, it was gratifying to discover confirmation in these pages from fifteen years ago.

I read on, but there wasn't anything else in the story to top what I'd just read.

I rolled the microfilm forward and read through the subsequent weeks' accounts. In the following edition, there was a story about

206

a woman claiming to have seen a girl matching Melissa Townley's description walking along Valley Shores Road around the time of Melissa's disappearance. The reporter noted that if the girl had been Melissa, she'd have been heading in the opposite direction from her girl friend's house, which would lend support to the police theory that Melissa had an alternative destination in mind, or even an assignation. I read the item over again, attaching some significance to it in light of what I now knew. Then I read on through subsequent weeks' stories, but for the most part these contained little of interest. One edition contained a story about the community of Old Valley Shores Estates having turned inward. It said neighbors were declining to talk to reporters out of sympathy for the Townleys, who had refused all interviews.

I flipped through the next few weeks, which contained no new information. Then, in mid-September, the paper published a lengthy update on the case, which contained several quotes from the police chief, Carl Bushong. He was quoted as saying that the case continued to take up a number of his working hours each day, and that the police were still talking to a number of people in connection with the case. He declined to call them suspects, and he emphasized that evidence from the crime scene had established no definitive link to any of the individuals in question. He wanted to be "real clear" about this in view of "rumors that were circulating."

"The bottom line?" he was quoted as saying. "We've not given up on it, and we're not going to."

I was skimming through the next few weeks and finding little else of interest when there was the sound of throat clearing at my shoulder. I looked up to see the librarian standing next to me with a middle-aged man wearing bifocals. She apologized for the intrusion, then she asked if I'd mind surrendering the machine for twenty minutes or so so this gentleman could read an item. I said I'd be glad to. I was stiff from sitting and concentrating, and I'd reached a point of diminishing returns. About the only other thing I wanted to read was the edition from the year following, on the anniversary of the killing, which might contain some sort of story.

I rewound the film, and turned the machine over to the guy with the thick lenses, thinking I might take a walk over to the police station and see if I could corral Dominic Cioffi, the officer who'd been on the force at the time of the murder. But I was hesitant to do this—it might be hard to explain what I was doing here—and I wasn't sure what else Cioffi could tell me. Besides, when Rich and I had spoken to him, he hadn't struck me as the sharpest tack in the box. So I was thinking I'd pass on this and go pay a visit to one Frances Bushong, whose number and address I'd found in the phone book earlier. I figured she was either Bushong's widow or his daughter.

I found the librarian between the stacks, returning books, and I handed the film over to her. She thanked me for being considerate, and I said it was no problem, then I asked her if she had microfilm for 1976. She checked, and she did, and I was about to ask her to put it aside for me because I'd be back later to read it, when she said, "I couldn't help noticing what you were reading. It was about the Townley murder case, right?"

I nodded.

She said, "I thought so," and I asked her if she was familiar with it.

"Oh yes."

"You've lived here a long time then?"

"All my life."

It occurred to me that I might have a valuable resource right here.

I said, "Yeah, it's an interesting case . . . did you happen to know the girl?"

"Only by sight. I was a few years older than her, but I had friends who knew her." She hesitated, then she asked, "Why are you so interested in the case?"

I took a moment to take a second look at her. She had an open, honest face, and I had the feeling she might be taking more than a passing interest in what I was doing. I told her I was a reporter.

"I thought you might be . . . but you're not with the *Gazette*?"

"No," I told her which paper I was with, and she asked the obvious question: "What are you doing out in this neck of the woods?"

"Well, the case was never solved."

"But you're from the city, and it's been so long . . ." Then she looked at me in an apologetic way and said, "I'm sorry. I didn't mean to pry . . ."

I grinned. "Curiosity's the name of my game."

She shot me an odd look as she returned a batch of books to a shelf. Then she smiled and said, "So what do you think, now that you've read all about it?"

I said I had a few thoughts, a few questions. I told her one of the stories I'd read had mentioned a lot of rumors that had floated around at the time. Then I said, "Maybe you could fill me in on a few things that weren't in the paper."

"Me?"

She looked at me in surprise.

"Well, you've lived here all your life."

She laughed and moved to another cartload of books. Then as she turned the cart around, she said, "I'm sure there're a lot of people who could tell you a lot more than I could."

For a moment, she seemed a bit flummoxed, and I wasn't sure if I'd made her nervous. I said, "Well, maybe you could help a little. I mean, you're the first person I've spoken to since I read up on this." She was still looking a bit startled, so I said, "Well hell, you are a librarian. Librarians generally know more than the average Joe on the street."

I didn't want to push, but she'd already given me the feeling that she might know a thing or two, especially in view of her sudden reticence. It was as if she'd suddenly begun to realize that she might have said too much, and she'd become uncomfortable. So I said, "Look, it's up to you . . . I guess they let you out of here once in a while . . . how about if I buy you lunch and we just talk?"

She stared at me in astonishment. Then she said, "You haven't even told me what this is about."

I grinned. "I'll tell you over lunch."

She seemed faintly embarrassed. Then she said, "I can't do that."

"Why not?"

"Well, I don't generally go off to lunch with strange men and talk about old murder cases . . ."

I stared back at her, and after a moment I said, "So live a little."

She just laughed this off, still resisting, but faintly amused. Then she said, "You still haven't told me what this is about."

"Okay." I looked at her, dead serious, and said, "It's about some new details that have come to light. About the case."

Her jaw dropped. She said, "Are you serious?"

I nodded.

"Something you've turned up?"

I thought I detected a chink in her armor. I said, "Well yes . . . but I still need to know some background."

Her eyes didn't leave mine for a second, then she laughed nervously. She said, "What makes you think I know anything?"

"I'm not saying you do. I just thought we could talk, that's all. It's the background stuff I need."

She was staring at me, and eventually she said, "I get the feeling this is serious. Maybe you should be talking to the police about this."

In a way she was right. And I thought about Richie when she said this. But it was hard to know what to say in response, and she was still giving me an admonishing look as she reached for another stack of books. I lingered, wondering if it was worth the effort to try to persuade her, and thinking there might be any number of people who could help me. Then I thought no. Persuading others could take just as long, and this woman might have something to say.

I saw her look off. A teenage boy had come into the library, and as he walked to the desk, she glanced at me, then walked off to tend to him. I sat down on a three-rung ladder and waited.

The teenager was returning some books, and I looked on as she stamped his library card. Then, when the boy left, she glanced back at me, and I was still staring at her, trying to suggest we had unfinished business. She hesitated a moment, then she came back over to me, and I realized from her intensity that she was still giving this some thought.

She stared at me for a moment, then she said, "I can't believe you got me talking about this."

I said, "Well, that's what I do for a living."

"What made you pick on me?"

I reminded her I didn't. She'd broached it with me, and she at least seemed to recognize this. Then she said, "I don't even know your name."

"Mike Kincaid. Yours?"

"Sally . . . Sally Garr."

We faced each other in silence for a moment, then she folded her arms and said, "Are all reporters as persistent as you?"

I grinned. "I don't know. Maybe."

She shook her head in a weary sort of way, then she looked at me like I was being exasperating, and I told her that anything she might have to say to me would be off the record. And to emphasize the point, even at the risk of being patronizing, I asked her if she knew what that meant. She gave me a baleful look and said, "Of course."

Then she said, "I still think there're lots of people who could tell you a lot more than I could."

I said, "Maybe. But I bet your memory's pretty good."

She shot me another of her looks, and at that moment I felt it could go either way. Then I said, "Not to scare you or anything, but I wonder what Melissa Townley would urge you to do right now."

I knew I'd hit something as soon as I said this: I'd struck some chord in her that believed that maybe a victim deserved a fair shake. And I seized the moment. I said, "Look, nothing you could tell me would ever be connected to you. All I'm asking is that you flesh out the rumors, the stuff that wasn't in the paper."

"Be the town gossip, you mean . . ."

"I wouldn't call it that."

She sighed and stood with one hand on her hip. Then she shook her head in the same way she had earlier, and finally she said, "They do let me out for lunch, and I generally eat at Dugan's—that's a coffee shop down the street. If you happen to be sitting there around twelve-thirty, maybe I could join you."

She smiled and I told her she was terrific, and she said, "I don't know about that." And she was still looking at me warily, but I had the feeling she wasn't about to change her mind. I said I'd see her at Dugan's, and I promised I wouldn't have a notepad on the table when she walked in. I'd just be the guy from the library.

She said, "Right . . . and if my husband walks in, I'm dead." Then she added she was only kidding. She said her husband worked up the island twenty miles away.

When I walked into Dugan's five minutes later, I took a seat at a corner table, as far away from other customers as possible. The waitress came over, and I ordered a bowl of chowder, and while I waited I glanced at the newspaper from time to time, but I was no more able to retain a sentence than I had been earlier that morning. My mind was still going a mile a minute, and I was now putting myself through an internal debate, speculating about what Sally Garr might be able to tell me, and hoping, after all this, that I wasn't going to be disappointed.

I had a couple of nervous moments, until quarter to one. Then she finally walked in and apologized for being late. She said the library closed from twelve-thirty until two, but she'd been on edge since I'd left, and she'd forgotten about the man at the microfilm machine. "I'd already locked up when I remembered he was still back there."

I asked how long she'd worked there, and she said, "Six years." Then she told me she lived nearby, so it made for an easy schedule. She told me she had two kids. Then she gave me one of her baleful looks and said, "I still don't know why I'm agreeing to do this."

The waitress came over and she ordered a tuna salad and coffee, then she changed her mind and said she'd have iced tea. Then the waitress walked away, and she gave me another look. Then she said, "So where do you want to start?"

I asked her to tell me what she knew about Melissa Townley.

She took her time, playing with the sleeve of her blouse for a moment, then she said, "Well, like I told you, I didn't know her, except by sight. But I knew guys who dated her."

"Older guys?"

She nodded. "Couple of years older, maybe."

"What did they think of her?"

"They said she was nice."

I waited as a middle-aged woman appeared next to us and seemed

212

on the point of taking the next table. I scowled at her, a scowl that suggested that with all the other empty tables in the place, she didn't have to sit here. Then I lit a cigarette, and between the scowl and the smoke, I guess I got rid of the woman. She moved off and took another table, and I turned back to Sally Garr and got straight to the point. I said, "Do you happen to know if Melissa Townley ever dated a guy named Stephen Lister?"

Sally puzzled over the name for a moment, then she recognized it. "The guy from here? The photographer who was murdered?" I nodded, and her face took on an intrigued look. Then she asked, "Is that where all this came from?"

"Indirectly . . . this stays between us, okay?"

She said I'd better believe it.

Then I asked, "So did she date Stephen Lister?"

"I don't know. I didn't know him. At least I can't remember him. He wasn't in my year—I just read about him being killed—it was in the paper."

The waitress arrived with her lunch, and as Sally was squeezing the lemon into her iced tea, I asked her, "Do you know if Melissa ever dated a guy called Brad Palmer?"

Sally finished squeezing her lemon. She looked at me in a strange way, and at first I wasn't sure whether to attach any meaning to the look. Then she said, "Was that in the paper?"

My heart started thumping. I said no.

Sally lowered her fork, then she said, "Oh . . . wow." Then she said, "Yes, she did date Brad."

She was staring at me, and after a moment I asked her, "Why do you say, 'Oh . . . wow.' "

"Well, you scare me when you come out with things like that. I mean, I kind of have to wonder what else you know."

I said, "Not enough, clearly." Then I lit another cigarette and said, "So tell me about her and Brad Palmer."

"Well, I know she went out with him. When she was killed, the police came to the school and talked to all the guys who'd gone out with her. Brad was one of them."

"Was he a suspect?"

She hesitated, then she said, "I don't really know for sure . . . I guess he might have been . . ."

"Why do you say that?"

"Well, Brad wasn't seeing her anymore. And this guy I knew told me something. He said Brad had once called her a slut and said he wanted nothing more to do with her."

"Was this long before she was killed?"

"I don't remember . . ."

Sally looked around nervously. I said, "Do you see any guys in dark raincoats?"

She laughed and went back to her salad, and I asked her, "So was there any talk? About Brad?"

She took another bite of her salad. "Not really. I guess you know who Brad's father was." I nodded, then she said, "The real talk around town was about Mr. Delamere."

"Who was he?"

"Melissa's piano teacher."

I hadn't heard his name until then.

Then Sally said, "He came in for it more than anyone."

"Why?"

"Well, this is only what I heard at the time . . . but I remember someone at a dance one night telling me that some hair from Melissa's sweater had been found in his car. And the same guy told me Mr. Delamere didn't have a solid alibi." She looked thoughtful for a moment, then she said, "But when you think about it, that isn't much. The hair could have come from just sitting next to her at the piano."

I took a moment, then I asked, "So did people think he and Melissa had been getting it on?"

"I guess that was it. He was nice-looking man, kind of quiet . . ." Her voice trailed off for a moment, then she said, "I guess it must have been hard for him, because when word got around, nobody wanted him near their kids."

I could imagine the chain reaction. Piano lessons being canceled right and left. I said, "So you're saying everyone knew, and Delamere was hounded?"

She took a sip of her iced tea, and after a moment she said, "I don't know if I'd say *hounded*."

"But nobody ever laid any doubts to rest?"

"I guess not. I mean, nobody ever came forward and said so."

"So he was hounded?"

After a moment, she said, "I guess maybe he was. I mean . . ." She broke off for a moment, then she went on, "I guess *I* always thought there was a chance he'd done it."

"Do you know what happened to him?"

Sally shrugged. "He moved away eventually . . ."

"Do you know where he went?"

Sally shook her head. She was quiet for a moment, then she said, "Are you saying I should feel sorry for him . . . I get the feeling that's what you're saying?"

"Maybe."

"And what about Brad?"

"What about him?"

"Well, I get the feeling you know something about him."

"You mean, am I pointing the finger?"

"Yes."

The waitress put the check in front of us and I reached for it, and when I looked up, Sally Garr was still staring at me. In a slightly injured tone, she said, "So are you going to leave me dangling? Wham. Bam. Thank you, ma'am? Is that how it works?"

I grinned. "No."

She waited, and when I'd paid the tab, I told her I planned to be fair to her after what she'd told me. I said, "The night before this story runs, I'll call you, if that's okay. You can blow your husband's mind by telling him what's going to be in the paper the next morning."

She smiled, then she said, "When will that be?"

"I don't know yet."

"Can you at least keep me up-to-date?"

"Maybe."

"I mean, I won't sleep till I know."

I promised her she'd get the call. I asked her to give me her number, and she wrote it down. Then she crossed it out and said, "On second thought, you'd better call me at the library." And when she handed me the slip of paper, there was a hint of flirtatiousness in her eye.

I got the same impression once we were outside. As we walked toward my car, she asked me if I was coming back to read the other story. I said I'd pass. I told her she'd already filled in more than I could have hoped for, and I still had a lot to do. After a moment she glanced over at me, then she sighed and said, "I wish I did what you do. It seems like fun."

I said it wasn't all fun, and she said it seemed that way to her. Then she pecked me on the cheek and walked off. Back to the library.

When I left her, I picked up a soda at a convenience store and walked to my car. The day had turned humid and it was close to 90 degrees now. I started the car and turned the air-conditioning on and stood next to it for a while, with the doors open, letting the heat blow out. And when the temperature was bearable, I got in and drove over to Old Valley Shores.

I wanted a good look at the Palmer place. I felt a growing confidence that I'd be writing about it soon, and I didn't want to have to make another trip out here to get descriptive detail. I still had things to do later, but there was time, and driving over to the Palmer place gave me time to think.

Twenty minutes later, I drove in through the estates entrance and slowed to a crawl. Then I stopped and took a good look at the houses around me. For all the careful landscaping and neat lawns, there was a brooding quality to this area. Maybe it was the pines along the roads, which lent a touch of desolation even in the midsummer heat, or maybe it was the associations I now had, the fact that Melissa Townley had been murdered somewhere near here, but in any event I felt an absence of life here. No children seemed to be playing on the lawns, and there were no tires hanging from trees—I guessed the community had some sort of strict bylaws of its own.

I turned right at the third lane. It wound for a half mile, then I saw the Palmer place. It was a handsome yellow-brick mansion built in the twenties, and it sat on a low bluff directly overlooking Long Island Sound. I parked a short distance from it and took a moment to admire the view, and for a while I sat watching the gulls circling above the sound. Then I glanced toward the slate path that led to the front door, and as I looked on, a gardener in navy overalls came around the side of the house and began pruning roses.

He glanced at me once, and I felt a little conspicuous, so I took a notepad and pen from the glove compartment and acted as if I were a salesman catching up on his paperwork in a quiet place in an off hour. Meantime, I took a few notes. Then a few minutes later, the front door opened and Mrs. Palmer appeared. She began to direct the gardener. And as she stood over him, she looked even taller than on the two occasions I had seen her previously, at Lister's funeral and at Rich's office. She moved out along the slate path, and as she moved there was a vigor to her stride. I decided she was the kind of woman who hadn't gained an ounce since age thirty.

She went on directing the gardener, and I sat watching her, letting my mind wander. And as I watched her, I felt somewhat awed at her capacity to go about the ordinary tasks of life, given what I now believed she must have gone through. It was a strange moment, because for a second I felt sorry for her, then I felt anger. And it was anger I was feeling when she looked over at my car in a curious, challenging sort of way, as if to suggest that I had no business being here. It was a suspicious look, a look that said, "Maybe I should call the police," and then it was a look that said, "Maybe he is the police," and as I gazed back at her, I muttered to myself, "Sure. Go ahead, lady."

She turned back to her roses, as if dismissing me, and I had to resist the impulse to get out of the car and go make some casual inquiry, just to get a rise out of her. Then I locked the car door—an absurd thing to do—but I didn't trust myself entirely, and the thought of what I'd like to say to her ran through my mind:

"Mrs. Palmer? My name's Mike Kincaid. I'm a reporter, and I have one question for you. What can you tell me about the photo of a dead girl found in Stephen Lister's apartment?"

But I didn't do this. Instead, I made a note to check out whether

217

there were other Palmer children, then I put my notebook away, started the car, and drove out of the estates.

Glenville encompassed several smaller unincorporated townships, including Old Valley Shores, but most of the unincorporated villages were to the east of the main business district. I headed this way, following Route 25, because I felt a face-to-face with Frances Bushong would get me more results, more quickly, than any amount of research I could do on the former police chief.

I thought of calling Sally Garr at the library and asking her the one thing I'd forgotten to ask her—whether Frances Bushong was in fact Carl Bushong's widow or his daughter. Then I thought, "No, just keep going," and around four P.M., after a twenty-minute drive, I turned the car on to a tree-lined street named Dunham Drive.

I'd been following my sketch, which I'd copied down from the town map in the local white pages, and I checked the street number again—number 19. I crawled forward a block or two. Most of the houses here had been built in the seventies, custom-built on two-acre lots, and they were none too shabby. There were several handsome Capes and a number of sprawling ranches with fancy stone chimneys, and number 19 was one of these—a well-maintained, if tasteless, ranch.

A mint-green Cadillac sat in the driveway, and I got out and walked by it along a path that led between sculpted evergreens. When I rang the bell it chimed endlessly, hinting at other ill-conceived appliances within. It was still chiming when a woman in her early fifties came to the door. Right away I didn't like her. She had tinted blonde hair and an avaricious mouth, and she looked at me as if I were a salesman to be gotten rid of, which only reinforced my determination. I was going to fit in the last piece of the jigsaw, even if it meant conducting a charade.

"Mrs. Bushong?" I said.

"Yes?"

"Mrs. Bushong, my name's Jim Danziger." I showed her one of Danziger's cards, which I'd filched from his office during his press conference. Things such as these were often useful, and I'd made a habit of acquiring them. "I'm an investigator with the state attorney's office."

"Oh."

She seemed a bit surprised. Nothing more. I said, "Carl Bushong was your late husband, right?"

"Yes."

I flashed a brief smile and said, "I just wanted to make sure. Chief Hagstrom was pretty sure you were the right lady, but he's new in these parts . . . Can I come in a minute?"

"What's this about?"

"I'd sooner talk inside if that's all right, Mrs. Bushong."

I'd meant for my manner to seem a tad ominous, and for the first time I saw a flicker of concern at her mouth. She said, "All right," rather abruptly, then she stepped back. I followed her inside.

She didn't ask me to sit down right away, and I hovered awkwardly until she did. Then she sat down opposite me. I surveyed the living room and took note of the new TV and the plush carpeting, and my mind did a few calculations. Things weren't going badly for a woman living on a police chief's pension—I assumed she didn't work since she was home at four in the afternoon.

I said, "Mrs. Bushong, I'll get straight to the reason for this visit. The D.A.'s office is conducting an investigation . . . and although I don't want to alarm you, some questions have arisen in the course of it concerning your late husband's relationship with the late Congressman Walter Palmer."

I was watching her closely as I spoke, and I saw her jaw go slack. She didn't say anything, and I figured maybe she was too shocked to, so I went on, "I gather your husband knew Walter Palmer."

She said weakly, "The late congressman?"

I nodded and tried to look a bit sympathetic, at the same time maintaining my best D.A.'s office manner. I waited for her to respond, and after a few moments I saw her cover her surprise. She said, "Well, I think he knew Palmer. I'm not sure."

I had 90 percent of what I wanted already, but some little voice in me was saying, "Go for it. Go for it all." And I went on with the act.

I said, "Mrs. Bushong, I find it hard to believe you don't know that your late husband and Walt Palmer knew each other. And I'd appreciate it if you'd just be straight with me."

She reacted defensively. She said, "I am being straight. I told you, I thought he knew him. It's been a while."

"They were well acquainted, isn't that what you mean?"

I made a point of letting her know I was studying her. Then she said, "Well yes, they knew each other, like I said. You still haven't told me what this is about."

"It's about their business relationship. I guess that's what you could call it."

I said this with a hint of sarcasm, and this time I saw some color drain from her face.

She said, "What sort of business relationship?"

I said that's what we were trying to find out.

Then I sat looking at her deliberately, and finally I said, "Mrs. Bushong . . . there're any number of ways we can go about this . . . but when this information crossed my desk, I thought the best thing I could do for you was to drive out here and talk to you one-on-one. I don't want you to get the wrong impression, but I'm doing this for your sake."

I figured her head was spinning by now. She was staring at me, and I flashed a tight smile, then I asked her, "Do you mind if I smoke?" I wanted her to think the request betrayed a certain friendliness.

She said, "Er, no . . . go ahead." She got up nervously. "I don't have an ashtray, I'll get you one."

She went into the kitchen and returned a moment later with some souvenir from Florida. I glanced at it and flicked away my ash, then I said, "I want you to know your cooperation in this won't do you any harm. This office isn't out to recover monies from you . . . do you understand what I mean?"

Her brow furrowed. "I'm not sure I do."

She was still pretending to be astonished.

I sighed and stared at my cigarette, then I shook my head slightly as I waited.

Eventually she said, "What is it you're implying?"

"I think you have a good idea, Mrs. Bushong. Like I said, this office isn't concerned with taking a widow's money. Our investigation is focusing on how certain campaign funds were spent. That's why I say before we start subpoenaing bank records etc., it would be in your interest to help us."

She arched her back and said, "Well, I'm sitting here thinking maybe I should call my attorney." She was suddenly peevish. "I mean, you come in here—"

I interrupted. "That's your prerogative, Mrs. Bushong. But I'm sure your attorney will advise you to cooperate rather than open up a can of worms."

"Cooperate on what?"

I ground out my cigarette and looked at her and shook my head again, almost sadly. Then I stood up. I said, "Okay, I realize this has been a surprise. I can see we're not getting anywhere here." I handed her a card and said, "Why don't you take the evening and think about it? Call me in the morning." I got up, smiled my tight smile again, and I started out.

"Hey, wait a minute . . ."

I turned. She was not sure what to say, then she said, "Are you saying Carl took money from Walter Palmer?"

"That's what the evidence suggests, Mrs. Bushong."

"Well, if it's true, I didn't have anything to do with it." Her face had reddened. "Carl always took care of our finances—I had no part in that until after he died."

"I understand . . ." I hesitated, and feigned patience. "That's what I was trying to explain, Mrs. Bushong. In your case, there's nothing to be concerned about."

She had been fixing me with an indignant stare, but hearing this, she backed off a bit and said, "He never talked to me about police work either."

I smiled. "Like I said, nobody's blaming you."

I took out a pen and a scrap of paper, then I scribbled down a number and handed it to her. "This is my direct line," I said. "Talk to your attorney first if you like, then call me." I took the card back and handed her the scrap of paper, and she took it nervously. I said I was sorry to have to lay this on her. I realized it was upsetting.

"It certainly is . . ."

"I'm sure."

Then I glanced over at a coffee table, where there was picture of a jowly guy with sandy hair wearing a police chief's uniform. She saw me looking at it.

I said, "Nineteen seventy-five, Mrs. Bushong, that's when our information shows this started . . . that's a long time ago."

She didn't respond, and I said, "I'm sorry to use this word so bluntly, but do you have any idea what these payoffs might have been for?"

"No, I surely don't! And I don't believe it!"

She moved back to the couch and reached for a box of tissues. She was about to go wet-eyed on me, and I doubted it was because she feared her husband's reputation was about to be stained. Everything about this woman and this house suggested she was a very practical sort. She dabbed at her eyes, and I gave it a whirl—just to smooth the jigsaw surface.

I said, "Didn't you notice any surprising increases in money, Mrs. Bushong?"

She didn't answer, and I said, "All right, let's put it this way. Didn't you and your husband take some nice vacations around that time, or soon after?"

I nudged a shoulder toward her, urging her to answer. And when she didn't, I said, "Don't you see what I'm saying, Mrs. Bushong, the money's already spent."

I flashed my smile again, and after a moment she said, "Well, we did take a couple of trips. But Carl always told me he'd saved that money."

The jigsaw was smooth.

"You see what I mean," I said. "The money's spent. Nobody's coming after you for this." I glanced at the furnishings, then I indicated the piece of paper she was still holding and said, "Call me tomorrow, Mrs. Bushong. We'll talk some more."

I turned and headed for the door, but she came after me, and she was continuing to ask for reassurances. I told her not to worry, but it was another ten minutes before I got out of there, and only then because I insisted I had another appointment.

When she finally closed the door, I got in the car and drove three blocks, then pulled over, feeling like I might burst. I'd worked up such an intensity during the charade, I felt like an actor who couldn't shed a role. I decided I shouldn't feel sorry for her—even when I thought of her calling the number I'd written down, and getting God knows who. She was her late husband's tacit accomplice—I was sure of it.

I realized I was sweating, and it wasn't just from the heat. I turned the air-conditioning up and gradually I felt the sense of accomplishment seep through me. I had *everything*. If there weren't such a thing as libel laws, I'd have gone to the paper right then and there and written the story. In fact, I planned to start writing it just as soon as I'd spoken to Rich Bianco. I wanted it ready to go when the time came.

In the meantime, it was Rich's job to prove all this. But what I was handing him was a lot more than circumstantial, and ultimately, it would solve not one murder, but two.

—— CHAPTER EIGHTEEN ——

TEN MINUTES LATER, I pulled over at the first phone booth on Route 25 and called Phil Gutierrez at the 20th Precinct. He was in the middle of an interrogation and couldn't be interrupted, and so I asked for Larsen. He was out but he was expected back any minute, and fifteen minutes later I pulled over at another phone booth and called again. This time I got through to Phil, and trying not to sound too excited, I asked him when Rich was due back from Bermuda.

"Tomorrow."

I asked what time, and Phil said Rich had checked in earlier that morning and said he planned to take an early flight. He thought he remembered him saying he was leaving around seven.

"Do you know what time he gets in?"

Phil didn't know, and he did some calculations aloud to figure out if you gained time flying east to west. I said you did. Then I asked which airline Rich was taking, but Phil said he didn't know.

He asked if I was thinking of giving him a ride in.

I said, "Maybe."

"You're a nice guy, Mike, you know?" Then he chuckled and said, "I hear you got taste in women, too . . . least in the looks department." He laughed at his own joke, then he said, "Hey, congratulations, I'm glad it worked out."

I told him he'd have just as soon seen her fry, and he said, "Aw come on, Mike. Don't be like that."

I said I was only kidding. I could afford to.

Then he said, "Listen, I got a guy in the hot seat here trying to set a record for telling lies, so before he dreams up any more, I gotta get back in."

As a pro forma, I asked, "Anything new on the case?"

"Not really." He chuckled. "Some broad got off."

Then we hung up, and I got back in the car, and I drove back to New York with the radio blaring.

I went to my apartment first and made some calls to airlines and found out there was an American flight from Bermuda, leaving at 7:00 the next morning. It got into Kennedy at 8:15. There were no others. Then I stashed my notes, then I picked up the phone again and called Ann. I got her machine, which was disappointing, but it was still only 6:30, and I figured she should be back any time. I left a message, and an hour later she called back.

I said, "Let's get together."

She told me this sounded urgent.

I said it was. I planned to fuck her brains out.

"You're a little feisty."

I was holding a lot inside. I said, "You want to order in?"

"You want sex with takeout? Okay, what time?"

"Half an hour?"

"How's Chinese?"

I said we'd never done that. What was it?

"Boy, you are feisty."

I said I'd be there as soon as I took a shower.

I showered and shaved, but I took my time, and as I was getting changed, I couldn't resist taking the notes out of the drawer and waving them around with a war whoop, like some idiot. Then I fixed myself a drink and sat gazing out the window, savoring the scotch. I was feeling pretty pleased with myself.

Then around eight, I went downstairs and took a cab across town. It was just starting to get dark and the lights were going on in the big apartments along Fifth Avenue, a vast row of wealth I often envied, but I wasn't feeling envious that evening. I was feeling a strange sense of serenity and a glow from the accomplishment.

Then, as we drove along East Ninety-sixth, I spotted a liquor store and I told the driver to pull over. I hopped out and bought a good bottle of wine, and ten minutes later I was climbing the stairs to Ann's apartment, and crossing paths with the food delivery guy who was just leaving.

When Ann answered the door, she looked faintly amused. I did my best not to act too excited. She kissed me a couple of times, then she took the wine and went into the kitchen and asked if I'd put on some music. I found a good jazz tape, resisting an impulse to hear Sinatra sing "New York, New York," and to the strains of a sax, we sat down at the table and started in on the food.

I said, "So how was your day?"

She said it was fine.

"Mine was pretty good, too."

"You didn't go to work?"

"I did. Kind of."

"I thought you were going to take some time off."

"Not right away."

"Why not?"

"Because I've got a story to write."

I was doing my best to be casual, enjoying the buildup.

"What story?" she asked.

"Oh, little bitty thing."

But from my manner, she began to realize I was sitting on something. She said, "All right. How long are you going to keep me in suspense?"

"Maybe a little longer." I took another bite of food. "This is good."

"So's the story, sounds like."

"It sure is. It's a murder story. A double murder."

She looked a little puzzled. "When did this come up?"

227

I figured I'd milked this long enough. I said, "I started it a month or so ago, and I finished the legwork today." Then I said, "I know who killed Stephen Lister."

Her jaw fell. Then she set her fork down and looked at me steadily. After a moment she said, "This isn't a joke, is it?"

"It's no joke."

She blinked. "Wow . . ." She sat with her hands on the table next to her plate, and for a moment she said nothing. Then she said, "This was quicker than I expected."

"What was?"

"Well, when did this happen? When did the cops find out?"

"The cops didn't find out."

For a moment she looked confused again. Then she caught on and her mouth wavered slightly, then she said, "Mike, you're scaring me."

I said there was nothing to be scared of. I'd been working on the story and I'd pulled something off. Something big. "I got there before the cops did . . ."

She stared at me in astonishment, and I said, "In part because of something you said."

She looked really scared then.

"About Stephen?"

"No . . . about dinner reservations."

I grinned. But I could see she was ready to let fly with exasperation. She groped for words, then finally she said, "Stop speaking in riddles! What dinner reservations?"

"This coming weekend's."

Her mouth flapped again, and this time she got up. She couldn't take much more of this. She yelled, "Mike, if you know who killed him . . . for God's sake, tell me!"

She was standing with her hands on her hips, and I eased her back in her seat. Her body was tense.

"It was a woman called Isabel Palmer and her son . . . ."

She faced me in astonishment, and I said, "You don't know them . . . I'm not sure which one pulled the trigger, but it doesn't matter. They're both guilty as hell."

"Who are they?" She was still staring at me, baffled.

"A congressman's wife and her son. Lister was blackmailing them. He had been for years."

She was looking utterly perplexed, and in the ensuing silence, the music suddenly seemed intrusive. She got up abruptly and turned it off, then she sat down, looking impatient and frustrated.

"Start at the beginning!"

"Okay."

I started to speak, but before I could get beyond a phrase, she said, "And stop telling me this, like it's tomorrow's weather or something."

I grinned and said she'd have to be a patient audience, but she interrupted and asked, "How do you know all this?"

"Like I said, I've been working on it. I caught a couple of breaks."

"Do the police know about this?"

"They will by tomorrow."

"I mean, can this be proved?"

"Oh yeah. A good D.A. can make a case. And make a name doing it."

She started shaking her head. "Holy shit," she said eventually.

I asked if she was ready for me to start, and she said, "Damnit, yes." Then she said, "No, not yet. I need a real drink first."

She got up and went into the kitchen and poured herself a scotch. I'd set her head spinning, and only when she came back did it occur to her to ask me if I wanted one. I said I might as well keep her company. Then she snatched up her plate and said, "I can't eat any more . . ." and as she took the plate away, I said I was done too. She shook her head at me again, communicating her lingering astonishment, then she went out to the kitchen, and while she was fixing me my drink, I moved over to the couch.

I lit a cigarette, and when she came back in, I said, "You ready?"

"Yes, and go slow." She was still looking disconcerted.

She sat down next to me, and I said, "First you've got to bear in mind what the cops knew so you can see how this other stuff ties in."

"All right."

We were silent for a moment while I got my thoughts in order, then I said, "Okay, here's what they had. First, stolen license plates

229

found in Lister's car. Second, cocaine and heroin found in his apartment. Third, a lot of money in bank accounts. Fourth, a deal going down for him to run *City Magazine*. And fifth, a five-hundred-mile trip he made the Saturday night before he was killed. Okay, so far?"

She nodded, and I went on.

"They also knew he'd had lunch at the Russian Tea Room the day before he was killed, but they didn't know with who . . . So when you mentioned reservations for that restaurant up near your place, it jogged my mind . . ."

"What did?"

"Well, since he'd never made a lunch reservation there, I figured maybe it was the person he had lunch with who made it."

"Was it?"

"Damn right."

"Who?"

"Lisa Dennison."

"What?"

She looked utterly astonished.

I said, "You know who she is?"

"Of course . . ."

I couldn't resist a chuckle. I said, "You two have something in common. She had a little fling with Lister too."

"Are you serious?"

I nodded.

"But she's seeing Mitch Danbury."

"Not exclusively."

"Holy shit."

I chuckled again. Then I said, "You might like to know, she was his second choice, after you turned him down for the week on the yacht."

She was too preoccupied to see any humor in this. She started to say, "But how does this tie in—" And I interrupted.

I said, "Hold your horses." I took a quick drink, then I said, "The affair's a side issue. The point is, her name was on the reservation list for that day, and so she and I had a little chat."

I took a moment, realizing I had to back up a little. I said there were a couple of other things she needed to know first.

"Number one. Lister had made a call to an Isabel Palmer, in Glenville, Long Island, from his home phone, the day before he was killed. But when the cops spoke to Isabel Palmer about the call, she claimed Lister was a friend of her son, Brad, and that he'd called to get Brad's number in the city. That turned out to be bullshit, but I'll get to that."

I took another sip of scotch. "Then the cops found a photo of a dead girl in the back of Lister's files—I told you about that." She nodded, and I went on, "Well, they ran the photo through the NCII computer, and it turned out to be an actual photo of a dead girl named Melissa Townley, from Glenville, who'd been murdered fifteen years ago. Case unsolved."

Ann was looking puzzled again, and I said, "Just hold that thought, okay?"

She nodded, and I went on, "So I'm in the middle of talking to Lisa Dennison about Mitch. I'm thinking maybe, just maybe, that Mitch found out about her affair with Lister and did the deed. So I'm pressuring Lisa about whether Mitch knew about the affair, and in the middle of all this, Lisa tells me she overheard Lister on the restaurant phone getting tough with someone called Palmer. She thought his conversation had something to do with his business deal for getting control at *City*."

Ann was still staring at me, and I realized she still didn't get it. I said, "So I started wondering why the hell was he threatening Palmer. Then I remembered something Rich had told me, about Lister's uncle telling him that Lister was toting that camera around even as a kid. And it started to add up . . . I figured if Brad Palmer had been dating this girl, maybe Lister was sneaking around one evening, trying to get a peek—I mean, you told me he was voyeuristic. So I figured maybe he got a real peek—of what was really going on—he got to see a murder. And photograph it. Or if he didn't photograph it all, he got enough to compromise Palmer because, shit, he had this photo of the dead girl."

231

Ann said, "Jeezus Christ. I don't believe this!"

I said, "It's something, right?" Then I said, "So I guess he put the photos to work for him. I bet he sent a couple of shots to the Palmers, and then followed up with anonymous calls telling old man Palmer that if he didn't want to see his son go to jail, he should pay up. What was Walt Palmer going to do? He paid, and I bet he kept paying."

Ann was still staring at me. She hadn't touched her drink, and after a moment she said hesitantly, "How can you know? . . . How can you be so sure . . . of any of this?"

"Well, for a lot of reasons. For one thing, I spent today in Glenville."

She looked at me as if I'd said I'd gone to the moon.

I said, "I know Lister knew the girl. They were classmates. I found a little quote of his about her in the local paper."

"You mean . . . from when she died . . ."

"Right there, in black and white. From fifteen years ago."

"That's . . . unbelievable . . ."

Her voice trailed off, and I figured her thoughts must be racing. I asked if she needed me to go back over anything, but she shook her head and said, "No, no. Go on . . . I'm following."

I reached for my drink.

"Then I talked to a woman who worked at the local library. She'd lived there all her life, and she told me Palmer had dated the Townley girl, and not only that . . . at one time he'd called her a slut and said he wanted nothing to do with her."

"She remembered that?"

"She remembered a friend telling her that."

"Well, wouldn't that have made Palmer a suspect at the time?"

"If the world were a fair place, yes. But the local police chief was a guy named Carl Bushong. He's dead now. But at some point he let Walt Palmer know that his son was under investigation, and at that time money started changing hands."

"How do you know that?"

"Bushong's widow told me. Not in so many words, but I got enough out of her."

"She admitted it?"

I grinned. "Not quite. I posed as a D.A.'s investigator and leaned on her hard. She admitted she and her husband took a few fancy vacations in the late seventies, and she was still living pretty high off the hog. Palmer was loaded, so it doesn't take a genius to figure out what happened. The really dirty pool was Bushong wanted to make it look like he was still active on the case, so he pulled the wool over everyone's eyes and acted as if he was focusing on another suspect, some poor guy who happened to be the girl's piano teacher. Apparently they'd found some sweater hair of the girl's in the guy's car."

"And this guy was innocent?"

"Sure he was. But he took the heat."

Ann looked faintly disgusted. Then she said, "And nobody touched Palmer?"

"Not quite."

"What do you mean?"

"Stephen Lister did."

I let this resonate. And I saw Ann's hands shake slightly. For a moment, she seemed lost in thought, then she got up and walked to the window. I figured she was having a hard time with all this. And as I watched her, it suddenly hit me that we were talking about a guy she'd been involved with, a guy she'd gone to bed with—I guess in my enthusiasm I'd kind of put this aside.

Then after a minute or so, she said, "And all this came together for you after what Lisa said?"

"That's right."

She stared at me for a while, then she came back and sat down next to me, and after a minute she said,

"So what do you think happened? With the Palmers and Stephen?"

I said, "Well, I'm speculating a little here, but I think it all fits." I took a moment, then I said, "I don't know how Lister worked his blackmail over the years, but my guess is Walt agreed to pay him. And however Lister worked it, Walt didn't know who he was, of course. The way I see it, Walt was an old horse trader, so he decided he could live with the blackmail, because, hell, he could afford it. But when

233

he died, I think Lister went for the kill, and I think that's where he made his mistake."

"Why?"

"I think he underestimated the mother. I think he thought she'd be an easy mark. Only she wasn't."

Ann looked a bit surprised.

I said, "Why not? She's not a horse trader, like Walt was. And she's the type who thinks the sun shines out of her son's ass." I lit a cigarette, and Ann was still staring at me, and I said, "Right there, you're looking at the root of the problem."

"What do you mean?"

"Well, I got a look at mother and son one time, and they seemed pretty close. I figured Melissa Townley dumped Palmer, so he got furious and killed her. Maybe the mother's justifying it all along, saying the girl brought it on herself, got her poor little boy all crazy and bent out of shape. Now someone like that isn't going to have too hard a time justifying killing someone who's trying to soak her son. Or her, for that matter."

Ann was silent for a moment, then she said, "So why did Stephen go for the kill?"

"He had a big deal on the table, remember? The more City stock he could pick up, the better. And he's got visions of grandeur. He's renting yachts in the Bahamas. He's going for the big one. The way I see it, that's where the stuff the cops had ties in."

"How?"

"Well, what if he told Isabel Palmer he wanted a couple of hundred grand, and after that, he'd leave them alone? He might even have meant it, they don't know that. In the meantime, he's gotten used to the Palmers paying up. He thinks the mother's easy game, like I said, only the mother's not a horse trader. So Lister makes his demand and the mother gets with Brad and decides it's time to put an end to this."

Ann set her glass down and said, "Go on."

"So they lay a little trap. It's big money Lister wants, so they tell him he'll have to pick it up somewhere else. How about Washington? Maybe they tell him it's being drawn on an account there."

"Why Washington?"

"Because they know the town. Lister doesn't. But he's hungry, so he agrees. But they figure out some way to learn who the blackmailer is when he picks up the cash." I paused. "I'll bet it was Washington. Lister put five hundred miles on his car that night and he went through the Lincoln Tunnel."

"And the license plates, right!"

"Right." I smiled. "He's not stupid. He takes precautions. He makes damn sure to put phony license plates on his car in case they spot it." I drained my glass. "But they made him somehow."

My throat was dry. I got up to get another drink, and when I sat down again, she said, "So now they know who he is?"

"Right. And they don't screw around. One or the other, or both, they pay him a visit that Sunday. He still has the money at his pad—they take it back. They want the photos too, and he gives them up. All but the one that fell behind his file drawer. He thinks this'll buy him his life. Wrong.

"Then they cover their tracks. They put a load of flake in his refrigerator, leave a little smack in the bedroom, and jab him in the arm a couple of times with a needle."

"To make it look like a drug hit?"

"Right. Because they don't know whether Lister called them from his apartment. So they want to give the appearance of a drug hit, because they're smart enough to know that if Lister did call them from his place, the police are going to get his MUD and pay them a visit. So they lay a false scent, and they concoct a story about Brad running into him one day in New York and talking about them getting together. That can explain the phone calls to the mother. And just to put the icing on the cake, they make a point of going to his funeral."

I was quiet for a moment. Then I told Ann I didn't think I'd missed anything. I said I was making a guess, but I had the feeling it was both Brad and his mother who had dropped in on Lister that Sunday. She asked me how I thought they'd got in, and I said, "Lister had no reason to feel nervous. He'd probably open his door to a middle-aged woman, claiming to be a neighbor asking a favor—it might have been no more complex than that."

235

"What about getting in the building?"

I said that was easy enough. There was no doorman. A neatly timed arrival as another visitor was leaving would more or less ensure that the door would be held. Who wouldn't hold the door for a well-dressed middle-aged woman and her son visiting on a Sunday?

Ann said, "Do you think he hid the photo of the dead girl deliberately?"

I told her I doubted it. "I think it probably just fell behind the file drawer. Either that or it slid back there in his panic to hand the stuff over." I said I'd imagine he worked pretty hard to convince them this was everything, praying they just might walk out of there.

Ann said that wasn't a pretty thought. I said blackmail wasn't pretty either. And then we both sat in silence.

I don't know what I expected having told the story, but the net effect was not quite what I'd had in mind earlier. Ann seemed pensive, distracted, and I could hardly blame her. I'd said a mouthful. She asked what the next step was, and I told her I'd be talking to the cops the next day, and that I'd bring Cantor up to speed. I imagined he'd tell me to start writing.

She smiled and said, "You're going to win a Pulitzer for this one."

I said I'd take it.

"You're smart, Mike. You'd deserve it."

"Well, thanks."

I was feeling a bit abashed. Like I was taking my victory lap.

Then she said, "I mean it. You put it all together," and I reached across the couch for her, and she drew her knees up and curled up next to me. Then she sat with her head resting on my shoulder and said, "God, my head's still reeling."

I said I wasn't surprised.

Then she pulled back from me a bit and with a kind of weary flourish she said, "I'm exhausted! No, I mean it . . . I feel . . . mentally exhausted."

When I came out of the bathroom, she was already in bed, lying with her hands behind her head, staring at the ceiling. I got in next to her, and she looked at me and smiled faintly, then she shook her head in a kind of awed way. I lay watching her for a while, then I stroked her hair a couple of times, and she rolled over and curled close. It wasn't a passionate move, it felt as if she were seeking refuge or protection, and after a while she said, "God, the world can be an awful place."

I said I guess I'd painted it that way.

Then she reached for the light, and I felt a little disappointed. Weren't conquering heroes allowed to partake of their desires to their hearts' content? But I could understand her reticence. I'd really laid some heavy stuff on her, and I was still bearing in mind that she had dated this guy.

I did get my "rewards" a few hours later. I woke up and felt her stir, and I nudged her a little. And in the ambient light from the street, I smiled at her as her face turned toward me, and after a moment, she said, "I think I know what you want."

── CHAPTER NINETEEN ──

IN THE MORNING, I took a cab over to the West Side and picked up my car. And by seven A.M., I was on my way to Kennedy Airport. It was a morning much like the one before, with a mist hanging over Flushing Bay and clinging to the leaves of the ailanthus trees along the Grand Central Parkway.

I was at the airport in plenty of time, so I grabbed some coffee and a bagel, and when I checked the arrivals board, Rich's flight was on schedule. I stood at the window, watching the plane nose toward the gate and shut down engines, then, as the passengers disembarked, I stood to the side of the line until Rich and Jeannie stepped out. They both looked relaxed and tanned.

Rich spotted me right away. He pointed me out to Jeannie, and after the first greeting, as Jeannie fussed over me, he said, "Hold on. I know this guy. This ain't a social call."

"Sure it is."

He believed me for a moment. Maybe. Then he said, "So, nothing happened on your end, huh?"

"Not quite."

"I knew it."

I said I'd saved him cab fare at least.

We waited for their bags, with Rich standing next to me, giving me a look once in a while, and asking, "Any clues?" I told him no clues. I figured once I got going with the clues it would set his wheels spinning, and I wanted to tell this story in one sitting. We collected the bags and headed out to my car, and I kept the conversation on the subject of Bermuda as I drove them to their apartment in Jackson Heights.

When Rich had changed and showered, he came downstairs wearing his professional attitude, as if he'd left it hanging in the closet all the time he was away. He told Jeannie he might have a full day, he wasn't sure, then with a pointed glance at me, he kissed her good-bye and we left. Before we even got outside, he was trying to wring something out of me. I asked him if he wanted to take his car, and he said he generally did. So I told him in that case we should meet somewhere in Manhattan because I wasn't leaving my car in Jackson Heights only to have to come get it in the evening.

He said, "Okay," then he asked me, "Is this worth the price of breakfast?"

I looked and him and said, very deliberately, "Count on it."

We drove into Manhattan in our respective cars and met at a diner on Eleventh Avenue. And once we'd ordered, I began with the story. I was up front about everything, starting with my maneuverings at the Russian Tea Room, and when Rich started to roll his eyes, I told him to chill out, the payoff was worth it. Then he was quiet for a long time. As I spun out the story of the conversation with Lisa Dennison, he got even quieter. Then, when I hit the punch line about Lister threatening someone called Palmer, his mouth twitched.

He said, "Holy shit."

He sat back, reacting for a moment as if this was all I had to tell him. Then, he started to draw some conclusions, and I said, "Hold on a sec, we're only at first base. Your pal here's been busy."

He stared at me, and I said, "Think one word. Blackmail."

At first he didn't get it. I said, "The photo. Of the dead girl."

Again it took him a moment, then his eyes narrowed and he said, "You're kidding me."

I shook my head.

"Does Phil know about this?"

"Uh-uh. I called him last night to see when you were coming back."

Then I started in on my trip to Glenville. I told him about the library, and the librarian, and about dropping by the Palmer place and getting a look at it and at Isabel Palmer as she oversaw the gardener. Then I told him what I knew would be a tough part for him—about my subterfuge with the police chief's wife. It raised his hackles a little. At one point he said, "Jeezus Christ, Mike," but by then he was so caught up with what I was telling him, he wasn't about to make an issue of it.

When I was done, he sat as still as a statue. And then, when I mentioned a possible payoff in Washington, his mind went to work, tying in piece by piece the things he already knew, much as I had done—the plates, the mileage, the drugs—he was thinking along the same lines exactly. I let him continue, then I pointed out how careful the Palmers had been to cover their tracks.

The waitress came over and stood holding the coffeepot, but Rich's thoughts were clearly elsewhere. He said, "Yeah," to the waitress finally, and when she'd filled his cup, he said, "Well, I guess we start by getting a look at Palmer's bank records." He looked at me, and after a while he grinned and shook his head side to side slowly, and after a minute he said, "I told you, years ago, you missed your vocation."

I grinned, and he leaned across the table and punched my shoulder and said, "Fucking A, ace, way to go. I knew you'd pay off one day."

I said, "Tell me the truth, You think you can put this one away?"

He thought about it. Then he said, "Yeah . . . but I doubt we're gonna get these people holding a gun, or any pictures." He left his coffee untouched and stood up. "Come on, let's go lay this on Phil. I wanna see his face when he hears this."

Ten minutes later we were at the 20th Precinct, and I was sitting at Phil's cluttered desk, running through the story once again for Phil and Larsen. When I'd finished, they were stunned, and I had to go over a number of points again, this time with Rich making various interjections. It was around one P.M. by the time we were done, and at that juncture Phil said, "Unbelievable. Fucking unbelievable! Let's go buy this guy lunch."

Rich said, "I already bought him breakfast," and Phil said, "Jeezus, Rich, you got no sense of occasion."

I solved the matter by saying I wasn't that hungry.

Rich wanted to stick around, get things moving, but Phil wanted a sandwich at least, and the three of drove to a deli on Broadway. And as we rode in the car, I was thinking I still had to tell this story one more time—to Cantor. I figured that could wait until morning. I'd call him from home later.

I'd already told Rich that my goal here was not to jump any guns but to let fly with one huge salvo of a story when charges were filed. He said he liked the fact that I was thinking positive. And as we came out of the deli and got back in the car, I asked him which assistant D.A. he might choose to work with. He said he was thinking about going with Marilyn Moline. I knew her well. She'd worked in the D.A.'s office about ten years, and she was a real pro. I said, "Great, she won't give me a hard time."

But Phil shot Rich a look, and said, "You're going with her, huh?"

Rich said, "Why not? . . . she's good."

Phil scoffed.

"Yeah?" He continued to stare at Rich, then he said to me, "This guy says he's happily married? Gimme a break."

Rich glanced around at me, and his face creased into a slow smile. Then he said to Phil, "Okay, we go with Steve Wolf then?"

"Oh fuck no!" Phil was beside himself. "Don't do that to me. I gotta watch him balling snot across the room for hours on end. No fucking way."

Rich said, "Okay, it's Marilyn then." He turned to me. "What's your take on her?"

I said not only was she good, I bet she looked all right in her underwear. Phil glanced at me and said, "Two of a kind, you know that?"

Rich chuckled, and we started back.

He was still giving it to Phil as we got back to the station house, suggesting that Phil was the only Cuban he'd ever known who could go without sex indefinitely. And when Rich spotted Larsen, he wanted to continue the joke, engaging Phil's partner in it. Only Phil ducked into the men's room, and Larsen said he needed to talk to Rich alone, and the two of them went off to the rear of the station, and the jokes ended there.

I stood in the corridor waiting. I figured as soon as Rich came back I'd take off. Then Rich and Larsen appeared again, Rich striding ahead of him toward me with his jaw set. I started to say I was leaving, but Rich said to me, "Where's Phil?" And when I told him he was in the john, he brushed by me and said, "Go get in the car, Mike, I'll be right there."

His face was flushed as he handed me the keys, and his attitude had done a one-eighty.

I called after him, "What's up?"

"Go get in the car!"

He marched into the men's room, leaving me baffled.

I figured he'd eventually emerge and apologize. I assumed he was mad at Larsen about something. And so I tossed the keys hand to hand for a moment, then I decided that rather than be around when he was reaming Larsen, I would head outside to the car. I figured he was planning to give me a ride back to my car in midtown.

I walked outside, got in the Caprice, rolled the window down, and waited. Five minutes later, Rich came out with Phil and Larsen in tow. They were all looking grim, and I figured something must have come up. Phil and Larsen went to one car and Rich came toward me. He held his hand out for the keys, and I handed them to him through the window, and I saw that whatever his problem was he hadn't calmed down any.

He got in and started the engine, and I said, "Where're we going?"

"You'll see."

He was in one great mood. Then he started out east along West Eighty-second Street, following Phil and Larsen.

"What happened?" I asked.

"Nothing good, I can tell you that."

He glanced over at me and shook his head, and I decided whatever it was, I'd play by his timetable.

We took the Seventy-ninth Street transverse across Central Park, and as we slowed for the light at Fifth Avenue, I took another shot. I asked him, "How long you gonna keep me in the dark?"

"Couple more blocks."

Then the light changed and we turned down Fifth Avenue and made a left on Seventy-seventh Street, and as we drove toward the light on Park Avenue, I saw police dome lights up ahead. Phil and Larsen's car had pulled up next to these, and I thought, "Shit. Something's up." I still had no idea what.

Rich parked behind Phil and Larsen, and when he'd turned the ignition off, he turned to me and rested his hands on the steering wheel. Then he said, "Guess who lives here?"

"Who?"

I figured it must be some luminary who'd been killed. He had to be looking at an eighteen-hour-day schedule to inspire his present mood.

He said, "Brad Palmer."

"Whaat?"

I felt the sudden ringing in my ears. It got louder and louder and then it slowly faded away, and in the interim I realized for the first time that Rich's attitude was directed solely at me.

I heard him say, "You heard." And I felt something reach in and squeeze my heart. Then my throat got dry, and I said, "What happened?"

Rich took a deep breath and said, "Did you speak to the Palmer woman, or Brad?"

"No."

I was adamant, but he was glaring at me, and I told him again no, and once more I asked him what had happened. He didn't need to answer. I already knew. I glanced at up at the lights of the radio cars, then I turned to him and I said, "He's dead, isn't he?"

Rich lit a cigarette and said, "What do you think?" Then he got out of the car.

I got out too, feeling really shaky as we crossed the sidewalk. My day was crumbling fast. Then we ducked under some yellow police tape and took a flight of steps up to a brownstone.

Inside, we met up with Phil and Larsen, and they both gave me looks such as I'd never seen—strange looks, part accusing, part sympathetic—as if they couldn't quite rid themselves of the congratulatory spirit of earlier. Rich marched on ahead. He seemed to be having no such trouble.

He glanced back at me once, and when a cop on the stairwell wanted to see badges, Rich turned back again. He indicated for the cop to let me through, and from his look, I had the feeling he absolutely wanted me to see this, and it was not for the usual reason. Then we climbed a second flight to an open apartment door, where a knot of cops stood. A group of neighbors peered down from an upper landing, their faces horror-stricken.

I could see the body from the open door. The late Brad Palmer lay at the foot of a chair, his head angled back on it, his legs stretched out in front of him. His right arm was crooked at an angle, and I could see a gun in his right hand. A .22 automatic. I could see only the left side of his head, the undamaged side.

Detectives moved around him, dusting.

Rich spoke to a detective across the threshold, and the detective indicated a small floor area, which had already been dusted. Rich stepped inside, and the detective then glanced up, saw the neighbors, and eased the apartment door closed. I was feeling confused and angry, and slightly sick.

I turned to face Phil and Larsen. They stared back at me, and I couldn't decide if their looks were critical, or if they were asking themselves what the fuck I'd been up to. Phil said, "Well, Mike?"

I said, "Beats me."

Larsen said, "Conscience, maybe?"

I thought he was referring to me. I said, "Fuck you, man. Get off my case." Then, a moment too late, I realized he was referring to Palmer.

Larsen let it go, and Phil hunched his shoulders slightly and said, "Let's wait downstairs."

They moved off ahead, and eventually I followed. I stepped outside and waited with them on the stoop.

For a few minutes, none of us spoke. Then Phil drew Larsen aside and huddled with him, and I sat down on the stoop and lit a cigarette. Eventually they came over to me, and I apologized to Larsen, and he said, "That's okay, Mike, you're entitled."

I said, "I'm just stunned, is what I am."

Larsen said, "Me, too. I heard about it, ten minutes after you guys went for lunch."

"When did it happen?"

Larsen shook his head, and Phil said, "Couple of hours, most." Then he glanced at me and said, "Any theories, Mike?"

There was no hint of accusation, and in an even tone I said I had no idea how Palmer could have known anything.

Then Rich came out of the building.

He walked down the steps slowly and sat down next to me. I could tell his mood hadn't improved, although he seemed a bit more resigned than earlier. After a moment he said, "One shot through the temple. Powder burns on the chair. Some on his wrist." He lit a cigarette and said, "A neighbor thought she heard something. Didn't take it for a gunshot."

Phil asked, "When?"

"Around eleven-thirty."

Rich looked at me and asked what everyone wanted to know, "So how did he know?"

I said, "How did he know what?"

There was an edge to my voice, and Rich caught it. For a moment he backed off, then he looked at me, and his eyes narrowed slightly and he said, "Nobody else knew, but you, Mike." He glanced back up at the apartment and said, "Somebody told him."

Phil said, "His mother, maybe."

There was an exchange of glances all around, then Rich asked me, "Tell me again, what you did at the Palmer place?"

I sighed. Then I said, "I drove by, parked. I took some notes. She came out with the gardener. She saw me, but I could have been any salesman catching up on paperwork."

"Then you left?"

I nodded.

"And you went to see the chief's wife?"

"Right."

"And you mentioned Palmer to her?"

So this had to be it. I said, "Yes." Then I added, "But I didn't get into any reasons why the money changed hands."

Rich tossed away his cigarette and said gruffly, "But she probably knew, right?" I didn't answer, and eventually he said, "Either way, it was a mistake, Mike."

Phil glanced at Rich. Then he said, "You think the chief's wife called the mother? Mike scares the shit out of her, she calls the mother for a heart-to-heart? That it?"

Rich looked at me. "How bad did you scare her?"

"Badly enough, I guess. Who else could it be?"

They were all silent then, and I was feeling sick to my stomach. I was also frustrated as hell, and eventually I said, "How the hell was I to know the son of a bitch would kill himself?"

Nobody said anything for a while. Then Phil indicated the apartment and asked Rich, "Any of these guys spoken to his mother yet?"

Rich said he'd check, and he got up and went inside.

As he walked off, I was about to remind him that the mother was in on everything, but I figured I'd said enough for one day. I kept quiet as he went inside the building, then I looked at Phil and he said, "Anyone else could have told him, Mike?"

I shook my head.

"What about the librarian? She wasn't an old flame, or anything like that?"

I said no.

"So that's it then. The chief's wife to the mother. The mother calls the son to let him know." He glanced at Larsen. "Hey, it figures."

I was still thinking about the Bushong woman's attitude when I'd left her the previous afternoon. I'd scared her plenty, but she wasn't scared when I left. If anything, she was reassured. Why the hell should she call Isabel Palmer? Then I decided maybe the Palmers and the Bushongs had been closer than I thought. Maybe the woman couldn't resist making the call. Maybe she wanted to tell Isabel Palmer to get rid of certain records.

Phil sat down next to me and put a hand on my shoulder. Then he said, "Mike, maybe this was something you shoulda left to us." I felt grateful to him for at least saying it.

A few minutes later, Rich came down the steps. He said, "We'll play this one by the book." Then he looked at me and said, "You know what that means, Mike?"

I said, "Sure."

"You don't write anything. You don't do nothing, okay?"

He said this in a quiet, weary way, and I felt the sting of his criticism. I nodded slowly and said, "I hear you."

I could sense Phil and Larsen reacting uneasily, but this was between Rich and me. They were staying out of it. Then Rich said, "You'll be home tomorrow?"

I nodded.

"I'll call you there. Once I've had a chance to think about this."

He turned and started for his car, and I figured I wasn't getting a ride after all. Phil rested a hand on my shoulder, then he and Larsen got in their car and backed up the street. I watched them go, then I shuffled off toward Lexington rather than have to endure Rich's look as he went by.

My day was in ruins, and I was about as depressed as I ever could be.

——— CHAPTER TWENTY ———

LIKE I SAID earlier, it never pays to celebrate too soon. Still, if there was one day in my life I figured I'd be enjoying, it was this one. No such luck. The best of days had turned into the worst, and I could only shake my head at the irony.

I found myself walking block after block, trying to shake off the worst of the gloom. But it didn't work. And finally, I hailed a cab and rode down to midtown and picked up my car, and as I drove home I was saying to myself, "Well, you never saw this one coming."

It was around five when I got home, and I poured myself a brain-fogging-size scotch and sat at my desk, staring at the river. After a while, I tried to sift through the story to see if there was any way I could write it without embarrassing myself. But I kept hearing that conversation with the Bushong woman, and I knew I'd kind of stepped out of bounds on that one. I assumed it had to be her who had called Isabel Palmer. Who else could it be?

I wondered if the mother knew yet, and if she did, how she felt about it, and I asked myself a couple of times what her conversation with her son, Brad, might have been like. I doubted she'd have suggested he take the honorable way out. I figured this was something he must have done on an impulse. Still, it surprised me he'd done it so quickly—after all, I'd told Mrs. Bushong only that the D.A.'s office was looking into payoffs. I'd never really said that I knew what the payments were for. Then again, maybe Frances Bushong had gone a little nuts and told Isabel Palmer that she was planning to fess up to everything. In which case, what would Isabel Palmer have done but to call Brad, give him warning at least?

As for Brad himself, I didn't feel too bad about him. He was a double murderer, and his past had simply caught up with him.

All the same, as I sat there, I recognized that I'd been far too caught up in all this. One way or the other, I felt I'd fucked up, and in the midst of the gloom, I decided I might as well get a little drunk. I went into the kitchen and poured myself another scotch, and as I was sitting back at my desk, the phone rang.

I figured it was probably Ann, and I wasn't sure if I wanted to talk to her just yet, so I left the machine on and screened the call. A woman's voice came over the machine, and it took a moment before I recognized it as Sally Garr's.

At first I didn't pick up. Then I decided I might as well. She'd be reading about Brad Palmer in the paper in the morning. I lifted the receiver and said, "Hi, Sally," and she said, "Oh," a little breathlessly. "You're there?"

I said I'd just walked in.

"I hope you don't mind me calling you. I tried you at the paper, but they said you weren't there, so I looked up your home number, and there was only one Michael Kincaid."

"No, it's okay."

I was having a hard time talking to her.

"Anyway," she said. "I just called . . . not for anything really . . . I just sort of wanted to thank you for yesterday. It was kind of fun, and I just wanted to make sure you would call . . . when something happened."

I took a deep breath and said, "Something already has, Sally."

"Oh . . . really?"

"Not what I expected. Brad Palmer shot himself this morning."

"Oh my God!"

She was silent for a moment, then she said, "Why? Because he was about to be arrested?"

I said I assumed this was the reason. Then I decided there was one thing I'd better check with her. I said, "Sally, don't read anything into this, but you didn't tell anyone about what we talked about, did you?"

"No, of course not." She sounded injured.

"Okay," I said. "It's not important. Don't read anything into it."

I didn't want to talk any longer, but she said, "Why did you ask?"

"Sally, forget it."

"Okay . . . just tell me this. Is it going to come out that he killed Melissa Townley?"

"I guess so . . . eventually."

"Well, I won't say anything until then, I promise."

I said I was grateful to her. Then she said, "When do you think you'll write the story?"

"I don't know exactly."

She was silent for a moment, then she said, "Well, I'll tell you one person who'll be grateful to you. Mr. Delamere, the piano teacher. He'll be vindicated after all this time."

"I guess so."

I didn't elaborate, and after an awkward silence she said, "Well, I didn't mean to bother you, but I'm sort of glad I did." She laughed, then she said, "Oh my God, I've got to run, I should have closed the library ten minutes ago."

I thanked her for her time the previous day, and she said, "Oh, that's fine. Like I said, it was fun," and when she'd hung up, I gulped the rest of the scotch and walked back to the kitchen.

I started to pour another drink. Then, for some reason, I stopped in the middle of it. And before I knew it, I was staring at a pool of scotch, spilling onto the Formica counter. I remember gazing at the Dewar's label, and my mind was whirling.

I thought of calling Sally back, but then I decided no, I wouldn't do that. And I don't know how long I stood at the kitchen counter, but I do know this: There are certain realizations—epiphanies, if you will—that can work wonders at reducing the alcohol in the bloodstream.

Because by the time I got to my car on Riverside, I was incredibly sober.

— CHAPTER TWENTY-ONE —

As I DROVE north that evening, miles seemed to roll by during which time I was unaware of the act of driving. Every so often, I'd snap to and remind myself that I was on a parkway, in traffic, then my thoughts would drift again, and it would take a passing car or some necessary maneuver to serve as a reminder.

It was about five forty-five when I left the city, and the humidity had diminished, leaving a clear sky and a long evening ahead. The traffic thinned out once I got beyond Westchester, and it might have been a pleasant drive at any other time, but my thoughts were racing, and I felt skittish, and I wasn't paying attention to the scenery. I was staring fixedly ahead, hearing only the drone of the engine and the voices inside me.

I made good time, and when I turned off the parkway, it was barely seven P.M., and at that point I even thought of driving on up to the cabin and thinking about all this overnight. Then I decided no, that would serve no purpose. I'd probably only toss and turn through a series of jagged dreams and wake up in a cold sweat with the sheets pulled up around my neck. Still, part of me wanted to delay, and I knew why. There was a war going on inside me, the desire to know versus the desire not to know, and you know me well enough by now to know which one would win. Still, I was having a hard time with this. The feeling was akin to not being able to admit something out loud. It was like coming out of a nightmare and not wanting to talk about it because you're afraid the nightmare might be a premonition.

I drove on, aware of the potential for internal collapse if my suspicions were confirmed, and as I got near my destination, I felt the urgent need for fortification. I spotted a bar and pulled over and went in, and took down a large scotch alongside a group of guys in plaid shirts who were watching a ball game, and whose lives seemed far less complicated than mine. Then I set the glass down and left, envying them, and drove the next mile to the McArdle Nursing Home.

I'd already rehearsed what I would do, but I expected the patients would be inside by now. They were not. At least not the group I saw as I drove in. It was still light, and they were seated on a screened side porch facing a grove of woods, and among them I recognized Mrs. Raymond.

I parked and went inside and spoke to one of the administrators at the desk. I wasn't sure if it was the same woman I'd seen Ann speaking to when I was last here, but when I announced I was Ann Raymond's boyfriend, it turned out she was the same woman. She smiled and said, "Yes, I remember you. You were here a few weeks ago." I said that's right. Then I told her I was en route to New York from Pittsfield, and since the clinic was on the way, I'd taken a moment to stop in, with the idea that I could surprise Ann by telling her that I'd stopped in to see her mother. I said Ann was busy in the city, and she was feeling bad about not being able to get up here for the coming weekend.

The administrator smiled and said, "Well, that's very nice of you . . ." She started out from behind her desk and said, "You understand, of course . . . there's no chance she'll remember you." I said I was aware of the extent of the disease and that I was really doing this for Ann, and the woman smiled again and said, "You want to sit out on the front porch? I'll send someone to get her." I said that would be fine.

I took a seat on the old front porch in one of the rockers, and a few minutes later a nurse escorted Mrs. Raymond toward me from the side porch. As they approached, I heard the nurse say, "This is Ann's friend, Margaret . . . Mr. Kincaid . . ." and I saw Mrs. Raymond look over at me with a glimmer of curiosity. She sat down next to me and said, "Oh yes . . ." Then she smiled, but it was not a smile of recognition.

Still, she extended her hand. Then she brushed a lock of hair back, smiled at me, and said, "Ann. . . . my gosh, it's been a long time."

The nurse smiled at me helplessly and left us alone, and I felt I should at least try and get us off on the right foot, no matter how hopeless this might be. I was already saying to myself, "Was I mad to go this route? What did I expect?"

"No, Mrs. Raymond," I said. "I'm a friend of your daughter, Ann. We came here together a few weeks ago."

"Oh, that's right. These things . . . I was just talking to Mrs. . . ." She broke off and smiled. "How are you? Did you have a nice trip? Did you have something to eat?"

I said I'd eaten, yes, and, yes, the trip was fine. I told her I'd wanted to stop in and chat for a while.

She said, "Oh good. I love to chat."

I asked if I could get her something to drink, but she said no, she was fine, then she pointed off at a tree in front of the porch and said, "That's a very messy tree. What kind of tree is that?"

I said it was a horse chestnut.

She smiled again and said, "Aren't these grounds beautiful?"

I agreed they were, and I had no idea where to take the conversation next, and I was still feeling this was probably crazy. Then we sat in silence for a while. She seemed quite content. Suddenly she said, "Arthur was here . . ."

I gazed at her. "Who is Arthur, Mrs. Raymond?"

"Arthur . . ."

"Is he your late husband?"

"No, Arthur . . ."

Arthur could as easily have been the grounds keeper. I was unlikely to find out.

I asked her if she was happy here, and she said the people were very nice. And again I felt stumped. I knew very little about Alzheimer's and I was flying blind, not knowing what she might remember. I even thought of going inside and maybe asking a casual question of the administrators, but I couldn't come up with a strategy that didn't sound forced, and eventually I asked Mrs. Raymond, "Do you like living in the country?"

"Oh yes."

I told her I lived in the country too, not far from there. She smiled and said, "How nice." But she didn't elaborate, and when I realized she wasn't going to, I said, "Did you always live in Massachusetts?"

"Yes, Massachusetts."

She smiled again, and after a moment I said, "Did you ever live in Glenville?"

I saw something cloud her face.

"Glenville," I said. "Old Valley Shores Estates?"

She shook her head wisely and said, "Nothing good can come of that place," and at that moment I felt like the breath inside me had stopped.

A few minutes later, I summoned my strength and got to my feet. I went inside and thanked the administrator, and as I came out again, I walked over to Mrs. Raymond and said good-bye. She smiled at me, and I kissed her on the forehead. Then I walked to the car, dragging my feet, feeling a sadness for myself, for her, for Ann, for the whole damn world. I started crying. I couldn't help it. I had to wait a few minutes before my eyes cleared and I felt like I could drive.

— CHAPTER TWENTY-TWO —

IT WAS DARK by the time I reached the parkway, and as I drove south it was a toss-up all the way whether I should pull over and call Rich. I felt anger, pain, betrayal—and a deepening awareness that whatever proved to be the outcome, some part of me had changed forever. I felt I could draw a line between my life until then and any life I might have subsequently, and the thought left a hollow feeling inside me.

I made it to the city. And as I turned off the East River Drive, I was stopped in traffic. In the lane opposite was a family, their car all loaded up for an August vacation. I thought of my brother in Westchester and remembered that he, too, was due to take off on vacation that week with his family. I thought about the normalcy of his life in comparison to mine—something I'd always been a little smug about, until then. And for a moment there, I was ready to turn the car around and go off myself. Sell everything, move out west, leave the paper and my entire New York life behind, start anew. Then the light ahead of me changed, and a horn sounded behind me, and I drove on—up the incline on East Ninety-seventh Street and made the turn south on Lex.

I couldn't find a parking space, and I didn't care. I left the Buick next to a hydrant. Then I got out and marched up the familiar steps of the brownstone and rang the buzzer, and when Ann's voice came over the intercom, asking who it was, I heard my own voice say, "It's Mike."

She was waiting for me at the landing outside her apartment, and I guess I shot her some sort of look as I came up the stairs. But she said, "Hi," and sounded very casual. Then she said, "I called you a couple of times, you weren't in."

I said, "Right," and marched by her and into the apartment, and since I didn't hear her move for a moment, I figured she was scrutinizing me. She'd have to know I knew about Palmer's death, and I assumed she was thinking that this alone was enough to account for my mood.

I heard her close the door and I turned. Her hair was still damp from the shower, and she had a comb in her hand. She stared at me a moment, then she said, "You look furious. What's up?"

I didn't say anything.

Then she said, "You want some wine, they just delivered some?"

"You celebrating?"

She couldn't ignore the sarcasm in my voice. She blinked and calmly said no. Then, just as calmly, she added, "I just felt like some wine." Then she looked at me with concern and said, "What's wrong with you?"

"Oh, I've had quite a day."

I cackled a bitter laugh, and she continued to stare at me for another few moments, then, with the same calm in her voice, she said, "Sit down. Have some wine. You look like you need a drink."

I sat down and watched as she poured a couple of glasses. I found her calm amazing. Remarkable, and unnerving. And despite what was churning inside me, some of her calm seemed to have infected me— I've no idea why.

She brought the drinks over to the couch, and I resisted an urge to move away. Then she handed me my glass, and in the same calm voice, she said, "So let's hear about this day you had."

That did it. The remark—just the way she said it—it set me off.

I felt something black welling up in me. And in a voice that didn't sound like mine, I said, "Let me ask you a question. Why did you have to *kill* Brad Palmer?"

"What?"

Something came over her face, but she hid it well. I had already imagined what her reaction would be, but she didn't look scared, or even worried. She simply went on with the pretense, making as if she were baffled, and when she half smiled, I felt something creeping up my spine.

She said again, "What did you say?"

I said, "You killed Brad Palmer this morning. And I know why."

There was another drawn-out moment while we stared at each other, then she started to act as if I'd made a joke. And for a moment I wanted to hit her. Then I couldn't look at her. I looked away. I looked at my hands instead. They were shaking.

She uttered a little laugh then, and she said, "Mike, this really isn't very funny."

"I agree," I said.

"Then why did you say it?"

I looked up at her and didn't respond. And eventually she made a little movement of her shoulders and she said, "All right. Let's just forget about it."

I could see her marshaling her thoughts, trying to decide if she should regroup her defenses, or if it was already too late. And in the silence that followed, I kept seeing her going into Palmer's apartment, producing the gun, sitting Palmer in the chair, blowing his brains out, then making it look like suicide.

Finally I said, "I know everything. You lived in Glenville. You killed Brad Palmer for revenge because a man name Delamere was your father. He changed his name, right?"

She returned my gaze, this time with a cold stare, and the silence seemed to go on for ages. First her look was critical, then her eyes flashed with anger. Then the anger went away, and after what seemed like an eternity she sighed and said, "Well then. There's nothing more to say . . . is there?"

She leaned forward and made a small adjustment to the coaster where her wineglass sat, and as she did this, I noticed that her hands were unsteady too. Then she leaned back on the couch and didn't look at me directly, and after a while she asked, "Have you told the police about this?"

I didn't answer, and she said, "Or are you planning to *write* about it?" Again I didn't answer, and she said, "Because if you do, I think you'll be making a big mistake."

"Do what?"

She did not respond. She got up abruptly and went in the kitchen, and when I heard her open a cabinet, I felt a moment of apprehension. Then I heard her put a bottle on the counter, and a minute later she came out with a couple of drinks. She took away my wineglass and set a scotch in its place. Then she went back in the kitchen and ditched the wine. Finally she returned, and as I sat looking at the scotch, she said, "Don't worry. It isn't poisoned."

There was a sort of face-off. And when I looked away she said, "Mike, don't do this. Don't ruin everything. This has nothing to do with you."

"What?"

"You heard what I said."

I had heard, but I couldn't believe I was hearing it. I glanced back at her for a moment, then I got up and walked to the window, aware her eyes were following me. Then I turned back to her and said, "You're a killer."

She sat calmly, not saying anything in response, and eventually I said, "You're a killer, and you used me. I'm an idiot, but you're something else. You planned all this—"

"That's not true!"

"Getting close to me . . . after Lister got killed . . ."

"That's not the way it happened!"

"Bullshit." I came back to the couch and stood over her, then I said it again, "You're a killer."

She sighed and didn't say anything, and there was an empty look in her eyes I'd never seen before.

After a moment, I said, "You knew you'd made that phone call to your mother! You strung me along, and the cops, and the attorney . . . !" She started to interrupt, and I yelled at her, "Don't lie to me!"

"That's only part true—"

"You knew how to get me in your corner! You knew I'd be telling you everything about the case! You wanted to stay hands-on after Lister got killed . . . you still thought it might have been Lister that killed that girl . . . !

"You're mixing it all up!"

"Bullshit!"

I was glaring at her, and she was glaring back at me, and I could feel the blood rushing in my ears. I cursed her out, and throughout this she sat in silence, then she said, "I understand how you feel. But it was something I had to do."

"No kidding? I just fell into your lap, didn't I? I was pretty convenient, right?"

"No!"

"The fuck I wasn't."

She glared back at me, and after a moment she said, "Think back, Mike. Think back to when I met you at the City party. I liked you then . . . Stephen wasn't dead then."

"So what?"

Her mouth wavered for a moment, then she said, "I wasn't using you then . . . I wasn't using you even when you interviewed me . . . I was falling for you, but things happened, and, yes, even though I was falling for you, I took advantage of the opportunity. I had to."

I scoffed, then I said, "It never pays to be an easy fuck."

I watched her face redden. Then she rose to her feet, and for a second I thought she was going to throw her drink in my face. Then, bristling with anger, she looked me dead in the eye and said, "Don't you trash our relationship like that!"

The remark threw me.

"Our *relationship* . . . ?" I laughed aloud. "Our relationship . . . ?" I swallowed a mouthful of bile, then I said, "Don't talk about our relationship. You're a killer . . . one who thought she could get away with it!"

She stood facing me, hands on hips, then her lower lip started to quiver. For a moment I wasn't sure what she was going to say or do, then she sank back down on the couch and stared at the floor awhile, then she looked up and said, "I don't care if I get away with it or not, but if it takes all night, I'll make you see."

"Make me see what?"

She didn't answer, and I said, "Let's talk about what you did this morning."

"Why?"

I laughed aloud. "Why?"

"Why do we need to talk about it? I don't want to, and you know what happened."

Her voice was very calm now, and I stared at her, amazed. I stared at her in disbelief, then suddenly a thought occurred to me. I said, "Did you kill the mother too?"

"Don't think I didn't try."

She glared at me defiantly. I couldn't believe it. I shook my head and slumped down on the couch.

We were silent for a long time then. Then we both started to speak at the same time. She kept trying to say something, and I wouldn't back off. I kept saying, "No, let's talk about it. Let's talk about what you did. Come on. Let's talk about it . . ." and finally she yelled, "Shut up!"

She grabbed hold of me. "Shut up and listen to me! If you'd listen, I just might get through!" She took up her stance again, hands on hips. Then she said, "Yes, I thought it might have been Stephen . . . why do you think I was hanging out with him? I read the same things you did."

I sat down on the couch, feeling that things could fly out of control at any moment, and eventually I asked her, "How long had you been working on this?"

"Never mind that. If you'd been in my shoes, you'd have done the same thing I did!"

I said, "Oh yeah?" But something was puzzling me. How had she made the assumption about Lister? We were still facing each other and she didn't seem about to say anything, and after a while I said,

"Some kid with a camera? That wasn't enough reason. You didn't find out about the photo of the Townley girl until I told you about it . . ."

She faced me deliberately. Then she said, "That's right. But I had something you didn't have."

"What?"

I waited, and she didn't say anything, and finally she huffed her cheeks and said, "Why should I tell you?"

"You're right," I said. "Don't bother."

I started to get up, but she shoved me back down, and maybe she saw me react, saw a dark look in my eye, saw that I was ready to come out of my seat, knock her aside, and head for the door, because she quickly said, "I'm sorry . . . I'm sorry . . ."

She stood in front of me, playing with her hands like a little girl, and I kept looking at her hands, and flashing on what they had done hours earlier. But I stayed where I was, and when I next looked at her, she said, "I found a letter after my father died . . . when my mother was hospitalized . . . it was from a county detective. He'd written my father to say there was a witness who saw a kid with a camera going into the woods that night . . ."

I said, "Go on."

"Well, the witness changed his mind. He claimed he saw the kid the night *before* Melissa was killed . . . I can show you the letter . . ."

I didn't say anything, and she went on, "I think the detective didn't believe the witness, and he just wanted my father to know . . ."

She broke off again, and I said, "That he believed him!"

She nodded. "The detective said they'd talked to a kid named Stephen Lister, but that he claimed never to have been near the place."

I was silent a moment. I wasn't even sure why she was telling me this. Then I said, "But you thought he might be the one?"

"I made a point of meeting him, yes."

"Getting real cozy? Letting him take nude photos of you?"

"I wanted him to trust me."

Her face took on a hard look, then she said bitterly, "You didn't see what happened to my father, Mike. You didn't see how he fell apart because of all this. You didn't see how he slunk around all that

263

time, feeling disgraced . . . because of people's lies!" Her voice rose a notch, and she went on, "And you never saw what happened to my mother after he died! You haven't been living with her disintegration like I have . . . !"

She broke off, and her eyes shot full of tears, and I stared at her, and after a moment I said, "But it wasn't Stephen . . . And you found out who it was by using me . . ."

She looked at me defiantly and said, "Well, what the hell would you expect me to do? Those Palmer scum destroyed five lives—Melissa's! Her parents'! My parents' . . . ! I made damn sure their money couldn't buy them out of it this time . . ."

She broke off, and eventually she sighed and shook her head. Then she said, "What do you care? You're only interested in how I used you . . ."

She marched away then and got herself another drink, and when she came back, she picked up the phone and handed it to me. She said, "Go ahead. Call the cops."

I didn't react, and she set the phone in my lap and said, "Go ahead. It's all up to you anyway."

I didn't move, and she said, "Go ahead, Mike. Let the Palmers ruin a couple more lives. Let's see how long we can keep this up. . . ."

She turned and started from the room. But as she approached the bedroom door, she stopped and looked back, and when she saw I was still staring at her, she said, "That's right, Mike. Yours too."

"What?"

"*Your* life."

"Why mine?"

She looked at me as if the answer should have been obvious. Then she said, "Don't lie to yourself. I'm good for you. It's up to you to choose between me and your story." She hesitated a moment, then she added, "You decide. I'm going to lie down."

And with that, she went into the bedroom.

I stared at the phone in my lap. I can't remember the exact course of my thoughts for the next few minutes, but I know at some point I started thinking about that elderly woman I'd kissed on the forehead in a Massachusetts clinic only a few hours earlier. What had I meant by that? Was it some benediction, or did I feel sorry for her, or was it some gesture signifying that I'd make things right, that I'd take care of her daughter? I guess it meant something.

Then I thought about how I'd been used. I thought about the lengths she'd gone to for her revenge, all the scheming prior to when I'd met her, all the acting the week the cops were focusing on her. Then I rehashed conversations we'd had, conversations after making love, conversations when she'd been blatantly lying to me.

Now there was this.

I got up and went to the bedroom door. When I looked in, she was lying on her back, with the pillows stacked behind her. She glanced at me, but I couldn't read anything in her look, and I just stood there for a long time.

Eventually I said, "It must have blown your mind when Lister was killed."

She uttered a little sardonic laugh in response. Then she looked off and didn't say anything.

I said, "Why were you resisting going away with him?"

"I had copies of his keys. I planned on searching his place." She said this as if it had very little relevance to the larger issue we were facing. Then she said, "Nothing was going to stop me, Mike—that's what I've been trying to explain. You're taking this personally. I'm telling you, my mind was made up."

I thought about what she'd said, that I was taking it personally. That seemed like the least of it.

We faced each other in silence, and I drummed my fingers on the doorjamb. I couldn't think what to say. I kept thinking that maybe a buildup of hate over the years could ultimately legitimize any deed. Wasn't that one of the lessons of history?

But I didn't want to get into that, nor did I want to speculate on whether the years of hate had driven her over the edge permanently, or whether she felt a sense of release now that the deed was done. And so I just continued to stand at the door, and after a while she patted the bed next to her, inviting me to sit down. I didn't move, and she said, "Please," and after a moment I stepped into the room.

I sat on the far corner of the bed, away from her, and she gazed at me for a moment, then she said, "I won't blame you, no matter what you decide to do."

I didn't respond, and she said, "I mean it. I just think it would be a shame, that's all. For both of us."

I looked at her steadily, and eventually I said, "Did it occur to you that I might not be able to live with this?"

"I wasn't counting on you putting it together."

She managed a brief smile, then she angled herself slightly across the bed, and as she moved, she seemed thinner than when I'd last seen her. She was still looking at me, and I tried to avoid looking her in the eye, and I found myself idiotically studying a scar on her neck. Then she sat up and moved across the bed right next to me, and as she leaned against me, I felt her hair brush my cheek. I didn't move.

I was thinking of all the other stuff, of the days and nights spent together. I remembered how I'd felt that first time we'd gone upstate to my place. How it all seemed so fresh and new, and how I'd wanted it to go on. And now it couldn't, and yet I still wanted it to, and as her hair brushed my cheek again, I began to feel a bit like a prisoner on a scaffold. For a moment I half expected a crowd to gather.

I looked at her and realized I'd been thinking that we might grow old together. I could see us lying in bed Sundays, and recommending books to each other, and tiring of each other's jokes. And I realized then, I should get up and move away. But I didn't. I remained, anchored.

Then her face touched mine, and a moment later her hand brushed my fly. Slowly, without anyone seeming to be the guide, we lay down on the bed. I felt an odd moment of fear, like I was being led to an execution, then I gave in. Our clothes came off, and for a moment I wondered if I might be able to get an erection. But fear and hesitancy vanished under her touch. She said, "I know what you want," and we made love, and as we did, she did not take her eyes off mine.

— CHAPTER TWENTY-THREE —

THE BUSHONG WOMAN, of course, denied calling anyone. When Rich talked to her, he pressed her hard, and she did mention her visit from the D.A.'s office investigator, but she maintained she'd had no contact with Isabel Palmer, and in the face of her adamant denial, there wasn't much Rich could do.

Subpoenas were filed to obtain Isabel's and Brad's bank accounts, but it turned out the money that had been paid to Lister and retrieved—$250,000—had been drawn on an account in Brad Palmer's name, so there was no direct evidence tying the Palmer woman to it. She was not intimidated by Rich's questioning, and although Rich tried to make a case against her, the D.A. wasn't interested.

Nor was the gun found that killed Lister. And so the only details linking Brad Palmer to Lister were the phone calls and the money—which wasn't much. I wrote a story about Lister's blackmail of Palmer—and about why Palmer killed Lister—and then shot himself—but it was largely speculative, a complex mix of police theory and circumstance, and when I handed it in to Cantor, he passed it on to the lawyers, who jumped all over it.

Their real concern was that Isabel Palmer would sue. I doubted she would, since she was still under investigation, but the lawyers needed to be satisfied, and three weeks went by before the story finally ran. By then the lawyers had made me hedge it with all kinds of confusing source material, and the Lister-Palmer connection was advanced as only one of several theories the police had been following. I doubted many people bought it, and by then I didn't really care. Everything had changed, and I had already decided that my professional life had to change too.

I think it would have changed no matter what. But I guess the shift really began about three days after the night of Ann's admission. I was still anguishing over what to do, but the longer this went on, the more composed I began to feel about doing nothing. I'd had some time to think. And I'd spent some time on my own, away from her. I'd listed the pros and cons, and I'd run through my mind the various scenarios involving a decision either way. I even sort of acknowledged the power of the sexual attraction, and believe it or not, from time to time I felt I could put this aside.

I'd considered what it would be like if I did tell the cops, and I even envisioned Ann's trial, and my part in it. And for some reason, I kept seeing Aaron Hoffman at the sentencing hearing claiming that it was unlikely that Miss Raymond would ever kill again. I wasn't sure about that, and one afternoon as Ann and I sat in Central Park I made a point of telling her that if she ever went near the Palmer woman, that would be it. She said she knew I meant it, and that she understood.

I remember the conversation vividly. We were seated on a bench in Central Park, and there were children playing in a playground nearby, and she was sitting next to me in silence, gazing at the kids. Everything seemed strangely normal. Then, when I'd finished what I had to say, she looked over at me and said, "You're calling all the shots here, Mike."

I didn't say anything, and eventually she asked, "Have you reached any decision yet?" I said I hadn't, but I just knew that no matter what I did, everything would change.

She seemed to understand what I meant, and as I glanced over at her, she also seemed strangely at ease with herself, too much so for me to believe I was being manipulated, and at that moment I kind of recognized that she wasn't over the edge after all.

I know I didn't say so at the time, but I guess at that moment I made the decision. And to tell the absolute truth, to this day I really don't know how or why.

But I made it, or at least I made some resolve to take things one day at a time. And from then on, our lives went on in a strange way. We had several more conversations about what had happened, but they were spun over various evenings, and the revelations didn't lead me to backtrack. She claimed that a couple of things Lister had said about a fascination with snuff films had caused her to heighten her interest in his possible involvement in the Townley killing while she was seeing him. And that after he died, and she learned about the money in his bank accounts, she had thought of blackmail as a possible source of the revenue. After all, she was sure the money hadn't come from drug profits—she knew he wasn't dealing.

She said she had wondered hard about the drugs in the refrigerator. She guessed someone might have been laying a false trail, and she had even wondered if maybe Lister had had an accomplice all those years ago back in Glenville. And so she had felt it wise to keep on top of the case to learn why he had been killed, which was why she played out her hand when the cops showed an interest in her—to keep me on board, telling her everything—yes, she admitted it.

She always said, "It was something I had to do, Mike."

I asked her once why she had gone to the funeral, and she said simply, "It was expected. Virginia asked me to go." And in other conversations, she told me more about the humiliations her father had suffered—the pursuit, the disgrace, the loss of work, the unending suspicion. How it had driven him from Glenville, led him to change the family name, move to another state. She saw it shorten his life.

It was all understandable.

When she had told me all about it, I let it all sift for a couple of weeks. And during that time, I began to put myself in her shoes from time to time. I began to ask myself certain questions.

Would I have been capable of it? What if some bastard had caused my father to suffer? What if they'd shortened *his* life and gotten away with it? Would I have pursued his nemesis with the same single-mindedness, knowing I could exact revenge? Would I have cared, ultimately, if I'd been caught or not?

I guess you never know what you are capable of until you are in that situation. It's easy to say, "The law should take care of it."

In any event, after those first few weeks, we began to talk about it less and less. But it still weighed heavily, and there were reminders everywhere, and it more or less became obvious to both of us that the main thing to do was to get away. And so we decided to move, and when I suggested California because my son, Jackson, was there, she told me, "Like I said, Mike, you're calling all the shots."

And so one day in November we boarded a United flight with Ann's mother, and we installed her in a pleasant clinic in a small town not too far from San Francisco. And over the next several months we made several trips back to New York to dispose of our respective properties. We pooled our money and set up house, and all in all life hasn't been too bad for two people living on limited incomes. Ann still makes a living as a writer. I get by making periodic trips to Los Angeles and writing the occasional television script, but I have little enthusiasm for reporting. I find I am no longer of the mind-set that rejoices in public disclosures—in fact, I tend to guard secrets much more closely.

Sometimes I think of New York, and I miss it—terribly at times, especially when I think about fall colors and the view from my place upstate. I miss the city and its energies, its magic whirl, the life at the paper. I get sentimental for it at times, and in one of these moods I even wrote an apologetic letter to Virginia. She didn't answer, but as they say, you can't win all the rounds. I still get Christmas cards from Rich.

Is this a trap I dug for myself? Maybe.

Once in a while, I'll be driving home on the freeway, and something will go off in my head, and I'll remind myself, "You're living with a murderess." But then I get home, and there isn't any murderess, there is simply Ann, and I say to myself, "Hey, she is what I ordered."

I can't exactly define what there is between us. I guess it's love.

I know it works. I also know when we argue, there are certain subjects off-limits. In this respect, I guess we're not so different from most couples. There remains, of course, the question I sometimes want to ask her—a perverse one, I'll admit—but I feel that maybe I ought to know what it was like for her, the day she got into Palmer's apartment and pulled the trigger.

I've never asked her that. I guess I never will.

If I've learned one thing, it's that curiosity has its limits.